Hit on the House

Also by Jon A. Jackson:

The Diehard

The Blind Pig

Grootka

Deadman

Dead Folks

Man with an Axe

La Donna Detroit

Hit on the House

Jon A. Jackson

GROVE PRESS

New York

Published simultaneously in Canada
Printed in the United States of America

FIRST GROVE PRESS EDITION

Library of Congress Cataloging-in-Publication Data

Jackson, Jon A.
Hit on the house / by Jon A. Jackson
ISBN 0-8021-3705-9
I. Title.
PS3560.A216H58   1993   813'.54 — dc20   92-22723

Grove Press
841 Broadway
New York, NY 10003

00 01 02 03   10 9 8 7 6 5 4 3 2 1

I'd like to acknowledge the assistance and inspiration of
the following people by dedicating this book to them. They are
S. Clay Wilson (for the title), Mike Gouse (for the guns), my
brothers for their technical and artistic input, and my son and my
daughter and my sweetheart for their variously wry, caustic, and
loving support. Thank you.

Hit on the House

One

"**Y**eah," said a man after a single ring.

"This is Hal. I got a message to call."

"Oh, right. Just a minute, Hal. He's waitin' to hear from ya."

After a moment another voice came on the line. "Hal! Hey, how are you?"

"Me?" he said, as if surprised. "I'm just fine. I, uh, got a message..."

"Yeah. Say, that's pretty quick service, Hal. Where you calling from?"

"Does it matter?"

"Well, it could, Hal. See, I got a kinda rush job for you, and it's here, in Detroit. If you're in Alaska or some place like that, you won't be able to make it. But you sound like you're right next door."

Hal considered for a moment, then said, "What's the problem, Fat?"

The Fat Man chuckled, a thick, gurgling sound that wasn't necessarily mirthful. "Jeez, you don't take no chances, do you, Hal? Whata you, paranoid or something?"

"No, I'm not paranoid, Fat," Hal said without a trace of annoyance or disrespect, "but I have my system, you know."

"Oh, that's all right," the Fat Man assured him. "I like that. Better safe than sorry. But listen, this is really a rush thing. Twenty-four hours. Can you do that?"

"Just about anywhere that has a phone is within twenty-four hours of Detroit," Hal said. "But it's never a good idea to rush."

"You got a point, kid. But the deal is we got something goin' down here, and we don't got a lotta time. It's worth a Benjy. Can you make it for a Benjy?"

"I'm practically there, Fat Man."

The Fat Man gurgled. "That's my boy. You want me to pick you up . . . the airport, maybe?"

Hal thought for a moment. He was extremely interested in what the Fat Man wanted, but he knew it wouldn't do to seem too available. This was not a business that could be conducted by telephone normally.

"Why don't you call me back," Hal suggested, "from some other phone." He knew the Fat Man would understand that he meant from a pay phone.

"I can do it," the Fat Man said, "but I don't wanta be standing around outside all night. It's cold here, Hal."

"Call the service in the next fifteen minutes," Hal said, "and give them the number. I'll get back to you within twenty minutes. I wouldn't normally work this way, but you're the one who's in a hurry."

After he hung up, Hal went back to the bar for another drink. There was a large window beyond the bar that looked out onto the bowling lanes, but only a few people were bowling. The pins resounded faintly as the balls crashed into them. "I guess people don't bowl so much anymore," he said to the bartender. For some reason he felt like small talk. Idly he wondered if it was simply a way of putting off thinking about what he was sure the Fat Man would be asking of him. But then he dismissed the thought.

"It's always slow on Sunday night," the bartender said. "We're between leagues. Come in here tomorrow night, and it'll be jammed," he said. "The new leagues'll be starting."

Hal sipped at a beer and chatted a bit about the Tigers. Spring training was starting. The bartender felt that the Tigers didn't have a chance. "They don't want to pay the money for the big guy" was his theory. "Well, you can't blame 'em—it's gonna cost 'em four, five mil. That's what you gotta pay these days. But so what? You gotta pay money to make money, right? So come August and we're five, six games out and then they'll be thinking pennant, but where you gonna find the big gun? You can't buy him then. Who's gonna sell you a hammerman, or a stopper? The Yankees? Get serious. Am I right?"

Hal looked thoughtful. He knew nothing about baseball and cared less, but he nodded sagely.

"Yer damn right I'm right," the bartender said. " 'Cause when you come down to it, it's always one guy is the right guy. And if you didn't get the right guy in the first place, then yer ass is in a bag. Right? You gotta have the guy who can do the job, not some dipstick who can maybe do the job. So you saved a few bucks in the spring . . . big deal. Now you gotta pay twice as much. Whaddidyou save? You gotta spend money to make money. Am I right?"

"You're right." Hal carried his beer back to the phone and called his service in Los Angeles. He rarely called this service direct. It relayed messages to a service in Omaha, which routed them on to Miami and thence to Fort Smith, Arkansas. The system was cumbersome, but Hal preferred it that way. It was more expensive and slower, but the security was worth it. In this instance, however, time was pressing, and the potential breach of security had to be risked.

"This is Harold Good," he told the Los Angeles operator. He gave her his account number and instructed her not to forward the message this once. Then he called the Fat Man in Detroit.

"Hey, that was fast," the Fat Man said. Hal could hear traffic noises in the background. "Well, what we got is Sid."

Hal felt a chill. Somehow he had known it would be Sid, but he must have suppressed it. "Sid?" he said carefully.

"Yanh. Big Sid. You know him, you know where he lives. It's gotta be tomorrow night the latest. You got any problem with that?"

"I don't think so," Hal said, "but I can't guarantee anything on this short notice. Um, it would be helpful to know what the rush is."

"I thought you didn't like to know the details," the Fat Man said. "You always say you don't wanta know."

"Usually," Hal said, "but it helps to know if Sid's going to be on his guard."

"Nanh, he thinks he's pulling a fast one. But . . . he might be a little jumpy. He's gonna run, see. He's s'posed to be taking a little vacation to the inlands only he didn't buy a round trip ticket. It might not be so easy to find him once he flies. He's over at Carmine's right now, blowing smoke."

"I understand. I'll get right on it. Normally I'd have to have half up front," Hal said calmly, "but under the circumstances it'll have to wait. I'll get back to you."

Hal hung up but didn't immediately leave the phone booth. It was an extremely delicate situation, he realized, absolutely vibrating with danger. A part of his mind said, "Trap!" Sid was talking to Carmine? Hal knew Sid too well . . . and Carmine. Sid couldn't talk to Carmine without letting something show. Maybe it wasn't a trap, but how could he be sure? Well, he'd soon find out. He reminded himself that he'd always felt he was in this game for the sake of the game, the thrills, not for the money. The money was nice, but he really got off on the game. What he felt this instant was that if he'd wanted a game, this was the Big Table.

There was no point in trying to see Sid again, Hal thought, except for the big moment. If the Fat Man wanted Sid, that was it. Either they knew he was in on it, or they didn't. He didn't believe that they were kinky enough to play games. They had called him because he was their ace, the stopper, the hammerman. Hal liked that thought.

He drove back to Kercheval in a light rain. It was nearly eight o'clock and traffic was nil. He turned a block before Sid's street. He knew Sid's place well enough, but he chided himself for not having paid professional attention to the neighborhood. Now he had to spy it out. It was all residential, small single-family frame houses on this street. Most of them had garages on the alley, but they all must have had a couple cars apiece because all the spots on both sides of the street were filled. There was just a narrow driving lane. Everybody was home, it seemed, eating dinner or watching television.

He turned onto Sid's street. Compared with the streets around it, Sid's was at least twice as wide, almost a boulevard. No shortage of parking places here, not that he'd park on the same street where he'd do the job. The houses were correspondingly larger as well. Some of them were in fact mansions, set well back from the street, with enormous lawns and a towering old tree or two. It was interesting, he thought, that this fancy street was here, like an island of luxury and privilege in a sea of modest working-class homes.

Sid was into plenty, of course. But this didn't really seem like Sid's style. Not flashy enough. This was an older neighborhood, originally the homes of lesser executives in the auto industry, just a few blocks from Grosse Pointe, where the real big shots lived. He cruised slowly by Sid's house. It was much like the others: a massive brick pile of no remarkable style, square, ugly, with a broad veranda. It was surrounded by a wrought iron fence, and a brick path curved across the lawn. There were heavy drapes on the front windows, but Hal could see the glimmer of lights. There was no way of telling if Sid had returned home. There were no cars in the drive, but as Hal recalled, there was a large garage, practically a stable, in the back that had been remodeled into apartments for Sid's men. Not more than a half-dozen cars were parked on the street.

He cruised the flanking streets again, but there were still no parking places. It was just as well, he decided. He parked two blocks away, on Kercheval, in a supermarket parking lot, and sat in the car for a long moment.

Now what? Might as well go take a closer look, he thought. He toyed with the idea of leaving the gun in the car. This would just be a preliminary walk-through. But he decided to take it. You never knew. He got out and locked the car, then opened the trunk. It was chilly and damp, but no wind. He drew a pair of dark gloves from his raincoat pocket and slipped them on. They were thin, like another skin. He liked the feel of them. He had tried many kinds of gloves, but these were the best. They were some kind of man-made fiber and had a tactile quality that silk gloves, which he had sometimes used, lacked. These were never slippery like silk, even when wet.

He glanced around. It was much too light here. From the trunk he took the slim case, rather like an attaché case. He set off through the misty rain, swinging the case in a casual manner. He thought he must look like an insurance agent or perhaps like someone's husband coming home late from the office, and the idea pleased him. But then he remembered that it was Sunday night, and he was disappointed. The temperature was about forty, he thought, but the chill was penetrating, nasty, as it often seemed to be in Detroit. But he didn't mind. A good night for something. He smiled.

He stepped into an alley and went about ten paces before stopping to open the case. He picked the revolver, a Smith & Wesson K-22 Masterpiece, out of its molded foam bed and checked to be sure it was loaded. Well, of course it was loaded. He'd loaded the shells himself: .22 Super Vels. He slipped it into his coat pocket along with a couple of HKS Six Second speedloaders. It wasn't particularly noticeable despite its long barrel. He closed the case and set it next to a brick wall. It was invisible in the shadows, and he noted its position from the utility pole. He returned to Kercheval and turned toward Sid's street, gloved hands deep in his coat pockets.

It was after eight. There was no traffic on Sid's street. That was neither good nor bad. Of course, he told himself, he'd choose a later hour to do the job—when people were not walking their dogs, as an old lady was doing across the street. She was heavy and bundled into a long coat and wore a kerchief on her head. The dog, a waddly hound, was practically dragging his ears on the sidewalk, and he stopped to cock a leg at nearly every tree. The old woman tugged him on without stopping. She never saw Hal.

The block was very long, and when he was five or six houses away from Sid's, Hal was pleased to see that there were still no cars parked in front, though a Chevy Suburban sat across the street and down a few houses. The gate to the brick path was padlocked, Hal observed, as was another gate across the drive that ran up alongside the house. Two huge evergreens stood on either corner of the house, and the light still glimmered through the heavy drapes.

He wondered again what fantasies of respectability had motivated Sid to prefer this old neighborhood, and he strolled on. It wasn't usual for him to know the target, but it had happened before. He had no strong feelings about it, but he felt now that he had been foolish to get involved with Sid. The man was not stable, he realized. Impressive at first, in a loud and blustery way, very palsy-walsy. From the instant the Fat Man had said the word, Hal had known that he'd miscalculated. He'd be out some money, but assuming it wasn't a setup, which he told himself it couldn't be, the Fat Man's fee would be ample compensation. Obviously, however, it made the approach to Sid more difficult.

The layout looked promising. The fence was no problem, and with all the trees . . . hell, it was practically like a farmhouse in the country. Nice and private. He couldn't remember if there was a dog, though. No sign of one. He should have paid more attention, he realized. Not very professional of him.

He turned up his collar and strolled on, shoulders hunched against the cold and the mist. He wished he'd worn a hat. A street like this, he felt, you had to be careful not to attract attention. You didn't want anybody looking at you too closely. But except for the woman with the dog, who was gone now, there wasn't a soul in sight. Not a car had passed.

He stopped before reaching the end of the block and turned back. No reason not to check out the front again before taking a look at the alley. The alley would put him in a position to check out the garage quarters. He had a hunch it might be the best way to go in, but he wanted to check again for signs of a dog.

As he approached the gate, his attention wholly concentrated on the yard, a large car swept up behind him so silently that he was surprised when it abruptly pulled across the sidewalk, practically at his heels, and stopped at the closed gate.

He whirled around to see the door of the car open and Mickey Egan bounce out from behind the wheel, evidently bent on opening the locked gate. Egan glanced at Hal and stopped as if noticing him for the first time. His mouth fell open in surprise.

"Hal!" Egan cried out, his face opening into a smile of recognition. "Hey, I thought you was going—" And then he came to his senses. "Oh shit," he said. He jammed his hand into the left shoulder of his coat.

There was nothing for it. Without hesitation Hal drew the .22 and fired. There was little noise, not much more than a sharp pop. Mickey went down. Before Hal could stoop and look into the interior of the car, Sid piled out of the back on the opposite side. He ran out into the street, hunched over but scrambling for his life.

Hal looked over the roof of the car. Of all things another car had chosen this moment to come sizzling down the wet street toward them.

Sid straightened and planted his feet widely, waving his arms as if to halt the oncoming car. Hal swung the long barrel past Sid's head, then back, steadied, and squeezed off three shots. He was certain that all three had hit Sid in the head. The man stumbled forward aided by the impact.

Brakes squealed, and the car swerved to miss the stumbling man. It struck the parked Suburban, then ricocheted across the street, and ran up the sidewalk to slam into Sid's wrought iron fence. It stalled.

Hal looked down. Mickey Egan lay on his side, at Hal's feet, his mouth and eyes open. He looked as if he were frozen in midstride, except that one foot was turned in an awkward way.

Hal thought he was surely dead. But he didn't hesitate to lean down and fire two more shots into the cranium through the left eye. That sure ought to do it, Hal thought. He stepped over the body and into the street, shucking out the empty shells and dropping them into his coat pocket in the same motion with which he withdrew the speedloader and punched six fresh rounds into the cylinder of the K-22. He rolled Sid over with his foot and fired a shot into each eye and one into the mouth. He turned to survey the scene. No movement from the car that was stuck in the fence. That was good. But there was something odd about Sid's car. He couldn't make out what it was. There was no movement. Just something amiss.

Mickey? he thought. But no, Mickey was surely standing on the porch of hell, blind in one eye. Hal watched for a moment, but there was no other movement. He toyed with the idea of walking back the hundred feet or so, to make sure, but he decided it wasn't necessary, and now it was time to go. Anyway, he hadn't contracted for more than Sid, and already he'd tallied one extra in Mickey. Forget it. Move.

He continued on across the street, away from the scene, walking as casually as he could manage. Porch lights were flicking on. Hal glanced back over his shoulder at the car that had hit the fence. The driver's door was being forced open with a creak, and somebody was groggily clambering out. Hal kept walking. In a curious way he seemed only now to hear the sounds of the car's impact with the parked car and the tinkling of glass, then the whump as it hit the fence, even though those things had occurred several seconds earlier. Obviously the noise had penetrated beyond the lawns and muffling pines. Detroiters are sensitive to the sound of a car hitting another car, especially when they have one parked nearby. People stepped out onto their porches. They peered into the gloom and called back into their houses to unseen questioners.

Hal suddenly felt the coolness of the rain on his face, and he shook himself, his head clearing as if he had walked out of a matinee and found himself in unanticipated evening. Then he felt alarmed and anxious, but he controlled the feelings. He quickened his pace until he was out of the range of the disturbance behind him, the porch lights and the cautiously calling voices. He slowed down to a normal pace. He could hear distant sirens.

When he came to a storm drain in the curb, he flung the pistol into it, along with the empty cartridges and the remaining speedloader. A little farther along he peeled off his gloves and tossed them into the branches of a large evergreen.

It was an incredibly long block. At the moment it looked like a mile to the bright light of the through street at the end. He saw the flickering blue lights of a patrol car as it turned onto Sid's street and then came rushing past him. He did not look back but strode resolutely on. He was only a few paces from the corner when a large Chrysler cruiser skidded past the end of the street, halted, and backed up. It turned slowly onto the street and moved ominously toward him. It drew up and a window rolled down. A very bright light blinded him.

"Hey, you!" a voice commanded. "Come over here."

"Me?" To Hal's dismay his voice squeaked.

"Yeah, you. Who the fuck you think? C'm'ere." The front passenger door opened, and a huge man in a raincoat and hat got out. Another man, also in civilian dress and nearly as large, unfolded out the back door of the cruiser. The speaker shined an enormous flashlight full in Hal's eyes. He considered running, but only for a second.

"What is it?" he asked, his voice under control now. He raised a hand to block the light.

The big detective moved closer, not lowering the light. "You just come from down there?" He gestured down the street with the light.

"Down there?"

"What is it, some kinda fucking echo around here?" the voice demanded harshly. "Down there! You see the accident?"

"Accident?"

"All right, that's it," the giant detective said. "Up against the car, asshole. Arms out. Spread your legs. Spread 'em!" He kicked at Hal's legs, the toes of his shoes cracking painfully against Hal's ankle bones, the heavy hand planted firmly in the middle of Hal's back. The detective handed the light to his partner, then roughly ran his hands up and down Hal's ribs and legs, not neglecting to bang against the testicles. Hal winced. The detective snorted and reached around to check Hal's chest and pockets. Finally he released the pressure on Hal's back and stepped away. "All right, get in the car, asshole."

The junior detective held Hal by the wrist and forced his head down with a broad palm so he'd miss the roofline of the car, forcing him into the backseat of the cruiser, next to yet another large plainclothes detective. The smaller detective crowded in next to him, and the boss jumped into the front, making the car sway. He ordered the uniformed driver to go on down to the accident.

When they got there, the boss got out, ordering the others to stay put. He strolled over to the scene. There were two patrol cars now, their lights flickering, casting a weird blue light on Sid's car, the wreck, the bodies, the people gathered across the street on the sidewalk, the young man sitting on the curb. Uniformed policemen were talking to the people, talking to the young man. Hal sat silently, trying to look mildly interested but not too interested. The boss man stalked about, talking to the cops, to the people, gesturing, occasionally laughing.

To add to the circus atmosphere, the ambulance arrived with flashing red lights and a dying siren. Then another car drew up, a black Checker, and two detectives got out, one of them a tall, young black man and the other a somewhat older, good-sized fellow wearing a raincoat and hat. He smoked a cigar. The others deferred to him, pointing out one thing or another, while he said little or nothing but just looked on. Hal concluded that this must be the detective in charge.

More cars arrived with more detectives, and still Hal sat, squeezed in the back of the cruiser between his bulky keepers. A van nosed up to the scene, and more plainclothesmen got out, setting up lights and starting to take pictures of everything, using strobe lights to make it a real light show. The cruiser boss laid a hand on the cigar smoker's arm and pointed back toward the cruiser. The detective listened absently, not looking at the cruiser boss but watching the men around the body of Big Sid. He had a long face with a narrow nose and hooded eyes. His mouth was thin, and when he grimaced, he revealed long, slightly spaced teeth.

A uniformed officer approached the two detectives and called out, "Mul! The medical examiner's here." The detective started to move away. The cruiser boss looked annoyed. "Mul!" he roared, "what about this jerk?" He pointed toward the cruiser.

"Take care of it, Dennis," the detective called back over his shoulder; "you know the procedure." And he disappeared into the throng of men around the body of Sid.

The cruiser rocked as the boss folded himself back into the front seat. "To the Ninth, Stanos," he growled. "Fuckin' Mulheisen, in a cloud as usual."

The driver placed his arm across the back of the seat and backed the cruiser at a reckless speed, dodging around squad cars and police vans, occasionally shouting jocular obscenities at cops who scuttled out of his way. He had to back up for nearly the entire block, but finally he was able to turn around, and they sped away, toward the Ninth Precinct.

As they drove, Hal made one attempt to save the situation. "I didn't see a thing, officer," he said to the big man in front.

The detective responded by saying, "Read him his rights, Doug. Also," to Hal, "shut the fuck up."

Two

"**G**ood riddance to bad rubbish," Detective Inspector Laddy McClain said. He travestied a child's fluttering good-bye wave at the ambulance that was hauling away the remains of Big Sid Sedlacek and Mickey Egan. "And good-bye to you, Mul," he added.

Mulheisen didn't acknowledge that remark. He looked at his cigar, which had gotten wet and no longer tasted very good. He was reluctant to heave it away, however. It had cost too much and was only half-smoked.

"You know something, Laddy . . ." he said finally. He bared his teeth in a grimace that could have been a smile but almost certainly was not. It was these teeth that had earned him the street moniker Sergeant Fang. "Whenever you've got a case you don't like, you shuffle it off on the precinct. I don't complain. But now here's this mob shooting, and you don't even suggest we do the prelim. Now why is that?"

McClain patted him on the shoulder. "I know how overworked and understaffed you guys are, Mul."

"No. That's what you guys are," Mulheisen reminded him. "I've got a couple guys in this outfit who are pretty good. A case like this can make a young detective like Jimmy," he nodded toward a young black man standing nearby, "and it wouldn't hurt promotion chances for some of the older guys either. Now I seem to recall a case about six months ago, where a gunman got shot down in a garage and—"

"That was years ago," Laddy said.

"OK, two years ago," Mulheisen said. He struck a match and held it to the cigar for a moment before puffing it back to life. It still didn't taste right. "But you still owe me for that. And then there's—"

"All right already," McClain said. He laughed and punched Mulheisen's shoulder playfully, but hard. "Do the prelim. Then we'll see."

"Fine. And you'll do the press?"

"I'll do the press," McClain said, rolling his eyes with mock exasperation.

"And keep Buchanan off my ass?"

"Buchanan's your boss, your problem, but I'll have a word with him." He turned and looked up at Big Sid's house. "Isn't this something? A fine citizen like Sid gets blown away in his own driveway, and nobody even comes out to see what happened." He shook his head.

Mulheisen waved Jimmy Marshall over, and the two of them stepped over the knocked-down fence and trudged up to the house. They rang the doorbell and waited a full three minutes, by Jimmy's watch, until someone came. It was a small, dark woman, about thirty years old. She was pretty, or normally she was pretty, Mulheisen felt, but at the moment her eyes had a hollow look, and her face was drawn. With no preliminary she said, "He is dead." It may have been meant to be a question, but it came out a flat statement.

Mulheisen figured if a person were going to be that blunt about it, he could respond as bluntly. "Both of them," he said. "Who are you?"

She said her name was Helen Sedlacek, daughter of the late Sid. Her mother was unable to see them, she said. She had collapsed. A doctor was coming.

Miss Sedlacek was clearly enraged, but she was containing herself admirably. She had a story and she told it straightforwardly.

"We didn't hear anything until we heard the car hit that other car," she said. "I ran into the living room—Ma and me were in the kitchen, getting some food ready in case Papa wanted something when he got home, and—"

"Where had your father gone?" Jimmy Marshall interrupted.

The woman shrugged, her arms crossed under her breasts. She wore a black turtleneck jersey and black jeans. Her face was somber and composed, but her deep-set dark eyes glinted. "We wouldn't know," she said. "Papa doesn't tell women where he's going. It was business, I guess. Or maybe he went to see his whore."

"And who would that be?" Jimmy asked politely, his notebook ready. He glanced at Mulheisen, who moved his head slightly.

"You ask me?" she spat back. "You damn cops don't know? You watch us all the time, I thought you knew everything."

Jimmy did not respond. Finally she said, "Germaine Kouras. She says she's a singer."

"What did you see out the window?" Mulheisen asked while Jimmy scribbled in the notebook.

"I saw Papa's car with the doors open. The trees are in the way. I didn't see Papa or Mickey . . . I thought they might have gone to help the guy who hit the fence. But then I saw somebody lying in the street, and I thought maybe Papa had been hit by the car."

"You didn't see Mickey Egan?" Mulheisen asked.

"No. I started to go out there, but Mama . . . she started to wail. And then Roman came in and told me to take care of her and not to go out."

"Who is Roman?" Mulheisen asked.

"Roman Yakovich," she replied. "He's a . . . an associate of Papa's." She was clenching her small fists and pacing a few steps to one side, then another. Suddenly she asked, "Would you like a drink?" The detectives said no, but when she stalked to a liquor cabinet and poured a large shot of something from a dark bottle, Mulheisen called out that just a couple of fingers would be fine. She threw a wry glance over her shoulder, her black hair flying. "It's slivovitz," she said. "Plum brandy. How about you?" she asked Jimmy.

"He's driving," Mulheisen said. When she brought the drinks, he asked, "What else did Roman have to say?"

She gulped the brandy, then closed her eyes for a second, the muscles of her jaw visibly clenching. After a moment she opened her mouth, and at first she couldn't speak, but finally she said very deliberately, "Ma wanted to know if Papa was dead. Roman just shook his head. Then Ma collapsed."

"Where is Yakovich now?" Mulheisen asked.

"Upstairs, with Ma. Well, what are you going to do about this?"

Mulheisen ignored this. "Your father was shot. You didn't hear any shots?"

"No. Just the crash."

"You didn't see anybody else on the street? No car driving away? No gunman? Nobody walking?" Mulheisen asked.

"No, no, no, for the last time, no. If I saw something, don't you think I would tell you?"

"If you wanted to," Mulheisen said. He drained off the brandy. He almost gasped but managed to ask, in a whispery voice, "You heard a crash?"

"Two crashes. The second crash was the car running into the fence. It wasn't so loud."

"So you ran to the window, and you saw your father's car with the doors open, but you saw no one."

The woman shook her head, a cloud of heavy shoulder-length black hair eclipsing, then exposing, her bone-white face. "I saw Papa's car. At first I thought it was part of the accident. Then I saw the other car in the fence and the car across the street—it was knocked sideways. Then I saw someone in the street."

"Someone lying in the street, you mean?" Jimmy said.

"Yes."

"What about Egan?" Mulheisen asked. "He was lying by the driver's door of your father's car. You didn't see him?"

"No, . . . I don't think so. I don't recall seeing him."

"Do you live here?" Mulheisen asked.

"No. I have a place in Bloomfield Hills," Helen Sedlacek said. "I come over every Sunday, to help Ma with the food."

"Every Sunday?"

"Just about. Ma insists on cooking every Sunday. Friends and relatives drop in and out all day. Some Sundays quite a few. Not so many today."

"How many?" Mulheisen asked.

"I don't know . . . a dozen maybe."

"A dozen people drop by," Mulheisen said. "What do they do?"

"They eat, they talk, they watch television, and of course, with the situation in Serbia, they argue about politics. The kids play, mostly downstairs."

"The situation in Serbia?" Jimmy Marshall said.

"The war. We're all Serbs."

"Was your father involved in politics?" Mulheisen asked.

"No. Well, all Serbs are interested in politics." She sighed. "Too much. But this had nothing to do with politics."

"No?"

"No. You know what it's all about. Not politics."

Mulheisen considered this, then looked at the woman more closely. She was about five feet tall but looked taller on account of the way she carried herself. She was really very pretty, he decided. She was compact and athletic looking, a trim figure.

"So every Sunday you come and help your Ma put on a spread for the folks," Mulheisen said. "Are you married?"

"He's dead," she replied, "a long time ago."

"Mmmm. What kinds of things do you cook? Canapés? Cookies? Little wieners on a toothpick? What?"

She looked at him as if he were crazy. "What kind of food is that? No, no. Liver dumplings, pierogi, *klenedljine od sliv*–plum dumplings. You don't know any of this food," she said with a mixed air of contempt and pity. "It's Serbian. And then there is *sarma*–that's minced ham and pork with onions and garlic and rice, wrapped in cabbage leaves–and there is walnut *povitica* . . . oh, lots of things. It's a lot of work. Ma actually starts cooking on Saturday night."

Mulheisen was intrigued. He would have loved to sample some of these exotic-sounding dumplings–surely there were some leftovers–but there was no way to suggest it, given the circumstances. He sighed. "Was there anything unusual about the guests today?" he asked. "Any strangers? No? What time did they all leave?"

"They were all gone by six, as usual," she said. "This wasn't a Serb thing." She stared at Mulheisen. Then, her voice harsh with bitterness, she said, "You aren't going to do a damn thing, are you? You know who did it. But you don't care. Just a bunch of thugs killing each other off. 'Good riddance,' you say."

"I have no idea who did this," Mulheisen said, "but I expect to find out. Who do you think did it?"

She looked at him with palpable disbelief. "It was Carmine," she cried. "Who else? Not Carmine personally, but one of his hired killers. But they're too big for you, aren't they? You don't mess with the big boys, do you?" She was working herself up to a real blowout, Mulheisen thought, perhaps as a vent for her grief.

"Why would Carmine want to do this?" he asked reasonably. "Was Sid on the outs with Carmine?" She didn't answer. "The last I heard they were good buddies, friendly business associates. Not so?"

She glared at him. Mulheisen sighed. "Look, Miss Sedlacek, I'm not real current on organized crime . . . this, this Mafia dance. I'm just a precinct detective, but I'll be working with the Racket and Conspiracy Squad on this. If you have anything that could help us, why don't you tell me? I can't just go and bust Carmine, or any other citizen, because you say he hired a killer."

"But you know all about him," she burst out. "You watch him and the rest of us all the time! You know everything about us, you . . ." Suddenly she was incapable of speech. Her throat seemed to lock and her eyes blazed. She stepped forward and punched Mulheisen right in the chest, just where the abdomen meets the rib cage. Her tiny fist was like a rock, and Mulheisen reeled, staggering backward, gasping for breath.

Jimmy Marshall pounced. He whipped the woman's arms behind her back, and before Mulheisen had recovered, Jimmy had her cuffed and was holding her by the hair with her hands yanked up between her shoulder blades. Her neck was long, and her throat pulsed, her breasts thrust forward, heaving.

"Whoo!" Mulheisen wheezed, leaning against the wall with an outstretched arm. He looked over his shoulder at the little woman who stood firmly but belligerently in Jimmy's grasp, her legs set apart, her chin thrust out. "Hang onto her, Jimmy," he warned hoarsely. "I'm going upstairs."

It was a dodge, to get out of the room so that he could lean against a wall and knead his thorax and indulge the pain out of sight of its inflicter and his young assistant. When he felt better, he climbed the stairs. By now the doctor had arrived and given Mrs. Sedlacek a sedative. She was a dumpy, gray-looking lady, tucked up in a large bed with a satin comforter. She was sound asleep, snoring slightly. Roman Yakovich sat in a chair by the door, watching her stolidly. He looked hewn out of granite himself. He stood to greet Mulheisen.

"I didden know nothing aboudit," Yakovich said. "I was watchin' TV in my room. I didden even hear nothing."

"So how come you ran out to the street?" Mulheisen asked. He was fairly certain that Yakovich was packing a large pistol in a shoulder holster.

"I didden go down to the street," Yakovich said. "Just down the drive a liddle. I dunno why. I just all of a sudden it was like I knew the boss was in trouble. I ran oudda the door, and I seen Sid's car at the gate, with all the doors open. I seen Mickey on the ground. And then I seen the boss in the street. There wasn't nothin' to do. I come in the house to see if Mrs. Sid and Liddle Helen was OK. Then the cops came."

It was a nice compact statement. Mulheisen admired it. It was hewn out of granite, too, not a seam showing.

"Who else did you see?" Mulheisen asked. "Did you recognize the gunman?"

"I didden see nobody, just a car smashed into the fence and some kid trying to get out. I thought I better see about Mrs. Sid and Liddle Helen."

"No other car?" Mulheisen asked. "What about Sid's car? Who was with him?"

"Mickey," Yakovich said.

"You said the car doors were open," Mulheisen said. "All the doors?"

Roman frowned as if focusing his thoughts. "Well, most of 'em, anyways."

"Most of them? Which doors were open?"

Yakovich's frown faded. He had decided what he'd seen. "All the doors was open except for the passenger door in the front. That's right. The boss always sits in the back."

Mulheisen digested this. "So who opened both the back doors? Sid didn't get out both doors."

Yakovich shrugged. "Maybe it was just the driver's door and the back door on the right . . . or the left." He frowned and looked down at his hands. "The back door on the left, if you was looking at the car from the front."

"Not both back doors, then?" Mulheisen said.

Yakovich looked uneasy. "I think so, but I dunno. I guess not."

Mulheisen nodded. "Little Helen," he said, "is she always so, ah, feisty?"

Roman grinned. "She gotta temper, eh? But she don't mean nothing by it. Liddle Helen is an angel. She must of said something, eh? She's mad, I guess. So would you."

"What's your theory, Roman? Who did this? One of the Serbs, maybe? Carmine?"

Roman's face had set like concrete on a dry August day. He shrugged. "Who knows. Kids, maybe?"

Mulheisen didn't know whether to laugh or spit. "OK, Roman, let's go."

"Go? Whadda you mean? To the precink? Who's gonna look after Mrs. Sid?"

"The angel," Mulheisen said.

Downstairs Mulheisen stuck his head into the living room. Jimmy was still holding onto Helen Sedlacek, though not by the hair. He stood to one side behind her, grasping her firmly by the arm to avoid any kicks to the groin.

"Roman is coming over to the precinct with us," Mulheisen said. "Miss Sedlacek will have to stay and look after her mother. You can let her go . . . as soon as I'm out the door."

Three

They called the precinct doorman Jellybelly, and Hal could see why. He had an enormous belly, and his name tag read Lovabella. He was an amiable man and quite capable, treating the prisoners and witnesses with an admirable combination of efficiency and simple, if rough, courtesy. He didn't yell at the prisoners, he didn't buddy up to the detectives and the patrolmen, he didn't ignore you if you had a legitimate question, and he paid no attention if you were just being a pain in the butt. But he was tremendously busy. Hal wondered if all Sunday nights were like this; he wouldn't have thought so. The little booking room of the Ninth Precinct was bustling, however, and from the adjacent holding pen Hal was able to observe the whole process.

This business engrossed him and served at least two purposes. It stirred him from a dangerous passivity, which had set in the minute he had been picked up, and it engaged him in the necessary process of escape. It had the further virtue of preventing the onset of anxiety. That's the way Hal saw it. Perhaps some of these reactions were the normal result of killing another human being; Hal wasn't sure what *normal* meant. In the past he had experienced many different reactions, most frequently a manic exhilaration, which could possess him for hours, sometimes longer. After his second—or was it his third?—killing he had roamed the streets of Chicago for three nonstop days, getting drunk, sobering up, getting drunk again, eating four or five meals a day, around the clock, until he finally fell down in exhaustion. Since then it never gripped him for more than a few hours, and when it wore off, he would be mildly depressed and quite tired. Once he had simply forgotten the whole business about a half hour after the killing—once he was safely away. He'd eaten dinner, gone back to the motel, and slept peacefully and then taken a plane home. Sometime during the day it had struck him that he hadn't actually thought about the killing since it had been accomplished. He had never encountered actual danger to himself in the aftermath of a killing, and it irritated him to have to endure it now. He was glad to distract himself by observing the minute details of the booking and holding process.

It was already ten o'clock and the pen was full. The few benches that ringed the room were occupied, and several men were standing; one man was slumped on the floor, drunk to the point of insensibility. Most of the men were at least a little drunk, and some of them were angry and aggressive—perhaps they had been arrested for brawling—but there were four men besides Hal who had been brought in as witnesses, sober and rather disdainful of their chance companions. Hal assumed that, like himself, some of them had been picked up simply for being in the neighborhood of the Sedlacek shooting. One in particular, a short, noisy fellow with a bristly mustache, was constantly and loudly haranguing Jellybelly and any other officer within hearing range: it was all a mistake, the loudmouth claimed; he was an important man; he knew even more important men who would make life a misery for the cop who didn't let him out, right away; he had a lot of money; he had places to go, things to do, people to see; he had to make another phone call; he demanded to see the precinct commander.

Officer Lovabella had tolerated a lot in his time. He had accepted the nicknames; he didn't wince at Fatso, or even at Lard Bucket, but he was damned if he was going to put up with "Hey, I'm talking to you, you fat fucking tub of guts. Is your head so full of lard you can't hear?" He called for a detective, and when he came, Jellybelly said, "Get this noisy son of a bitch out of here before I slip and fall on him." And that was the last they saw of the crank.

Hal considered the tactic. It had a definite effect, but since he didn't know where the loudmouth had been taken or what was happening to him, he didn't think he could chance it. It seemed unlikely that the police would simply let him go. But time was pressing. Hal had to get out. He had already been cursorily interviewed by a booking officer, who had done little more than read him his rights and determine that he had no good reason to be discharged without talking to a detective. Hal did not want to talk to a detective. He wasn't too concerned about his identification; it would hold up to a preliminary inspection and perhaps even to a second look. They hadn't fingerprinted him, and the cards and driver's license in his wallet, which was presently in a manila envelope in the property locker, would identify him as Harold Good, a resident of Iowa City, Iowa. Law-abiding, no criminal record. He praised his own good sense for not having traveled with his real ID. He was also glad that, as usual, he'd had the foresight to place a hundred-dollar bill in each shoe. But he knew that any lengthy interview with a sharp detective would raise some questions, and in a murder investigation, especially one as splashy as this one promised to be, he would be held until the police were satisfied they knew who he was and what he had been doing on Big Sid Sedlacek's street at the time Sid had been shot to death.

Hal had made no phone calls. He hadn't even considered calling the Fat Man and asking for a lawyer; it just wasn't done. You don't call. The Fat Man wouldn't know him. And there wasn't as yet any plausible reason for an innocent stroller to call a lawyer. Anyway, even if he knew the name of a lawyer in Detroit, he didn't think one would be useful to him. No, the options were, one, try to chat his way out of custody when he got to see a detective, or two, get out right now.

Watching Jellybelly as he bustled about, mildly joking with patrolmen or responding patiently to the detainees' entreaties, Hal concluded that bribery was no go. Too many people around, too risky, poor odds. He caught himself staring longingly at the booking card that bore his name, nestling in the iron rack with twenty others. If he could just get that card and his personal effects, . . . but that was a silly dream.

He began to hear, however, snatches of conversation from the booking room concerning the crowded condition of the holding pen. Evidently they anticipated another influx of prisoners from some scheduled operation—a raid was going down later that night. Jellybelly was talking to a higher ranking officer, who suggested moving some of the prisoners to the inner cells, but the doorman vetoed that. There wasn't enough room there either. The captain came over and peered into the bull pen, his nose wrinkled against the odor of vomit and urine and unwashed men—there was only a single open urinal in one corner, and it was partially clogged with paper towels and cigarettes.

"Black Hole of Calcutta," the captain said. "Get 'em out of here, and maybe we can hose it down before the next bunch arrives."

"I'll call for a wagon," Jellybelly said. "We can send the drunks downtown to night court, and the rest of them, with the ones from the sweep, can go to early sessions."

The captain agreed. Hal was unsure what this meant, but he sensed an opportunity. He turned to a man who looked to be sixty years old but was probably younger, leaning against the bars. "Looks like they're going to move us," Hal said.

The fellow, unshaven and reeking of some alcohol-enhanced wine drink, opened a bleary eye. "Yanh? Tha's good. More room downtown." He closed his eye and groaned softly, sagging against the bars.

"What happens downtown?" Hal asked.

"Nothin'. Judge fines you. Public intox."

"Really? What's the fine?"

The alky shrugged. "Don' know. Never paid it. Ten days in DeHoCo . . . maybe more, maybe less. Sometimes they get busy and just dismiss it . . . throw you out." The old guy grinned faintly and lapsed back into a kind of upright slumber.

Hal sighed. He wondered how accurate this bum's information could be. No way was Hal going to the Detroit House of Correction, but if it was just a matter of a fine . . . There was an element of chance, here, but he decided it was worth it. He surveyed the remainder of his cell mates. Most of them were black, and he wasn't; the rest were a pretty raggedy and sorry-looking lot. Except for one man. A man in a suit and a white shirt, his tie presumably taken from him, as Hal's had been. Not a bad suit, either . . . off the rack, but an expensive rack and with some essential tailoring to fit the bulky torso of the wearer. The suit was a mess now, flecked with food and dirt, even a little blood. He appeared to be in his early forties, tousled and tumbled and stunned drunk. He'd been brought in a half hour earlier, mumbling and dazed. He'd had a hell of a lot to drink somewhere, and probably not with the people he'd started out with, certainly not with people who knew him or cared about him.

Jellybelly had cleared a spot on the benches for the man and had more or less propped him in the corner. He could not have stood up, or even sat on the floor, without simply toppling over. His fat face was tomato red, and he breathed like a foot pump. His puffy hands lay open in his lap.

Hal took his time working his way over. He looked down at the raggedy man who was crunched in next to the fat man and said, "What's the matter with your buddy? He sick?"

The raggedy man looked up, his eyes yellowish in a face as dark and grainy as an old football. He had a scab forming on his cheek, and he was wearing three shirts, all of them foul. He looked at the fat man, then back at Hal, and shrugged. "Ain' mah buddy."

Hal leaned down to the drunk and said in his ear, "You OK, bud? You all right?"

"Hanh?" The drunk struggled to lift his head, one eye cracked to a slit. "Wha'sa matter?" he said. "I'm all ri'. Gimme a . . ." He cleared his throat and straightened up slightly, opening the other eye. ". . . I'll have a little Scotch." He spoke this last with surprising clarity, adding, "Uh, make it a double while you're at it." Then he collapsed, his eyes clanging shut. The raggedy man grinned through missing teeth and looked up at Hal.

Hal stared back at the black man until he looked away, nervously. Hal leaned down to the drunk again and said, "What's your name, pal?"

No response. Hal took the man by the ear and twisted it until the man yelped and looked at him. "Lea' me 'lone," he said.

Hal twisted the ear harder. "What's your name?" he asked.

"My name?" Even with the pain the eyes merely flickered open and shut, but he finally said, "Fogarty. Nice to meetcha."

Hal released the ear, and the man slumped back into oblivion. Hal straightened up and stared down at the black man again. The black man did not look away this time. There was even a hint of a smile on his lips. He had a high, receding forehead and tight ridges of hair. "What are you grinning at, steeple head?" Hal said.

"I'm jes' natcherly happy, bro," the man said.

Hal gazed at him for a moment, then turned away and squeezed through the standees until he was able to lean against the wall. After a while he ruffled his light brown hair with his hands, leaving it disheveled. A few moments later he eased his shirt tails out and unzipped his fly until it was half-open. After that he concentrated on the activity in the booking room.

Eventually Jellybelly pushed up to the rack that held the booking cards and began to pluck several out of their slots. He examined them briefly and stuffed two or three back, including Hal's, and selected replacements. He scanned them all and then went to the personal-effects locker and ruffled through the envelopes while consulting the cards. When he had accumulated the matching envelopes, he signaled to a couple of patrolmen who came to assist him. One of them opened the door to the parking lot. Cold air wafted into the room, relieving the funk, and the men looked up expectantly.

Jellybelly approached the door of the holding pen. "Awright, listen up, fellas," he said. "Some a youse are going downtown. When I call your name, sing out and come forward." He unlocked the door and parked his massive hulk in the opening. He looked at his cards. "Carter!" A skinny fellow squeezed through to the door. Jellybelly took him firmly by the wrist and stepped aside to hand the man to one of the patrolmen who escorted him through the doors to the parking lot.

"Dexter! Fogarty!" Hal pushed forward and passively permitted himself to be led to the paddy wagon. He sat down on a bench in the wagon next to Carter. For the next few minutes he sat tensely, waiting for Jellybelly or one of the patrolmen to come out and get him. All it would take would be for the drunk to wake up or for Steeple Head to say something to Jellybelly. Then the fat would indeed be in the fire, for the detectives would be very interested to know why Hal had attempted to walk using another man's identity.

Steeple Head suddenly appeared in the door to the wagon. He peered in, searching the faces; then he was pushed forward by an impatient hand, and he sat next to the door. The door was slammed shut and locked. It was dark in the van, but a little light filtered in through the barred windows of the door. The raggedy man stared at Hal, grinning slightly. Hal relaxed. The officers' voices sounded outside, the front doors opened and closed, and the engine started. They began to move.

Within forty-five minutes they were downtown, processed, and let into a larger bull pen off a busy courtroom. Hal sat down on a bench and eased off a shoe to massage his foot. The raggedy man flopped down next to him.

"What it is, Fogarty," the man said. He grinned. His breath was stunning.

"OK, Steeple Head, what's your real name?" Hal asked, kneading his foot.

"Mowfitang," the man said.

Hal didn't get it. "Mowfitang? What kind of name is that?"

"Tha's mah name, bro. Maffitan."

"Maffitan? Malfitan? That it? Malfitan? So, what brings you to this cheery camp, Steeple Head?" Hal slipped the shoe back on and set his foot on the floor.

"Drinkin', bro," Malfitan said. He looked at Hal and waited, yellow and black stumps of teeth showing in his slack mouth.

Hal looked disgustedly at him for a long moment, then said, "Yeah . . . I'll see what I can do . . . brother." Malfitan nodded and moved away.

Not long after, they were mustered into a long line in the court-room itself and several young attorneys began to work the line, asking, "Need representation? Want an attorney?" When one of them reached him, Hal said, "Yeah. I want representation. What's the deal?"

The lawyer, a young fellow in a pin-striped suit, took him by the arm and drew him out of the line. "What's your name?" he asked.

"Fogarty." Hal tried to act a little dull, as if still slightly drunk or badly hung over.

The lawyer consulted a clerk. He turned back. "OK, Fogarty, it's public intox. They don't seem to have any record on you. You can plead guilty, and I can probably have you out of here in fifteen minutes. OK?"

"How much?" Hal asked, groggily, fingering the hundred-dollar bill in his pocket.

"Including my fee, probably fifty bucks," the lawyer said.

Hal nodded. "OK. Also my buddy back there . . . Malfitan." He nodded toward the black man. The lawyer glanced at Malfitan, then to Hal, and raised an eyebrow, but he went to talk to the man. He returned shortly. "It'll run you a hundred."

"Do it," Hal said.

A half hour later he was standing on the street in downtown Detroit, near 1300 Beaubien, police headquarters. He carried a manila envelope that contained the necktie, wallet, and ballpoint pen that belonged to Henry J. Fogarty. There was more than a hundred dollars in the wallet, along with credit cards. Mr. Fogarty appeared to be a businessman from Youngstown, Ohio, probably attending a convention, Hal surmised. He flipped through all the stuff while he waited for his buddy Steeple Head. It amazed him that no one had bothered to compare the picture on Fogarty's driver's license with Hal's face. The signature was no problem—Fogarty had been far too drunk to sign anything legibly, and Hal had not attempted anything fancy.

Malfitan appeared on the street. He looked a little surprised to find Hal waiting for him. He approached warily. "Hey, bro, thanks for jumpin' me out," he said.

Hal smiled and laid his hand on Malfitan's shoulder. It was thin, almost birdlike. Hal dug his fingers in, deep. The smaller man groaned and tried to pull away, but Hal held him fast.

"It's good to have brothers," Hal said. "I'm glad I could help." He dug his fingers in deeper. Malfitan fought down a cry of agony. Then Hal waved a bill in front of the man's face. "You recognize this dude, Steeple Head? It's Ben Franklin. I look just like Ben, don't I? Don't I? That's good." He released the pressure and tucked the bill into Malfitan's hand. "Just remember, Steeple Head, if anyone asks, I look a lot like Ben."

Within the hour Hal was eating sausage and eggs with hash browns at a little restaurant at Metropolitan Airport and perusing the morning *Free Press*. There was a ticket to Chicago O'Hare in his pocket, made out to Henry J. Fogarty. He put the paper down and sipped his coffee. He was fatigued after his long day and night. But he didn't feel bad. He felt good, in fact. He had faced up to a regular nightmare of problems, starting with his journey to Detroit in the first place, the meeting with Big Sid, the call from the Fat Man, the hit, the arrest, the escape . . . He had seen one hell of a day, and he'd coped right down the line. If he weren't so damn tired, he had every right to jump and dance and shout, "Hallelujah!"

In retrospect, he had only one regret. He hadn't killed Steeple Head. If only he'd had a gun. At one point he had even considered asking Steeple Head to get a gun for him. He had no doubt the man could have done it. But it would have involved more people, more time, more complications in an already hideously complicated day. And then he would have had to find a place where he could kill the son of a bitch . . . No, he had done the right thing in simply giving the man money. It wasn't the ideal resolution, but it was the best under the circumstances.

Four

Mulheisen wasn't so sure he'd done his men a favor in wheedling the investigation out of Homicide. Roman Yakovich's statement was unhelpful. He had no trace of powder or nitrates on his hands, indicating that he had probably not fired a gun lately. He had a valid permit to carry the Thermodynamics .357 revolver. Helen Sedlacek's statements supported his story that he had run out of his apartment at the back of the house only after the shootings. He had appeared in the house almost immediately. There was nothing to hold him on.

Detective Sergeant Maki had been to the hospital to interview the young man who had driven into Sid's fence. This fellow knew nothing. All he'd seen was a car drawn up to enter a driveway. This had been no problem to him, but then a man had run out into the street, waving his arms. The kid had swerved to avoid hitting the man and instead had struck the parked Suburban. He couldn't recall a thing after that, not even hitting the fence. He had not regained consciousness until he was in the ambulance. He had heard no shots. He hadn't seen anybody but the man waving his arms, and he couldn't even say for certain where that man had come from, although he naturally assumed that he'd come from the car by the gate. He had a vague impression that the interior lights of that car were on, that doors were open, and it may be that the driver was standing outside his opened door, . . . but he couldn't be sure. Maybe he'd dreamed it.

Sergeant Maki's preliminary report lay on Mulheisen's desk. The kid was almost certainly not a party to the shooting, but Maki was a methodical man who would dig until there was no longer a reason to dig. But as far as Mulheisen was concerned, the kid was already in the clear.

Jimmy Marshall, sitting across the desk, pointed out the importance of the kid's statement that he was quite certain he had not seen any vehicle other than Big Sid's car approaching or preceding him on the block.

Mulheisen agreed. "Sid was running. He was shot in the street. Maybe the killer was in the car with Sid when they drove up. Maybe he pulled a gun. Maybe Sid jumped out and ran. The killer gets out, shoots, and then does this eye-shooting business. But if he was in the car, why would he wait until just that moment to make his move? No, he was on the street, at Sid's gate—a perfect place to wait for his target. Obviously Sid was set up. The killer would probably have a car waiting, perhaps with a driver, on the next block or something, Maybe not. Jensen and Field made a list of every car parked within two blocks, just in case the killer wasn't able to get to his car before the patrol arrived on the scene—which was how quick, do we know?"

Jimmy consulted a sheet on which he had constructed a rough timetable of events. "Sager and Barnes were cruising up Mack, just a few blocks away. They were at the scene within one minute of being called. The Big Four also entered from Mack, a minute or two later."

"That's quick," Mulheisen said. "That's a long block. If you only have a minute to run or walk it . . . Well, Jensen is running a check on the computer now for something interesting on the cars. It's a long shot, but . . ." He picked up a sheaf of papers and flipped through them. "Now, here's a half dozen so-called witnesses picked up in the area. None of them saw anything. It looks like Dennis just scooped up anyone he saw walking." Under his breath he muttered, *"Schwachkopf."*

"Beg pardon?" Jimmy said. He was a slender man with a V-shaped face. His eyes itched from Mulheisen's cigars, and he wanted desperately to go to the bathroom and rinse his contact lenses, but he didn't want to say so. "Is that German?"

"NATO Deutsch," Mulheisen said. He flapped the sheaf of witness reports. "This is what comes of designating the Big Four as detectives." This was a sore point with Mulheisen. The unit in question consisted of squads of oversize plainclothes officers who cruised around town in big Chryslers with a Thompson submachine gun on prominent display in the front seat. All of the members were at least six feet four inches in height. Mulheisen understood their function as intimidators but resented their status as detectives. In the Ninth Precinct the Big Four was led by Dennis Noell.

Jimmy Marshall riffled through the Big Four's list of pickups. "Nothing familiar here," he said, "but they got there pretty quick. One of these people ought to have seen something." He stopped at one page. "Here's a guy named Good. Just a prelim. Did you talk to him?"

"Never heard of him," Mulheisen said. He looked at the sheet. "It doesn't say he was discharged. No statement. Check it out, Jimmy." He quickly sifted the remaining reports. "Nah. Not even Dennis the Menace would let a professional killer slip through his paws. These guys—and one woman, who was walking her dog, for crying out loud—they look legit. They saw nothing . . . but each other. Anyway, we've got their addresses." He paused again at the report on Hal Good. "Good's the one who's staying at a motel, out on Eight Mile? Doesn't say what he was doing in the neighborhood. 'Taking a walk.' "

"If you want, I can ask Stanos about it," Jimmy said. Stanos was the Big Four driver and Jimmy's former patrol partner. It was a curious relationship; the two men had nothing in common but a few months of sharing a squad car. But on one evening, responding to a man-with-a-gun call, Stanos had shot down the man just as the man was about to shoot Jimmy. It was not something Marshall would ever forget.

Mulheisen nodded. "Look into it. Where is Dennis, anyhow? He should have followed this up. Maybe he's talking to the guy right now. What you and I need to concentrate on is the mob end of this. I've got to talk to Andy, down at Racket-Conspiracy, but that'll have to wait until tomorrow. What time is it, anyway?"

"It is tomorrow," Jimmy said. "Nearly three."

Mulheisen sighed and got up. "Make a note to find out from Sid's girlfriend if he was over there this evening and what time and who was with him. It would be nice to know where he'd been just before he almost got home. And Roman, he said something that seems odd to me."

"What's that?"

"It doesn't sound like much, but he said all the doors of the car were open when he came down the drive toward it. He saw the bodies and he retreated to the house."

"You mean why didn't he go to his boss or at least go check out the street?"

"No. I think he understood the situation immediately. No way he was going out there. But he said all the doors were open. Then he corrected himself. Only the right front door was not open. Now that suggests—"

"There was a third man in the car," Jimmy said. "The killer wasn't on the street. He was in the car."

Mulheisen shook his head. "I don't see it. If he's in the car, even if for some reason he wants to do it at the gate, why let Egan out, or Sid? Why not shoot them both, Egan from behind, before they get out? Egan actually had his gun half out of his holster when he fell, you know."

"Well, you've always said that these hoods aren't as smart as people seem to think," Jimmy observed.

"That's true," Mulheisen said, "but contract killers can be different. I don't think you've had any experience with hired killers, have you? They're not necessarily Mensa members, but at least a few have the sense not to associate full-time with the mob, which argues a certain intelligence. It wouldn't pay to underestimate them. What this guy was up to we may never know, but it looks like something went wrong. It's too soon to speculate."

"We should have brought the broad in," Jimmy said. "She's not telling us everything. She had to have seen something."

"She's not a broad," Mulheisen said. "And anyway, we can always talk to her tomorrow. Let's finish this up and get out of here. Let me get some coffee first," he said. As he went out the door, Jimmy followed and locked it behind him before nipping down the hall in the opposite direction.

Out in the reception area there was little going on. An officer stood listening to a heavyset black woman, who was bending his ear about "bad boys." Otherwise there was just a white woman sitting on a bench beyond the railings, dozing as she waited for someone. Mulheisen glanced at her. She looked rather attractive, although with her head down it was hard to tell. He went on behind the desk to the squad room. Detectives Jensen and Field were hanging around a computer terminal. They looked up and shook their heads, simultaneously, as they did most things.

"What about the grounds search?" Mulheisen asked, draining a cup of sludgelike coffee from the urn.

"Ayeh's on it," Jensen said.

Mulheisen sighed and went out. As he passed the reception area, he took another look at the white woman. She lifted her head wearily. She was very attractive, he noted. She appeared to be in her early thirties and was well dressed in a modest, middle-class style. But her bearing was different from that of most people one saw in precinct lobbies— rather prim, but in a disciplined, acquired manner, as if she were a professional model, perhaps. She wore a new raincoat, which almost managed to conceal her figure. A bright kerchief was folded in her clenched fingers. A mass of champagne-blond hair surrounded a soft, pretty face, which was drawn with concern. She had nice legs, Mulheisen noticed.

She looked familiar, but not in any usual sense, not as if she were a woman he had seen any time in the past few days or weeks. He was sure he would have remembered her face if he had seen it before. Rather, he felt a kind of visceral lurch, as of something recollected from years before. It wasn't a pleasant feeling somehow, and he repressed it, walking on with only a faint nod in the woman's direction, as if he were embarrassed.

Jimmy had reopened the office and sat waiting. Mulheisen slumped down behind the desk. He started to say something but couldn't remember what it was. He thought about the woman. She was familiar. It seemed to him now that she was familiar in the way public personages seem familiar: you don't know them, but you've seen their faces so often—on television, on magazine covers—that you know their features better than you know those of your Aunt Polly, who moved to Cleveland ten years ago. No doubt that accounts for the notorious heritancy of the rube who spots a famous movie star in a restaurant. "Hey, didn't you used to be . . ."

He got up and went to the door and peeked down the hall. There was no one there, just a line of chairs with a shiny stripe of grease on the wall above them, where the heads of suspects and witnesses had rested. The reception area itself was not visible from this vantage.

"What is it?" Jimmy asked.

"Nothing. I'll be right back." Mulheisen walked back down the hall and looked around the corner.

The woman looked directly at him, then her face lighted up. "Mul!"

Mulheisen still didn't recognize her. She got up and walked toward him. The raincoat flowed open, and he noticed right away that it had, indeed, concealed a good deal.

"Oh, Mul," she said, coming right to him, "I'm so glad to see you." She was glad, too. Her eyes shone.

"Uh, yeah, good to see you, too," he said. "Is it . . . is there something . . . ?" She was a little older than he'd thought. Maybe thirty-five, possibly even his own age. But she wore it a lot better than he did. He knew he knew her, he just couldn't place her. But there was that little kick in the gut again.

"It's my husband, Eugene," she said.

"Unh-hunh. What's the problem?" The woman was fairly beaming at him, though a shadow of concern still played across her face.

"Do you work here?" she asked. She looked uncertainly from him to the desk sergeant, who was looking on.

"This is Mrs. Lande, Mul," the desk man called across. "She's been waiting for her husband since . . ."—he glanced up at the electric clock over the door—". . . about nine o'clock."

"Nine o'clock!" Mulheisen raised a hand to forestall the woman, walking aside with the desk man. "What's the deal, Larry?"

"Lande was one of the witnesses on that, uh, accident," the sergeant said in a low voice. They had their backs to the woman, who waited beyond the railing.

"Where is he now?" Mulheisen asked. He was still racking his brain, trying to figure out if he knew any Mrs. Lande. He couldn't think of any and wondered how in hell he could forget a face and a body like hers.

The sergeant shrugged. "I just came on shift at midnight. Barnes said he was . . ." He nodded toward the detectives' rooms.

Mulheisen turned back to the woman. "Mrs. Lande, I understand your—"

"Mul! You don't recognize me, do you?" She looked disappointed. "It's Bonny. Bonny Wheeler." She smiled at him plaintively.

He recognized her instantly, painting a teenage face over the one before him. It wasn't remarkably different, except that it hadn't been so poised twenty years ago, so well made up, so . . . glamorous. Bonny Wheeler's hair had been a darkish blonde, not champagne. But then she'd had that same plaintive look of helplessness, a maddening self-deprecation that had undermined her beauty. Mulheisen had hated that look. It evoked unworthy feelings, a kind of unjustified annoyance, even anger. He found himself wanting to admonish the girl, even scold her, for so idiotically denying her beauty.

Bonny Wheeler had made boys think bad things. No doubt it wasn't her fault, but there it was. She confused men. She seemed at once alluring and debased. There was an underlying innocence overlaid with an aroma of sensual experience. Bonny Wheeler had caused a lot of anguish to more men and boys than just Mulheisen.

"Bonny," he said softly. "I'm sorry, Bonny, I . . . I just didn't . . . It's the context . . ." He gestured around them at the grubby precinct house with its atmosphere of daily misery and criminality. "So, it's your husband, eh? What's his name again?"

"Eugene. Oh, don't apologize, Mul. I understand." She had the same old soft, yielding voice, always too apologetic. "It's all some sort of mistake. Eugene called me and said they were holding him for identification. Why, he couldn't figure out. He went out without his wallet, just to get me some things from the store. And then somehow he was stopped by the police. I brought his wallet down, but they haven't released him. I don't know what's going on."

Now, from the release of tension, having found a friendly and sympathetic face among all the unyielding ones she had encountered,

Bonny was on the verge of tears. Mulheisen came around the railing and led her back to her seat.

"Sergeant," he called, "bring Mrs. Lande some coffee. Not that old stuff; make some fresh. Listen, Bonny, you just sit here, and I'll go see what the problem is."

"Oh, thank you, thank you, Mul. You're so sweet, so kind," she murmured—too grateful, as ever. He hurried away.

Jensen and Field didn't know anything about Lande. Maki and Ayeh had gone, as had the Big Four. The blue men knew nothing about it. Jellybelly was busy with paperwork, but he responded promptly to Mulheisen's inquiries. He only had one man in the bull pen, a snoring drunk lying on the bench.

"That's Good," Jellybelly told Mulheisen. "I sent the rest downtown so we could clean the joint out a little bit. We got a blind-pig raid going down." He glanced at the clock. "They oughta be in here in about a half hour, forty-five minutes."

"That's Good?" Mulheisen said. "Where's Lande? Back in the lockup?"

Jellybelly paged through his cards until he found Lande's. He wrinkled his brow, staring at it. "Now where did I . . . he's . . . where in the hell did I put that . . . ?" Suddenly he clapped a hand to his forehead. "Holy shit! I forgot all about that little prick! He was makin' so much noise, Mul, I hada stick him in one a the 'terrogation rooms."

Mulheisen sighed. "All right, Art. Let me have him . . . and his paperwork."

"Detectives got the prelim," Jellybelly said. He removed Lande's personal-effects envelope from the locker and made Mulheisen sign for it, then led the way down the hall to one of the interrogation rooms. He unlocked it and stood aside. Lande was curled up on the floor, snoring, but he awoke quickly and bounced to his feet. He rubbed his eyes furiously, then immediately launched a tirade, in a rasping voice.

"Jesus Christ! What the hell time is it? How long I been here? What the hell is this shit? What time is it?"

Eugene Lande was a short, stocky man with a brushy mustache. He was the sort of man who always looked annoyed, but Mulheisen considered that he was tired and not unreasonably angry. Still, he hardly looked like the sort of man one would expect Bonny to marry. Mulheisen took him down the hall to his office.

Jimmy looked on, puzzled, as Mulheisen waved Lande into a chair, then opened the personal-effects envelope, and shook out a penknife, a book of matches from Maiolani's Bar and Grill, and a small amount of cash in bills and coins. "This is Eugene Lande," Mulheisen said to Jimmy. "Big Four." He uttered the last with a meaningful look.

Jimmy flipped through the list. All the while Lande continued to complain, demanding to know why he was being held, where was his wife, what time was it. Jimmy found the report. "He was seen by Doug it looks like," Jimmy said. He handed the report to Mulheisen. It appeared that Lande was meant to be discharged as having no relevance to the investigation, but Detective Doug Joseph had evidently not notified Jellybelly.

Mulheisen handed the report to Jimmy with a curt nod and went back down the hall to Bonny.

"Did you find him? Is he all right?" Bonny stood at the railing.

"Sure, he's all right," Mulheisen assured her, "but there are a few details. It shouldn't take long. Uh, you say he went out without his wallet?"

"Yes, I've got it here." She dug it out of her purse. "I tried to give it to them, but they said to wait, and I've been waiting and waiting and waiting . . ."

Mulheisen took the wallet and flipped it open. The face on the driver's license looked like the man in his office. Brown hair with a widow's peak; thick, dark eyebrows and a bushy mustache under a slightly bulbous nose; a narrow face. The ears were set close to the head. Height, 66 inches; weight, 148. Age . . . Mulheisen calculated quickly—thirty-six . . . a few years younger than himself and Bonny.

"How long have you been married to Eugene, Bonny?"

"Six years. Is anything wrong?"

Mulheisen looked up and smiled—an attempt at pleasantness that fell into a weedy garden of long teeth. "No. I don't think so." He was amazed at her appearance. She didn't look twenty years older . . . scarcely ten.

"You say Eugene went out to the store. What time was this?"

"It was . . . oh, seven. I had started dinner. Why? What's happened?"

"Nothing. He was picked up in an area quite a ways from your home." He glanced at the address on the driver's license, an apartment in Harper Woods. Not really that far from Sid Sedlacek's street in actual miles, but Lande must have driven past an awful lot of grocery stores to get there, even on a Sunday evening, if he was just popping out for a quart of milk. "What was he supposed to be getting?"

Bonny had to think. "Rosemary," she said finally. "I needed rosemary for the lamb chops. Mul, what's wrong?"

Mulheisen tried to calm her. "Now look, Bonny, don't get upset. It's nothing, just a matter of formalities. I'll take care of it. Just sit down, OK? It won't be long."

Reluctantly she allowed herself to be led back to the bench. Mulheisen hurried off with the wallet in hand. Lande was silent at last. Jimmy stood next to the door. Mulheisen sat down and flipped open the wallet.

" 'Eugene Preston Lande'," Mulheisen read. "That you?"

"Course it's me," Lande snapped back. "So, she brung it. She still here?"

"How long have you lived at this address?" Mulheisen asked.

"About two, three years." Lande cleared his throat.

"Occupation?"

Lande gestured vaguely with his hand. "Computers."

"What about them?"

"I'm in computers."

"What does that mean?"

"I work with special computer systems . . . sort of free-lance."

"Free-lance what?"

"It's kinda complicated," Lande said, rolling his beady eyes as if he despaired of explaining the intricate world of computers to an ignorant cop.

Mulheisen bared his teeth. "Try."

Lande shrugged his shoulders. They were broad and thick, as if he worked out with weights. "It's like . . . a guy has problems with his program—maybe for his business—he comes to Doc Byte—"

"Doc Byte?" Jimmy said with a near laugh.

"That's me," Lande said almost cheerfully, proudly. "Anyways, he comes to Doc Byte, and I check it out, and when I find the bug, I either fix it—if it ain't too big a bug, right?—or I work with the people he got the system from, and they maybe replace it, or, well . . . it just goes on and on like that. I mean, there's a million things can go wrong . . . maybe I make a new system for him, or . . ." He stopped, looking questioningly at Mulheisen, then at Jimmy. "It's real technical . . . I could go through some of it for you."

Mulheisen made a sour face. "I get the picture," he said unconvincingly. "You do this out of your home, or what?"

"Out of my home? Well, I guess you could, but I got an office. Doc Byte. It's on Nine Mile, in Warren. There's a card there, in the wallet. Go ahead, take one."

"Your wife brought this wallet in," Mulheisen said. "She says you went out this evening—yesterday evening—to the store. Is that right?"

Lande nodded.

"What time?"

"What time? I don't know. It musta been about seven."

"Why did you go out?"

"I went to the store. I forget what for. I been here for so long! It was some kinda spice she wanted. Rosemary. That's it! What is all this, anyways?"

"You went a long way for rosemary," Mulheisen said.

"So what?"

Mulheisen looked at the arrest report. "Where were you when the officer stopped you?"

"Where was I? I was on Kercheval."

"Where on Kercheval?"

"A couple blocks from Alter."

"Were you driving?"

"I was walking. Whataya think? An' this big ape comes along and says, 'Git in,' meanin' his squad car. So what the fuck, I'm a law-bidin' citizen, I says, 'What the fuck is this?' And the big ape says, 'Just git the fuck in.' So what am I? I git in. They bring me here, and the next thing

I know they leave me in this fuckin' office, and now I'm talkin' a you. OK?"

He was getting worked up. "Relax," Mulheisen said. "What was the arresting officer's name?"

"I don't know the guy's name. He was huge. Mean fucker."

"Do you want to file a complaint?" Mulheisen asked casually.

"I ain't complaining," Lande responded quickly.

"You have a right to complain," Mulheisen said.

"I ain't complaining."

"Was the arresting officer Noell?"

"How should I know. I didn' ast."

"All officers wear name tags, or if it was a plainclothes detective, he should have shown you his identification."

"He was plainclothes, but he had a 'Flyer,' " Lande said, referring to the wings painted on the sides of the Big Four's cruisers, "he didn' haveta tell me he was a cop. I never seen no ID."

Mulheisen sighed. He examined the report, the effects, the wallet for a long minute. Finally he said, "You went a long way for rosemary."

"I was lost," Lande said.

Many Detroit streets, perhaps especially on the east side of town, were confusing. They ran at angles to the basic grid-and-belt system, and some of them changed names, such as Cadieux's becoming Morang and leading into Moross. It had to do with the old boundary lines of the French settlers' farms, Mulheisen knew. But Detroiters never got lost—or, more to the point, they never admitted being lost.

"I thought there was a dago store, some kinda deli, around there. I parked and walked, but I couldn' find it. Then the flyer come along—"

"Where did you park?"

"In a rest'rant parkin' lot. On Kercheval."

"What restaurant?"

"I don' know. I never paid no attention. Hey, come on . . . what the fuck? Do I gotta call my lawyer, or what?"

Mulheisen was suddenly tired of this pointless sparring. Obviously Lande had nothing to do with this investigation. And if it turned out, by chance, that he did, he knew where to find him.

"Did the officer question you at all?" he asked.

"Some bird did. He ast me about what you ast me. He ast me if I seen a accident."

"Did you?"

"I didn' see nothin'. What is it? A hit 'n' run?"

Mulheisen shrugged. "If you didn't see it . . ." He replaced the driver's license in the wallet and pushed it across the desk with the other things. "You want to check this stuff? See if it's all there?"

Lande checked through the wallet quickly, counted his money, and slipped the other items into his pockets. "It's all there." He stood up.

"One minute." Mulheisen pushed the property-inventory form across, along with a ballpoint pen. "Sign this."

Lande looked at the paper suspiciously. "What's this? I ain't signin' nothin'."

"It's just a release form. It says all your personal property has been returned, that's all. Go ahead, read it." Mulheisen pointed to the form.

"I can see that," Lande said, picking up the paper gingerly. He held it before him, eyeing it warily. "You're sure that's all it is?"

"Well, you can read, can't you?" Mulheisen said, irritably. "Here," he handed Lande the pen, "sign by that X."

"X? I don't need no X. I can sign my own name." Lande bent to the desk and signed his name with a large, stylish script, writing carefully. When he finished he handed the pen back to Mulheisen. "That it?"

Mulheisen picked up the form. "Good enough for the Declaration of Independence." He showed the form to Jimmy Marshall. "Now that's what I call a John Hancock."

Lande frowned. "What's wrong with it?"

"Nothing," Mulheisen said, wearily. "You're free to go. Jimmy, show Mr. Lande out." Mulheisen felt a sudden diffidence about encountering Bonny again.

When Jimmy returned, he said, "What a touchy fart."

"I'm just glad to get him out of here without a signed complaint," Mulheisen said.

"Weirdo," Jimmy said. "Computer freaks! They talk like illiterates, some of them. You hear that? Sounded like a cross between a Valley girl and a pimp."

"You think he was lying?" Mulheisen asked.

"Oh, he was lying all right," Jimmy said, "but what about? Went to get some rosemary? Probably slipped out to see his girlfriend. Who knows? These computer freaks don't speak the same language, Mul. All they know is bauds and bytes. They think in numbers. Nowadays if you don't know computers, you're the illiterate one."

Mulheisen didn't want to get into that. He knew Jimmy was up on computers. Himself, he didn't know a baud from a byte. "Did you see the wife?" he asked.

Jimmy smiled and nodded.

"She say anything?" Mul asked.

"Not to me. She let out a wail and fell on the little drip's neck like he was Warren Beatty. Maybe he is. Women are funny. Now you take my wife—"

"Thanks," Mulheisen said, "but no thanks." He had a vision of the large, splendid Yvonne in her African robes and glittering bangles. An admirable person, but not one of Mulheisen's favorites, nor was he one of hers. She wouldn't thank him for Jimmy's late hours. "See you in a few hours," he said and left.

Five

It was midmorning before Mulheisen was alerted to the abscondence of Hal Good. A great hullabaloo ensued, and the unfortunate brunt of it was borne by Officer Lovabella. He it was who had allowed Hal Good to take the position of Henry J. Fogarty, structural-steel salesman from Youngstown, Ohio. The clamor was for Jellybelly to be severely disciplined, if not dismissed from the force.

Mulheisen took a different view. Although it did not come up in the foofaraw following the discovery of Fogarty in the holding pen, Mulheisen could not ignore the fact that he himself had looked in on Fogarty's inert form and when told that it was Good, had not raised any questions. Worse, just moments earlier he had read the interrogation report, which had not suggested that the subject was in any way inebriated and certainly not practically comatose. At any rate, Mulheisen's curiosity ought to have been piqued at seeing Good still present at 3:00 A.M. But he'd had Lande—and Bonny—on his mind. Mercifully, Lovabella did not reveal Mulheisen's appearance in the booking room. Therefore, Mulheisen defended Jellybelly by charging that Noell had mishandled Lande. (He did not find it necessary, of course, to mention that Jellybelly had forgotten Lande's whereabouts for several hours.)

Since when, Mulheisen demanded, does a detective bring in a suspect and then not follow through on the investigation, or having found no cause to detain the suspect/witness, fail to discharge that

person from custody? Both Lande and Good, he pointed out, had been
the responsibility of Dennis Noell, who had seen fit to pick them up in
the vicinity of the Sedlacek murder scene, and yet Detective Noell had
not followed through with the investigation. The report of Officer Doug
Joseph (one of Noell's crew) on Lande was slipshod and incomplete,
and of course there had been no questioning whatever of Good, whose
subsequent behavior seemed to indicate that he might be a very important actor, indeed, in the Sedlacek scenario. This, Mulheisen declared,
is what comes of elevating cruising squads to detective status.

Mulheisen's complaint did not play as well as he had hoped. The
precinct commander of the Ninth, Buck Buchanan, an unctuous dandy,
was a sworn life's enemy of Mulheisen's. He believed, correctly, that
Mulheisen despised him, that he ridiculed him, that he was insubordi-
nate, and that he had usurped the affection and the loyalty of the men
of the Ninth. It particularly bothered him that Mulheisen had success-
fully avoided taking the lieutenants' exam for several years now. Buchanan believed that Mulheisen had been able to do this, and to take
other irregular actions, because he had political influence at a very high
level, through his long-deceased father. Mulheisen, Sr., had been the
water commissioner for some thirty years, not an influential post, but
he had been well regarded in the Democratic party and by the United
Auto Workers, so maybe he'd had some political punch. None of it had
devolved upon his son, however, but Buchanan did not believe that. It
was Buchanan's further erroneous belief that the reason Mulheisen did
not take the lieutenants' exam was he would flunk it. In fact, Mulheisen
avoided the exam because he knew it would inevitably advance him into
an administrative position, whereas he much preferred to be a working
detective. Also, he didn't need the money. This kind of reasoning would
never penetrate the seal-like head of Buchanan.

But now it appeared that Buchanan might have a chance to force
Mulheisen to take the exam, which if he failed would ultimately get him
out of the force and if he passed would at least get him out of the Ninth.
Buchanan sent a memo to the district inspector of eastern detectives,
noting that Mulheisen was officially the detective in charge of the
botched Sedlacek investigation, regardless of the performance of his
subordinates and fellow detectives. The investigation was his responsi-

bility, not theirs, Buchanan insisted. The district inspector of eastern detectives could hardly ignore this memo, although he personally believed that Mulheisen ought to be allowed to do just about whatever he pleased. He didn't feel compelled, however, to act rapidly on the matter. In due time it would be passed along to the deputy chief of detectives, also an admirer of Mulheisen's. Some day it might even reach the office of the chief—whoever that might be (the present chief was under indictment). Maybe when the deputy was promoted, he might take the file along. Maybe not.

There was unpleasantness also with the honcho of the Big Four. Normally Dennis Noell and Mulheisen got along, mainly by avoiding each other. But now Noell jumped into the fray with both feet (or was pushed by Buchanan). He claimed to have had nothing to do with the mix-up. Oh, sure, he'd picked up both Lande and Good, but he had promptly turned them over to the doorman, to be held for Mulheisen and his crew. In fact, he had tried to get Mulheisen to interview one of the witnesses at the scene, but Mulheisen couldn't be bothered. ("Which one?" Mulheisen asked; Noell wasn't sure. "Where were these men picked up?" Mulheisen inquired; there was no indication, and no one could sort it out.)

Stanos, the Big Four driver and ex-mate of Jimmy Marshall, told Jimmy that they had picked up "half a dozen" guys that night in the space of an hour, one of them actually, if barely, on the street where Sedlacek had been gunned down. "Dennis was just snatchin' 'em right and left," Stanos said with a grin. "He calls it the Bubba Smith method—you grab everybody in the backfield and sort 'em out later." Like the rest of the crew he couldn't say who was picked up where, but if push came to shove, he wouldn't say anything to hurt Dennis. He was tired of driving the cruiser and wearing blue (they had to have a blue driver because one whole Big Four crew had been gunned down, though not killed, when they stormed a dope den, and the defendants in the court case had walked by claiming they had no idea who these big bruisers were, in civilian clothes, attacking them with ax handles and shotguns—they had shot in self-defense). Stanos wanted an ax handle, or maybe even the tommy gun.

Finally Mulheisen countered that he had never had an opportunity to see Good, and Lande had similarly been misplaced. Noell should have seen to it that a detective—some detective, even one of his own had interviewed this most suspicious of witnesses. But beyond that he managed to smooth the ruffled feathers by noting that the real culprit was the outmoded system of identifying and holding and dispersing witnesses and suspects. Most metropolitan police forces were adopting a bracelet system, he noted, similar to that used in hospitals (to identify babies and surgical patients and to prevent the dispensing of medication to the wrong person). The bracelet system would prevent prisoners from impersonating one another.

Mercifully all the squabbling soon began to die down. There was more than enough work for every detective in the city. Buchanan's complaint was still at division level. And Jellybelly, after a few days' vacation with pay, was back on the night door at the Ninth.

After a week the case was deader than Sid. They had not found the killer's gun, or even his gloves. Some lucky teenager had found the attaché case. He'd thrown away the foam so he could use the case to carry his schoolbooks. Maki cleared the driver of the car that had almost hit Sid. The medical examiner had nothing interesting to say, except that Big Sid was aptly named, in a genital sense. Frank Zeppanuk, from the Scientific Bureau, offered the marginally enlightening information that powder residues indicated that the gunman had not used standard loads, which suggested what they already believed: the hitter was a pro.

But, of course, they had the unrecovered personal property of Hal Good. A wallet containing a driver's license, two credit cards, and $179 in currency. Also a nice necktie, which carried a label from Cool Noose, a Chicago shop. In addition, Jensen and Field discovered an interesting vehicle parked in a lot within two blocks of Sedlacek's house. When they contacted the rental agency, they learned it had been rented at Metropolitan Airport on Saturday, the day before the killing. The renter: Harold B. Good. Mr. Good had presented a credit card from Chase Visa but had insisted on paying cash, making a hundred-dollar deposit, which had not been claimed.

Mulheisen examined the driver's license thoughtfully. It said Good lived in Iowa City, Iowa, on Governor Street. He was thirty years old, and the photograph was that of a pleasant-looking young man who wore photo-gray eyeglasses and had sandy hair. The license was due for renewal in four months. The credit cards were from two banks, First Chicago and Chase, in Wilmington, Delaware. They were issued to Harold B. Good, with a box number in Iowa City.

"This looks too easy," Mulheisen told Jimmy Marshall. He was on hold, on a call to the Iowa City police. He was soon proved right. The Iowa City police reported that they had nothing on Harold B. Good, except that he had died more than three years earlier. Mr. Good had committed suicide by ingesting numerous sedatives, presumably because he had begun to experience full-blown symptoms of AIDS. He had died intestate, no known relatives, and the police had not investigated further.

This information did not depress Mulheisen. On the contrary, he now felt that he had a real lead. He turned over the Chicago credit card and dialed the 800 number on the back, then asked to be connected to the Fraud Division. A pleasant-sounding woman was very interested to hear about Mulheisen's find. She quickly punched up Good's account on her terminal and was able to relay the following: Harold B. Good had a twenty-five-hundred-dollar credit line; he was fully current; he had changed his billing address some three years ago from the Governor Street address to a post-office box. Charges were infrequent but, curiously enough, all were made at businesses in the Detroit area—car-rental agencies.

The case officer at First Chicago was eager to cooperate. She said Harold Good's employer was listed as Quaker Oats, in nearby Cedar Rapids. She put Mulheisen on hold while she dialed Good's listed home phone number—it was no longer in service. She promised to fax all relevant material to Mulheisen immediately and to put an alert on all future uses of the card, with the notation that the user was not to be stopped or alarmed in any way but that the company should be notified instantly. This was just in case the current user had access to a duplicate card, although the case officer agreed with Mulheisen that it was unlikely to be used again. "Still, you never know," she said hopefully. "Sometimes these people aren't brain surgeons, and, then, people do occasionally get into a bind, an emergency, where they just have to use the card. We'll keep a special eye on it."

The fraud officer at Chase Visa wasn't so cooperative. He insisted on an investigative subpoena before relinquishing any information. "We've been burned on these before, Sergeant Mullhouse," he said. "An absolute career con man out of Jersey nailed us in court for violation of privacy. So, company rule—gotta have a subpoena."

That same afternoon Mulheisen faxed him the subpoena, signed by a judge who didn't even read the request. By the following day Chase's response was back: Harold B. Good had a two-thousand-dollar credit line; he was up-to-date on all payments and fees; he had used the account only five times in the past two years—to rent automobiles in Chicago; Los Angeles; Omaha; Fort Smith, Arkansas; and Dallas. The billing address was the same post-office box as for First Chicago, as was the employer's name and the home phone number.

The postal inspector's office in Iowa City reported that a Harold B. Good had rented the box and paid the rent regularly. Apparently he picked up his credit card statements promptly; no mail was in the box at present.

Mulheisen agreed with Jimmy that Good was the man they wanted. "Nobody goes to this much trouble to conceal his identity unless he's a professional criminal. He probably lives in or around Iowa City, but obviously he travels. What's in Fort Smith, I wonder? Any word on the prints?"

There had been a few smudged fingerprints on the cards in the wallet and in the rental car. Jimmy had sent them to the FBI, but the only response had been "will try further processes." Jimmy said he'd heard that the FBI was experimenting with a new computer-simulated system, in which they took the prime characteristics of the partial prints and tried to create a more complete version. Nobody knew if it really worked, but it was worth a try.

They checked the airlines for an arrival of Harold B. Good on the Saturday preceding the killing. No luck. Nothing for the preceding days, either. Mulheisen decided that Hal, as he had begun to call him, must have traveled under some other name. Perhaps he had paid cash. One thing they did learn, however: Henry J. Fogarty had presumably flown to Chicago early Monday morning—quite a trick, inasmuch as he was sleeping it off in the Ninth Precinct's holding pen.

There was the name of a motel on the sparsely filled in prelimi-
nary-interrogation form: the Windswept, on Eight Mile Road. Mulheisen and Jimmy drove out there. By now they had an eight-by-ten
blowup of Hal's driver's license photo. The register at the Windswept
indicated that a Harold Good had stayed there Saturday night, but he
had checked out Sunday morning, and the room had been cleaned. The
clerk said the picture vaguely resembled Hal, except that he didn't wear
glasses and maybe his hair was a little darker. Hal was friendly, she said,
even a little flirtatious—which seemed reasonable, given that the clerk
was quite attractive. In response to Mulheisen's suggestion, she ada-
mantly rejected any notion that Hal might be gay. They looked at the
room but could find nothing, nonetheless Mulheisen called in the Scientific Bureau to do a full-scale sweep. That turned up a couple more
smudged prints, possibly Hal's, on the flush lever of the toilet. They
were sent on to the FBI, which still hadn't come up with anything.

And that was that.

Andy Deane, of Racket-Conspiracy, had big ears on the street.
Those ears' tongues said that Big Sid had been popped by a heavy hitter
from the West. The tale was that Sid had been skimming the numbers
and the flesh forever, presumably without complaint from his masters,
but lately he'd gotten into entirely new venues—not content to razor off
the fat, he was now (or had been) hacking off whole steaks. The
commodities specifically were coke and crack, said the tongues, which
commodities Carmine had expressly forbidden to his minions. Further,
Big Sid had been making fluttering noises, like a bird expecting to
migrate, most likely to some warmer climate, where the business didn't
have a branch office.

"Do you believe this dreck?" Mulheisen asked Andy.

Deane, a large man with red hair, a freckle on every centimeter of
his body, and doll-like blue eyes, laughed. "It's one of those accepted
fictions, Mul. A few years back Carmine was supposed to have promised his dear old mom, or maybe it was his new dolly, or maybe it was
his beloved daughter, Ann-Mary, who'd had a brush with the law for
possession of grass, that the business was gonna get out of the dope
business. That's the line. For generations Carmine and his pals controlled heroin, grass, meth, coke, . . . but this new stuff, especially crack,

was evil. Carmine wasn't having it. He said. And, in a sense, it's true. Those aren't mob boys standing on the street corner waving baggies of coke and touting cat's-eyes crystals. The business is ostensibly run by the Colombians and the kids. But Carmine has got his wienie in there, too, no doubt about it. It just isn't so visible."

"And how did Sid fit into this?" Mulheisen asked.

"Carmine warned all these second-echelon goons off," Andy said, "whether out of piety or to make his piece bigger, especially including Sid." According to Andy, Sedlacek had got into trouble with Carmine years earlier for trimming too close to the bone. Bones, in fact, were broken. Sid had almost eaten the Colt then, Andy said, and it had taken him a long time and a lot of hard, unpleasant labor to work himself back into a position of uneasy trust—loan-sharking, auto parts, and jukebox marketing, not cushy work.

"I guess he didn't learn," Mulheisen said.

"These guys aren't good students," Deane agreed. "It must have been humiliating for him. But he made it back, . . . and as soon as he did, it looks like he started trimming again. But this time he must have taken some big slabs."

"How big?"

"Five mil? Ten? Those are the figures I hear."

"So where is it?" Mul wondered.

"That's the question," Andy said. "It's still out there, they say. Carmine's still on the prod. They say. It's probably all bullshit."

None of this was any concern of Mulheisen's. This was Andy Deane's beat. Mulheisen was just as happy to think Sedlacek's murder was a hit. Hal would not be easy to find, but he would no doubt turn up again, down the road. As his old mentor, Grootka, used to say, "The world is round." Being a hit, an internal matter, so to speak, the pressure was off. The press wasn't concerned, especially, when the business bopped its own. There was a lot more pressure when bystanders or honest Johns got knocked. The Sedlacek case was not looking like a boost for anyone's career.

* * *

About a week after these events, there came a message for Mulheisen at the precinct from Mrs. Lande. He sat and looked at the note with misgivings for some time, then reluctantly called the number.

Bonny was pleased to hear from him. "You were so nice, Mul," she said, "that Gene and I both thought we just had to thank you. We want you to come to dinner."

Mulheisen was caught off guard, but he quickly begged off. He thanked her but claimed it wasn't ethical to engage in social contacts with a witness in an ongoing investigation. Bonny was immediately apologetic and sounded embarrassed. She wouldn't have him think for a moment that there was anything irregular about the invitation. But they did want to thank him. If he couldn't come, well, . . . she was sorry.

The following day Lande himself called. He just wanted to assure Mulheisen, he said, that there was nothing "funny" about the invitation. "Just a friendly, you know, kind of thing," he said. "Hey, no offense, buddy. But it'd be a great favor to Bonny, you know. Bonny don't have no real friends around here, and I guess you guys used to go to school together and all. I mean, I thought you figured out that I didn't have nothing to do with that Sedlacek shit, anyways. Right? I mean, nobody could say nothing about having dinner for Chrisake, could they? It'd be a great thing for Bonny."

He went on and on in that vein until Mulheisen began to feel like a jerk for denying his old school friend a chance to be properly grateful. But what did it was when Lande finally said sourly, "Bonny told me you wouldn't come. I guess your old man was the water Commish, or something . . . not on our level."

Mulheisen couldn't bear for Bonny to believe he was snubbing her and her husband. He agreed to meet them on neutral grounds, so to speak, at a restaurant in St. Clair Shores, and he insisted on paying for his own dinner. He claimed it was departmental policy. That was agreeable.

Six

Joe Service said, "I'm not interested, Fat. I made up my mind last time—I'll never go back to Detroit."

The Fat Man just chuckled. "Whata thing to say, Joe. Sounds like some kinda pop song."

"I mean it, Fat," Joe said. They were standing in the Cannon Terminal, in Reno. Joe was feeding nickels into the slot machines, and to his annoyance he kept winning. He didn't hit the jackpot, but there would be a little shower of nickels, and he just couldn't get rid of them. "Nothing but bad news in Detroit," he said, punching in nickels. His refusal had to do with a series of bad experiences in Detroit, many of which were concerned with a policeman named Mulheisen. But Joe didn't mention Mulheisen. He preferred to chide the Fat Man about his organization's incompetence and inability to deal with their own people. The situation the Fat Man had just mentioned sounded like the same old tune. Joe Service was no fan of the Motown sound. "Guess I'll sit this dance out," Joe said.

"Too bad," the Fat Man said nonchalantly. "Lotta money involved."

"Well, I knew there would be a lot of money," Joe said, "otherwise you wouldn't have flown all the way out here. Damn!" Three grapes showed in the slot machine window, and another disgusting pile of nickels slithered into the tray just as Joe had stuffed in the last of the previous nickels. He moved to another machine and quickly began to load it up.

"Don't you wanta know how much, Joe?" The Fat Man was disappointed at Joe's lack of enthusiasm.

"Sure. Why not?" Joe continued to punch nickels and crank the handle. "No, . . . let me guess. Five big ones. Maybe seven. That about right?"

"Five big what?" the Fat Man asked.

Joe stopped what he was doing and looked at his massive companion. "There was something in the way you said that," Joe said. The Fat Man's face was smooth and shiny, revealing nothing. Joe pulled the handle.

Clang-clang-clang . . . three bells rolled up, and the jackpot bell clamored. Nickels were shooting out of the machine and onto the floor. Joe stared at the machine in horror. He threw up his hands, then grabbed the Fat Man by the arm and led him away.

"You ain't gonna leave all them—"

"Forget it, Fat!" They walked off down the concourse, leaving a circle of astounded travelers glancing from the puddle of nickels to the departing men, one of them obese and the other small and jaunty. A child laughed and fell to his knees, picking up the coins and letting them run through his fingers. Other travelers squatted to seize handfuls.

Joe and Fat stopped at a newsstand and stared at piles of magazines and newspapers. "Who is this Hal, anyway?" Joe asked.

"Just a mechanic. We use him off and on the last coupla years."

"What does he look like?" Joe picked up a copy of *Time* and flipped through it, not even seeing it.

"About five ten, brown hair," the Fat Man said. "He looks real ordinary, Joe. A little older than you, thirty maybe. Not a snappy dresser like you, but neat, . . . ordinary. He don't have your build—he's kinda skinny." The Fat Man was well aware that Service valued his athletic conditioning.

Joe frowned. "He doesn't have a mustache or anything? Glasses? Nanh? Teeth. He have kind of little, separate teeth?"

"Separate teeth? What does that mean, Joe?" The Fat Man
snorted

Joe tossed the magazine back on the pile and held his hands up
before his mouth, moving the fingers against the thumbs to simulate a
munching action. "You know, little teeth . . . little square teeth that have
tiny spaces . . . like those little ears of corn, little white kernels . . . no,
hunh?" Joe shrugged. "For a moment there I was thinking of a guy I
knew in high school. Well, of course, Hal isn't him, but for some reason
I got this flash . . . Where did this Hal come from, anyway?"

They walked on. "Oscar sent him to us. We needed somebody
fresh. This was two, three years ago. Oscar said he was OK. Now Oscar
says he never even saw the guy; he was just passing on something he
heard from Mitch, in New York. Mitch says he thought the guy's name
was Julius and he was from Florida. Mitch says he never heard of no
Hal." The Fat Man shrugged and muttered something that sounded to
Joe like *fuzzuguvuh* maybe. Joe had no idea what that was supposed to
mean—his Italian was weak; he'd been born Surface, but his father had
changed the name to Service.

They had come to a saloon, or a casino, a kind of drinking-and-slot-
machine place. The Fat Man waved Joe in. They sat at a table amid the
pinging of electronic gambling devices and the jangling of slots. The Fat
Man had a glass of red wine. Joe wouldn't have anything.

The Fat Man had set a leather briefcase on a chair next to him.
Now he opened it and fished out a manila envelope, which he passed
to Joe. "Carmine said to give you this. It seems we still owed you fifty
from the last time." He looked away and sipped his wine.

Joe Service didn't touch the envelope. He hooded his lids and said
evenly, "It wasn't fifty, Fat. It was more like a full Benjy."

"You still talking about them bearer bonds, Joe?" The Fat Man
shook his head in disbelief. "I told you about them. With the discount
and the commissions it didn't come to anymore'n I paid. You agreed on
this, Joe."

Joe pinched the bridge of his nose. "You are giving me a huge
headache, Fat." His voice was tense and it began to rise. "We always
have to go through this . . . this utter fucking *crap!*" He leapt to his feet
and rapidly walked away. The Fat Man remained seated. He stared at

his wine, then reached out and picked it up. He sipped it, rolling it around his palate and smacking his lips as if it were some incredible vintage instead of California jug wine. He didn't touch the envelope.

Five minutes later Joe Service returned. He walked in his usual bouncy way and seemed to have completely forgotten his rage. He picked up the envelope, opened it, and peeked inside. He stuck his hand in and ticked through the bills. He tossed the envelope on the table.

"They look all right," Joe said as if to himself. "You don't ever want to give me bad money," he said to the Fat Man.

"Stop it, Joe, yer bustin' my kazakis."

Joe laughed. "OK. Tell me, Fat, . . . is Detroit still there? I mean, you didn't lose it or something? Are you still in the business? How do you manage? I can't figure it out."

The Fat Man didn't rise to this. "Every business has its hitches, Joe. Up, down." He waggled his hand. "This is one of ours. This is why we got you. If these jerks didn't screw up from time to time, you wouldn't have no work. You look like you're doing all right, Joe. You allus made a good living off us. Course I know the other outfits help pay your rent."

"Understood, cap'n," Joe said cheerily. "So, what was Sid's sin? How come you sicced this Hal on him?"

"He was stealing."

Joe nodded. "Right. That's what Sid does. Did. That's what you all do. So?"

"He was stealing from Carmine. He set up some kinda rake-off with the distributors . . . We don't know how it worked—that's where you come in—and we don't know what happened to the money."

"So you had him hit," Joe said, shaking his head. "Why would you have him hit? Couldn't you at least wait until you got hold of the money?"

"We hada hit 'im," the Fat Man said. "This was the second time around for Sid."

"Oh, well, that figures," Joe said. "Gosh, yes, then you definitely had to knock him. But shouldn't you have gotten the money first?"

"Well, Joe, . . . the money's around. It's gotta be around. I mean, it was a lotta money."

"Five big ones," Joe said. "Five very big ones."

"More," the Fat Man said. "Maybe two, three m—" He stopped as Joe held up a cautioning hand.

"Don't say it," Joe said. He closed his eyes, thumb and forefinger on his brow, like a mind reader on stage. "It's an *M* word, . . . am I right? Yes, I see it . . . it's *m-m-m-m-mooooola!*"

The Fat Man laughed, his belly chugging against the table. "You are a card, Joe."

Joe popped his eyes open. "And my part, Fat? How much o' the moola is Joe's?"

"One a the *M*'s, Joe. Carmine says you get one whole *M* to yourself."

"That's nice. Real good of ol' Coach Carmine. That's just about what they pay a second-string shortstop these days. But who's complaining? You paid me today for last time; I guess you'll pay me next time for this time."

"You find the money, Joe, your part comes off the top."

Joe Service nodded. "That's right, Fat. Off the top. Now, about this Hal—"

"He's gotta be in on it, Joe. Some of the fellas went over to Sid's and talked to Roman—he was Sid's heat. Roman is a very solid gentleman, Joe. He took a little fist on this—no hard feelin's—and he's clean. He said Hal had been around, talkin' to Sid. Roman didn't know what it was all about, they didn't cut him in. Sid wouldn't. Sid had a ginch, name is Germaine Kouras, s'posed to be a singer. Calvin went to talk to her. She said Sid and her was gonna beat it, headed for the Cayman Islands first stop. Sid told her he was retiring. He was sick of the old lady, so him and Germaine would just buzz off. She believed it. She didn't know about the rake-off."

"Who else, Fat?"

"Could be a bunch, Joe. There's a lotta shakin' goin' on in Detroit. If we get something, I'll let you know. But I figured you can start on Hal."

Joe nodded. "How did you contact Hal?"

The Fat Man explained how he would call the service in Los Angeles and Hal would call back, usually within a few hours. It was a system much like Joe's and employed for the same reason: to maintain a safe distance between one's clients and one's locus of being.

"What did he say when you told him it was Sid?" Joe asked.

"Nothin'. Cool as a breeze. He just said it might take a day. I told him it hada be before Monday night. Sid was on ice within an hour."

"So he was already in Detroit. You think he was there to see Sid? So why did he pop Sid? When you gave him the contract, he knew you were on to something."

"Well, I wasn't on to him," the Fat Man said. "The way I see it now, Hal and Sid must've already made their arrangements for shifting the money. Maybe Hal had it. Then he gits the word from me. He goes around and pops Sid and takes off with the money. I don't know how he did it, but I know he ain't called back."

"You saw this Hal a lot," Joe said. "Did you ever get any idea where he was from, where he lived?"

"Nanh, I just figgered he was from oudda town. Chicago?"

"Why Chicago?"

"I don't know. Maybe the way he talked, kinda Midwest. He didn't sound like New York or California. Now you, I'd say you're California."

"Really? Why?" Joe was interested. "The way I talk?"

"Nanh. You allus got a nice tan. You talk about the West a lot."

"I do?" Joe hadn't realized that. He'd have to watch that, he thought. "A tan, hunh? Maybe I live in Hawaii, Fat. Or Puerto Rico. It's none of your business. Anyway, I'm glad I don't have to live in Detroit. A very bad environment."

"I didn't realize you was a enviramenalis, Joe. You oughta see Detroit these days. They cleaned up the air and the river a lot. You wouldn't recanize it. They say there's even fish in the Rouge."

A different sense of environment had prompted Joe's remark. He said, "Don't eat any fish out of the Rouge River, Fat."

"Speakin' of which," the Fat Man said, "don't Charlie Dee have some kinda rest'rant out here? He's a old Detroit boy. Lemme buy you some ribs at Charlie's."

Walking out to the cab, Joe said, "I need to remind you, and Carmine, Fat, . . . I'm just going to look for this Hal."

"And the money," the Fat Man said.

"And the money," Joe nodded. "But no hit. I'm not a hitter."

"Well, you let us know when you find him," the Fat Man said blandly. "Carmine knows you don't do that kinda stuff. You find the boy, you find the—whadjou call it?—moola. We'll take care of the rest. Hey, slow down, don't walk so fast," he wheezed, "I'm gittin' to be an old man."

In the cab Joe said, "Let me guess who's investigating this for the cops."

"Mulheisen," the Fat Man said.

Joe sighed.

Seven

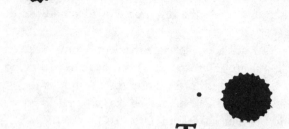

The Sunday before his dinner engagement with the Landes, Mulheisen was home alone. He still lived in the house where he'd been born. It was an old farmhouse on a quiet country lane, near the town of St. Clair Flats, some twenty miles from Detroit. It was against regulations not to live in the city, but like many other Detroit policemen he avoided the regulation by maintaining accommodations in the city, actually a kind of crash pad he shared with some other detectives. It frequently came in handy, and the caretaker, a cranky hillbilly from Tennessee named Speed, was adept at parrying departmental phone calls.

Mulheisen had lived at the apartment for a year or so, but he had eventually found that his colleagues had uses for the apartment that interfered with his peace and quiet, to say nothing of his own amours. There were only two bedrooms and that wasn't always enough. He found himself spending weekends at the old homestead, where his mother still lived. Soon he was leaving his laundry and then keeping a few books and records there. His mother said she was glad of the company, but they saw little of each other. She was active in Eastern Star and was an avid bird-watcher besides. Finally he had just moved back in.

On this weekend Cora Mulheisen was off on an Audubon jaunt. He was pretty sure she had said they were going to Point Pelee, Ontario, in the hope of catching the early migration. He was engrossed in a book about General Hull, who had surrendered the fort at Detroit to the British in 1812 without a shot being fired. But somehow Mulheisen's mind wandered, and he found himself thinking about Bonny Wheeler.

He sat in an old easy chair by the window of his room, looking out across the field toward the St. Clair River channel. The ice had gone out some days earlier, and there were a couple of Great Lakes ships passing, one of them displaying the black bear of Algoma Steel on its funnel.

He wondered if he still had a special picture of Bonny Wheeler. He smiled. Surely it was still around somewhere, although he hadn't looked at it in twenty years. He looked in the closet for a couple of old boxes filled with his old stuff. Then he remembered that when he'd gone into the air force, his mother had made him move it all up to the attic. The idea of poking around in a dusty attic wasn't appealing. To heck with it, he decided.

He went downstairs and sliced thick slabs off a cold roast beef and made a sandwich on rye bread with thin slices of onion, slathered it with Dijon mustard, and added some Canadian Black Diamond cheddar. He put too much salt on the beef for a man of his age and weight, but it tasted delicious with the fresh coffee he drank as he reread the Sunday sports section. Spring training had begun, and the Tigers' management was trumpeting a thirty-seven-year-old ex-National League third baseman, whom they'd picked up on waivers and was going to help them win the pennant—clearly a smoke screen for the fact that they had almost no front line pitching. Then he said, "Aw, what the hell," and went up to the attic.

There were a lot of interesting things up there, and he was amused to see that it was all neatly stacked and dusted. In one corner was his stuff: hockey skates and sticks, weathered duck decoys, fishing rods, a stick-and-paper model of a B-17 bomber, and an old aquarium. And many boxes. He looked into one and found it was full of school textbooks. After a few minutes he found what he was looking for in another box. He took the tattered magazine over to the light and opened it to the centerfold. Bonny Wheeler sprawled in all her glory.

In the article that accompanied the photo spread, she was referred to as Connie Ryder, from Windsor, Ontario. She named her favorite band—the Beatles—and said she enjoyed skiing and popcorn and playing with her kid brother. She said she was excited about her upcoming screen test. Mulheisen knew Bonny had never had a brother, and he wondered if she'd actually had a screen test; he wondered what, in fact, was a screen test.

The issue of the magazine had come out just a few months after Mulheisen had enlisted in the air force. He'd been stunned by the picture, and he'd excitedly told the other guys in his first outfit that he knew the girl. He was able to provide enough factual-sounding material about the real Connie Ryder for the guys to believe him, and she had quickly become the favorite pinup of the Thirtieth Air Division, NORAD. This centerfold was all over the base. Looking at it now, he tried to recall even one of the fantasies he'd had about Bonny. But they were too deeply buried in the sediment of the past. He seemed to recall that he had grown tired of the picture and had deliberately (he thought) forgotten her.

But, oh, what a body! All the guys had marveled—"Could this be real?" Could there really be breasts like that, so round, so firm, so perfectly projected? Were there legs so long and so magnificently tapered? A waist so tiny? Surely not. It must be the product of a photographer's craft, although the lush perfection of the buttocks and the monumental breasts seemed more the work of a cartoonist. Not that Bonny wasn't a terrific-looking woman. That had long been bountifully evident, although she hadn't been particularly popular in high school. He thought it had something to do with her downbeat personality, but she hadn't really bloomed yet either. Until the magazine had shocked him, Mulheisen had not imagined that she looked quite like this. And perhaps, after all, she didn't.

He felt unaccountably sad, looking at the picture. It didn't affect him at all as he'd expected. It was hardly erotic. He wondered if he was getting old. Hell, he was only forty. But it was more than that, he knew. The picture implied a way of looking at women that he no longer endorsed. All the pictures of the women in this magazine had a foolish innocence about them, despite an implied depravity. The girls, as they were invariably called, Bonny among them, grinned and postured in artificial, ludicrous ways that had nothing to do with decadence. They looked altogether too healthy and too wholesome for sin. Mulheisen considered that the sadness he felt had something to do with an embarrassment for the indignity of the posturing, as if a matronly housewife had been found playing with dolls.

He stuffed the magazine back into the box and put it away where his mother had stored it. Then he went gratefully back to General Hull and the fall of Detroit.

"What I wanta know is how come inna eyes?" Lande asked. His wife squirmed and looked bleakly down at her gnocchi.

Mulheisen sipped Chianti. He shrugged and took a bite of lasagna. This little restaurant was not even locally famous, but the food was good. It was the kind of place that made one realize what food should taste like before it deserved to be dubbed gourmet.

"I mean, is it s'posed to mean something? Some kinda warning? 'Don't be too nosy' or something?" Lande persisted.

"He used a .22," Mulheisen said. "Sometimes a .22 doesn't penetrate . . . it doesn't always kill. I think he was just making sure they were dead, and he figured a bullet had a natural route to the brain through the eye socket."

Bonny lowered her fork and held her napkin to her mouth. She looked at Mulheisen with disappointment.

"I'm sorry," Mulheisen said. He reached across the table and touched her arm. "Are you all right?"

She smiled bravely. "I'm all right. But I think I will excuse myself for a moment."

"Of course." Mulheisen stood as she got up and walked away. Lande looked up with surprise.

"Now what?" he asked. "Jeez, I never seen such a broad for a squeegee stomach."

"A what?" Mulheisen said.

"You know, squeegee tummy . . . like she's alla time wantin' to puke. She ain't herself lately."

"Queasy?" Mulheisen offered.

"Whatever. Say, since she's gone . . ." He leaned an elbow on the table and casually gestured with his sauce-stained fork, "I thought I oughta ast . . . you two didn't have a thing . . . when you was kids, I mean?"

Mulheisen looked at him with amazement. "You're kidding!" But then he raised a single brow and said, "If we did, would I tell you?"

Lande grinned. "Ha, ha! Hey, it's OK! I can han'le it. It don't mean nothin' to me, but I didn't wanta maybe make a joke or something and find out it ain't funny." He resumed eating his spaghetti.

"See, I know all about Bonny," Lande said, slurping up strands of spaghetti and chewing vigorously. "The centerfold and everything. It don't bother me. She's a hell of a wooman, right? I like that. I like a wooman who looks good to other guys. I mean, she better not cheat on me . . . I'd kill her! Uh-oh, I didn't mean that. I forgot the comp'ny I'm in. But I'd beat the living shit oudda her."

He said it as a matter of course, not viciously or jesting. Mulheisen took him at his word. He sipped Chianti and tried to look patient.

"One thing you gotta admit," Lande went on, "Bonny looks like a million bucks, but she ain't no genius, if you know what I mean. She thinks with her ass."

"That'll do," Mulheisen said quietly.

Lande's head came up sharply. He caught the tone in which it was said. He looked warily at Mulheisen, then nodded. "I just mean that she's, uh . . ." He struggled to find a word, waving his fork in desperation, tiny droplets of tomato sauce spotting the linen. Mulheisen drew back but said nothing.

"Gub—golly-something," Lande floundered.

"Gullible?"

"Is that like she believes everything she hears? It is? I thought so. I mean, I don't blame her if she got kinda screwed up. It ain't really her fault, right? Because she's so gubbil—gubbible."

Mulheisen frowned. "I'm not familiar with Bonny's history," he said.

"Well, sure you are. I mean, you seen the foldout, right? Every little jack-off in the country seen that. But I guess you mean after. Yeah, well, she kinda kicked around. I met her in Vegas myself. She was a whatchacallit, a hostess. Nothin' dirty. Well, pro'ly not a real, you know, professional. She just passed out drinks. But that's all over, see. That's what I'm driving at."

"I get it." Mulheisen picked at his salad. He sipped Chianti.

"Jeez, this is shit," Lande said abruptly and pushed the remains of the spaghetti away. He wiped most of the sauce off his bushy mustache, then shook out a cigarette and lit it.

Bonny returned looking better. Perhaps under the influence of her husband's remarks, Mulheisen couldn't help noticing how good she looked. She wore a silk flower-print wrap dress with a plunging neckline. The cleavage was deep, and Mulheisen unconsciously took a deep breath.

She immediately began to apologize, but neither man paid any attention to what she said, and she stopped in mid-apology. "Well," she continued brightly, "isn't this nice! We're so glad you could come, Mul. Gene and I owe so much to you." She looked pointedly at her husband.

"Right," Lande responded, puffing on his cigarette while Bonny picked at some manicotti that had grown cold. "You sure saved my tookis, Mul. I mighta been in that room till morning, or else they'da pro'ly thrown me back in with the jigs. Christ, what with all the pukin' and pissin' I don't know if I coulda taken that."

Bonny sighed and pushed her food away.

"I'm sorry you were inconvenienced," Mulheisen said.

"I'd like to pay you back," Lande said.

"Pay us back! You were the one who was put out. I apologize, Lande. It doesn't happen often, but there's no excuse for it. Anyway, I hope I made it clear—"

"I know, I know." Lande made calming gestures. "You cops are allus making a big show oudda how straight you are. But I got a feeling if you wasn't there and if Bonny didn't know you, I'da been gagging on my grub for a week. Mosta these cops, they just wanta cover their ass. I'm glad Bonny turned out to know a real big shot for once."

"Gene is just grateful," Bonny said. "We both are, Mul. I'm sure he doesn't mean anything that would cause—"

"I ain't talkin' about no bribe or nothin'. Don't get me wrong, Mul. Hell, I never had to pay a cop for nothin'! But if there's ever anything I could do for ya, . . . you just say the word, and you got Gene Lande in your corner. Get me?"

Mulheisen smiled. "I know you mean well, and I don't want you to think I'm ungrateful, but there really isn't anything. Maybe if I ever buy a computer, you could give me some advice."

"Gene knows everything about computers, Mul," Bonny said eagerly. "He's a real genius."

"Really?" Mulheisen said.

Lande made a show of modesty, pushing up his lower lip and wagging his head, but he couldn't sustain it. "Well, a lotta guys know computers, . . . but the troot is, most of 'em, they just know what's in the manual."

Mulheisen spread his lips in what might have been a grin, but there was a hint of malice when he said, "But you don't, eh?"

Lande didn't catch it. "The manual is for the workers," he replied, "and as a great man once said, 'Work is for saps.' "

"What great man would that be?" Mulheisen asked.

"Edward G. Robinson . . . *Key Largo*."

"You like gangsters, do you?"

"Inna movies," Lande replied.

"That's where I like them," Mulheisen said.

"Gene is nuts about old movies," Bonny said, but they ignored her.

"Or in the morgue, eh?" Lande asked. "Like Big Sid?"

"I had nothing personal against Big Sid Sedlacek," Mulheisen replied. "Nobody deserves to die like that."

"You don't think so? I never heard he was such a good guy," Lande said.

"What do you know about it?" Mulheisen asked coldly.

Lande shrugged. "I seen it on the news. Anyways, he caused me enough trouble."

"You? Oh, you mean getting picked up. Yes, well, still . . . On the other hand, I can't say the world isn't better without Big Sid Sedlacek around . . . not that he was the worst. There's plenty others I could do without."

"Like who?" Lande wanted to know.

Mulheisen shrugged. "Oh, I don't know . . . Charlie Evans, Perry Lewis, Tupman, Conover . . ."

"Marty Tupman?" Lande asked, interested. "The Snow Man?"

"You know Tupman?" Mulheisen elevated an eyebrow.

"Everybody's hearda Frosty Tupman."

Mulheisen said, "I don't think anybody actually calls him that. Some reporter just made it up, like most of these gangster nicknames. They got the idea from the movies maybe. It makes these jerks sound colorful. But they aren't colorful, believe me. They're just human dreck."

"Oh, I agree," Bonny said. "But it was awful about Mr. Sedlacek."

"Did you know him?" Mulheisen asked, surprised.

"Naw," Lande interjected. "I mean, we seen him on the news, that's all. Did you ever get anywheres on who done it?"

"We're working on it. The current theory is that it was a professional killer."

"Aren't they very hard to catch?" Bonny asked.

"It isn't easy. But there seems to be a lot of commotion in the crime community right now. I have a feeling this killer will surface again, and maybe we'll get a better shot at him next time. These fellows don't retire, you know."

"What kind of commotion?" Bonny asked.

"Well, apparently there was a good deal of money involved, and rumor has it that it hasn't been found. If it's as much money as we hear, it can't be easy to hide."

"You'll never find it," Lande said.

"You sound rather cynical," Mulheisen said.

"I don't know about that. I know about money, though. You see," Lande looked very canny, "a lotta people think of money as, . . . well, dollars and coins, . . . but it ain't."

"Ah," said Mulheisen. He looked at Lande with interest. He would not have suspected the man of philosophy. "What is money, then?"

"It's just data," Lande said. "Information. When you work in computers, you purty soon find out that everything is data. You tell the computer something, the computer does what it's gotta do. You tell a computer this is fifty bucks, the computer says OK. A guy sticks his card in a machine, the machine gives him fifty bucks. Who needs it? I mean, who needs the actual bucks? All you gotta do is get the machine to tell another machine that it's got fifty bucks." He stopped and crossed his arms with a triumphant look.

Bonny and Mulheisen looked at each other. She said, "But Gene, honey, you have to have fifty dollars at some point, don't you?"

"Nanh. Oh, somewhere, sometime, there's gotta be fifty bucks, but the machine don't care. Anyways, you wouldn't understand." He turned to Mulheisen. "So you think the guy, the hitman'll be back?"

Mulheisen shrugged. "My old partner used to say, 'The world is round.' He meant that even if you didn't catch the guy, the criminal, this time . . . just wait awhile. He'll be back."

Lande pondered this, then nodded. "It's a wonder someone hasn't already tooken out Tupman and Conover," he said. "Conover's a loan shark, a guy with a heart a stone. Now they say he's moved into coke. Slime like that don't deserve to live." He seemed genuinely angry.

Mulheisen shrugged. "So don't borrow any money from him."

Lande snorted. "Not me! I'm doing fine. I drive a Cadillac. I don't need no loan shark. Right, Bon?"

Bonny was quick to agree. "Gene's doing great! You ought to see our place, Mul. Why don't you come over for a drink?"

"Hey, yeah, come on," Lande said. "Y'oughta see how Bon's got it all fixed up. She could be a internal decorator, you know. Except she ain't a fag. But y'oughta see it. Come on, it's on'y a twenny-minute drive."

"I just can't do it," Mulheisen said, looking at his watch. "I've got so much on my desk now, . . . and I've got a precinct commander who is just waiting for me to screw up."

"Who?" Lande asked. "You mean that big ape who picked me up? What's his name?"

"No, you're thinking of Dennis Noell, the Big Four honcho. Buck Buchanan is about as different as you could imagine. He's a self-important little twerp . . ." Mulheisen faltered, aware suddenly that Lande's stature was identical with Buchanan's, but he quickly saw that Lande wouldn't even notice the remark, and he went on, " . . . but ounce for ounce he's more dangerous to law enforcement than a six-pack of Tupmans and Conovers."

Amazingly, Lande nodded his head in agreement. "I know the type," he said. "Some a these little jerks, they got what they call a little-man complex, you know what I mean? They gotta comp—ah, what's that word, Bon? You know, comp-something?"

Bonny hadn't been listening. She was staring into space, thinking about something else. Jarred, she said, "What?" Then, "Mul, you have to come over."

Mulheisen begged off. He had to be in court early. They seemed genuinely anxious for him to come over, but they eventually gave it up. They talked for another quarter hour, and finally Mulheisen was free of them, though not before he'd agreed to keep in touch. Privately he hoped never to see them again. But, after all, he thought as he drove home, it hadn't been all that bad an evening. The food was fine, Lande's habits notwithstanding, and Bonny was quite wonderful to look at. He felt sorry she had such a boor for a husband, but she was obviously devoted to him. When you came right down to it, it didn't look like such a bad deal for either of them. A lot of people would trade places with either one, especially with Gene, he thought. He wasn't among them, however.

Eight

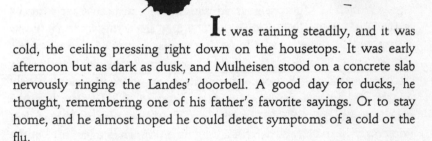

It was raining steadily, and it was cold, the ceiling pressing right down on the housetops. It was early afternoon but as dark as dusk, and Mulheisen stood on a concrete slab nervously ringing the Landes' doorbell. A good day for ducks, he thought, remembering one of his father's favorite sayings. Or to stay home, and he almost hoped he could detect symptoms of a cold or the flu.

The weather was reason enough to be uncomfortable, but he was uneasier still about this interview. Bonny had called the previous afternoon, the day after the dinner, and asked him to come by. She seemed near tears but wouldn't explain herself. She said it was serious. Mulheisen hoped to hell it didn't involve himself personally, but he hadn't been able to get a clear angle on what it was all about. He'd decided to treat it as a straightforward official visit, to complete the witness report on Lande. But he knew there were elements of emotional entanglement here—if he were being honest, he'd have to say it was sex that was making him so ill at ease.

Mulheisen belonged to a generation of males who believed sexiness was positive. Specifically, Mulheisen and his coevals believed that women, in particular, aspired to sexiness. The icon of this sexy generation was Marilyn Monroe. Her male counterpart was Marlon Brando. According to contemporary feminist theory, however, as Mulheisen understood it, through Marilyn all women were exploited for their

presumed sexual qualities. He understood that more than one generation of American males had been brought up to believe the best thing
about a woman was her sexiness and, by extension, her availability.
Evidently this was what the debate about "sex objects" was all about.
It was not clear whether Brando was similarly exploited or whether
men were thereby insulted. That notion never came up. Mulheisen was
a sensible man: he doubted that very many women seriously compared
themselves with Marilyn any more than very many men really aspired
to be like Brando. But it was nice to have a common ground on which
one could identify to some degree with Marilyn Monroe or Marlon
Brando. It was more fun than identifying with, say, the queen of
England or Senator Everett Dirksen.

As much as Mulheisen agreed with the feminists that such stereo-
typing was essentially negative, he couldn't shake his upbringing entirely. He still felt that Marilyn Monroe was a hell of a fine-looking
woman. Basically a pragmatic man, he sometimes felt like an aesthetic
moron: breasts and buttocks were attractive—why? He didn't think
somebody had just made it up. He felt there had to be a natural
attraction, and if so, why should he fight it? And because of these visible
emblems of sexuality, he had for a long time nourished a lust for Bonny
Wheeler.

Having looked at the old centerfold and thereby reassured himself
that he no longer harbored such callow notions toward her, he felt he
ought to be able to encounter her without any undue intrusion of sexual
attraction. At dinner she had been very attractive, even sexy, and she
hadn't made him feel at all uneasy. In fact, it was only her husband's
boorish remarks that had unsettled him.

So why was he nervous ringing her doorbell? Was it just that he
was alone and he knew she was alone? He was conscious of a suppressed excitement.

He had left Jimmy Marshall to review the list of passengers who
had flown into Detroit prior to Hal Good's rental of the car at Metropolitan Airport. The idea was to find the few, if any, who had booked
through from Iowa City. There was a chance that Good had used his
real name.

Mulheisen would have preferred to interview Bonny with Jimmy present, but she had asked him to come alone. He was anxious to avoid any false impressions, for instance that Lande was being given special treatment as a witness because of a relationship between Mulheisen and the man's wife. So he hadn't told Jimmy where he was going. With any luck nothing would come of it, and the whole thing would be forgotten.

He had driven out to the Landes' condominium, located in a cul-de-sac off Kelly Road. It was a duplex and looked moderately expensive. The cars parked on the street were in the Buick and Chrysler range, and quite new, with a sprinkling of Saabs and BMWs.

He had an irrational desire to be holding something, bringing something, a gift, flowers, candy. He had worn his best jacket, a very fine camel hair, and he had donned cashmere socks. Why? Just because cashmere socks always made him feel good? He didn't know and refused to think about it.

Bonny opened the door. She wore a simple chino skirt, a faintly pink-striped oxford cloth shirt with a button-down collar, and plain white Topsiders. She looked astonishingly youthful. Her curly blond hair was brushed out, and she wore the kind of makeup that made a woman appear not to be wearing makeup. The effect was charmingly innocent. She looked smaller, somehow. It was the schoolgirl outfit, Mulheisen decided. He was relieved. Nevertheless the shirt was nicely filled out, and the front was unbuttoned enticingly low, revealing a glimpse of a lacy brassiere.

"Mul, come in! Here, let me have that wet coat. Gee, imagine you in a hat." She took his things and hung them on a chrome stand in the foyer.

Mulheisen mumbled something about his hair getting thin and followed her into the living room. It was a pale champagne room—champagne shag carpet, champagne finish to the silk upholstery of the couch and chairs, pale blond coffee table. On a day this bleak it wasn't a charming place; perhaps on sultry days its coolness was soothing.

"Very nice," Mulheisen said.

"Coffee?" she asked.

Mulheisen followed her into the tiny kitchen. It was modern and shiny. Pans hung from a chrome and wood rack over the range, exposing their brightly scoured bottoms. Expensive-looking knife handles projected from a heavy wooden block on the tiled counter, and a fancy hardwood cutting board was scarred with real cuts.

Bonny chattered away as she measured ground coffee into a Mr. Coffee coffee maker. "Isn't this rain the pits? . . . I always think Maxwell House is best, don't you? . . . Do you like croissants?" She pronounced the word "cross-ants." She got out two bone china cups and saucers, poured the cream into the matching creamer, and set out the sugar. She had jam in a lovely little pot, and she put everything on a tray and carried it into the living room.

The television was on, showing a soap opera. It was a large set, and the sound was turned low. She seemed not to notice until Mulheisen looked at it. She picked up the remote control from the glass-topped coffee table and shut the machine off.

Mulheisen sat across the room in one of the matching chairs and drank from the little cup. It was not very good but better than precinct coffee. He refused a croissant.

He was puzzled by her seeming lightheartedness. Perhaps she was diffident. He decided to break the ice by attending to his own business—the report on Lande. It wasn't complete, he said. He took out his notebook. "I have to ask some questions," he said. He cleared his throat. "Nothing serious; routine, in fact. We're trying to clear off this case, you understand. The one Gene was picked up on. Mainly what I want to do is verify Gene's statement. According to my notes, he went out about seven. Is that right?"

Bonny frowned, thinking. "It's hard to be sure. I think it was earlier. It was still light out."

Mulheisen frowned. "Well, Bonny, it seemed to be quite clear when I talked to you and Gene that night. He went out about seven—you were making dinner, and he went out. Why?"

"Why did he go out?" Bonny looked blank. Then her eyes grew misty, and her face began to dissolve. She had looked bright and lovely, fully ten years younger, but now she looked her age, at least. "He . . . ah . . . I don't . . ." Her voice faded to a whisper.

Mulheisen picked up his coffee cup from the table and took a long drink, watching her over the rim. His heart went out to her, despite himself. She was in trouble.

"What is it, Bonny?" he asked gently.

She took a deep breath. "This is why I called you," she said. "He got a call, about five. He said he had to go out for a little bit."

"Who called?"

"I don't know. I mean . . . it was a woman. She called earlier, twice. Before Gene got home."

"What did she say?" Mulheisen prompted.

"She wouldn't say. When I said Gene wasn't home, she just hung up." Bonny mustered a look of bravery and offered, "I've talked to her before. I mean, she's called on other occasions."

"Do you have any idea who she is?"

Bonny gazed off to one side. She looked worn now, and to Mulheisen it seemed that her fresh complexion had grown sallow.

"I think I know who she is," she said. "I think she's a woman I met at a party once. Her name is Germaine something. She's a singer, I think. I know what she is. She's one of *those women*."

A dull silence crept upon the room. It wasn't a full silence—Mulheisen could see the rain falling steadily beyond the champagne curtains, and he could faintly hear the swish of automobile tires on the street, the ticking of a clock, the cycling of the refrigerator. There were words that needed to be spoken, but neither of them wanted to speak. He stared into his empty cup. Bonny noticed and gratefully got up and went into the kitchen for more coffee. When she didn't return, Mulheisen followed her.

She was leaning against the counter, her hands pressed down on the tiled countertop. Her back was to him, and he could see that her curly blond head was shaking. The kitchen window looked out onto an alley, and beyond it was a hedge; beyond that, the side of a house. The rain and the darkness made it quite awful.

"Bonny," he said softly and laid a hand on her shoulder. She turned to him automatically and buried her face in his chest. Quite naturally he put his arms about her trembling shoulders and patted her back comfortingly. She shook convulsively, soaking his shirt with tears.

After a while he grew impatient with her grief, despite his sympathy. But he didn't push her away. She was warm in his arms. She extended her arms under his jacket, around his back. She hugged him tightly. He quickly became aware of the pressure of her breasts. They seemed large and firmly resilient. He couldn't help envisioning the centerfold. Inevitably he was aroused.

Embarrassed, he attempted to extricate himself, but Bonny's arms were clinched tightly, and her face was buried in his chest. He had dreaded just this, of course; but on the other hand, he had fantasized something like it for some twenty years. The intervening time had greatly eased the intensity of that fantasy, but it was still there.

She lifted her face and looked into his. "Oh Mul," she said softly. Obviously his condition was known to her. He stared down into her face, and they might have kissed, but he realized then that this was not the sexy teenager of his dreams but a middle-aged woman married to someone else. The tears had marred the carefully laid on cosmetics.

Gently but firmly he pushed her away, saying, "We better slow down." He turned and looked wildly about the kitchen. "Where's that coffee?" His voice was absurdly high and raspy.

Bonny looked stricken for a second, then managed a forced "Whoo!" She raised a hand to her forehead, then wiped her eyes quickly. "I'm sorry . . . I, ah . . . I . . ." She took a deep breath. She smiled and said, "Yes, . . . coffee." She began to rinse out their cups, and Mulheisen strolled back to the living room. He desperately wished for a cigar, but this was not a room in which a cigar ever had, or could, be smoked.

When she rejoined him with the coffee cups, she looked remarkably bright and fresh again. Mulheisen stood up to take the cup and said, "I want you to know that, I, uh, like you, Bonny, . . . I always have, . . . but under the circum——"

"Oh, shut up, Mul," she said and seated herself across from him on the couch, smoothing her skirt. In a dry, frank manner she said, "I knew I never had a chance with you, Mul."

"Bonny!" Mulheisen's long face twisted in a grimace of concern.

"Let's drop it, shall we?" she said. "We were talking about Gene and . . . his girlfriend." She smiled wryly.

"Bonny, how did you come to marry a . . ."

"A dope like Gene? Well, he's not a dope, Mul. A lot of people make the mistake of thinking so, but he's really very bright. He just has that . . . that manner. Anyway, the answer is he asked me."

Mulheisen sat silently for a moment, then said, "And no one else . . . ?"

"No one. Well, a few drunks from time to time."

"But that's impossible, Bonny. Why, look at you—you're beautiful."

"Do you think so? Still?" She gazed at him calmly. "Or is it that I look like a great piece of ass?" Immediately she smiled in her old apologetic fashion and said, "I'm sorry, Mul. You didn't deserve that. It's just . . . well, that's the way it usually is and always has been."

Mulheisen was intensely uncomfortable. To his eyes nobody could be a more desirable woman than Bonny, but what did that mean? A piece of ass? And what happens when this desirable woman approaches the end of her career as a sex object? His face betrayed his dismay.

"How about you," she said, "did you ever get married? No? I would have guessed that." She arched a brow flirtatiously and said, "Not the marrying kind, is that it?"

Mulheisen shrugged. "I don't know. But you . . . how did you and Lande . . . ?"

"I met him in Las Vegas. I was working the gamblers in one of the casinos. I used to be in the chorus, but by this time I was bringing drinks to the big winners. I wasn't too old for that." She smoothed her shirtfront and smiled.

Suddenly she jumped up and went to a cabinet in the corner of the room. She took out a cut glass decanter and a glass, into which she poured a robust measure of whiskey. She turned to Mulheisen and hoisted the glass with a mocking gesture. "It's a little early, but"—she glanced out at the dark rain—"it looks plenty late enough." She drained the glass. "Whew! I needed that," she said. "You?"

Mulheisen frowned, then said, "All right."

He walked across the room to her. She poured for both of them. *"Nastrovya,"* she said. "That means 'nasty day.' " She drank half of hers.

Mulheisen sniffed the glass. "What is it?"

"Whiskey, dope."

"Yeah, but what kind?" He tasted it gingerly. It was some kind of blended rye.

"Who knows? It's something he buys." She refilled her glass and carried it back to the coffee table. Now, sitting back, she threw her arms along the back of the couch on either side. The stress on the buttons made the shirt gape.

Mulheisen eyed her from across the room. The whiskey had a metallic, artificial tang. He had a fleeting memory of visiting a friend's house after school and sampling the father's forbidden whiskey. This was a moment much like that—perhaps it was the same whiskey.

"You must have known I had a crush on you, Mul," she said after a spell of silence.

Mulheisen shook his head with a sad smile and set the whiskey aside. "No, and I'm not sure I believe that. Anyway, that's past. Now you're married to Lande."

"Yes, and I'm faithful to him, although I shouldn't be, obviously." She gazed at Mulheisen frankly. "I can imagine a situation in which I wouldn't be."

Mulheisen refused this lure. "How long have you been married?" he asked.

"Six years . . . three months."

"He was a gambler then?"

"He was gambling, anyway. I don't think he's really very interested in gambling. I carried some drinks to his table. He was winning. Management likes winning players to drink. But he kept winning, and I kept bringing the drinks, and finally he tossed in his cards and said something like, 'Guys, I can't stand it! Dis broad is too pantageous!' " She laughed.

"Pantageous?" Mulheisen frowned. "Pantages?" He had a vision of the old Pantages Theatre on Mack Avenue, now long torn down, and a whiff of velvet ropes and carpets and popcorn caught him.

"I think so," Bonny said, tilting her head as if catching the same long-lost odor. "Like the theater. It's one of Gene's words. I suppose he means fantastic or outrageous or glamorous, perhaps." Then she shrugged. "Anyway, we went off to his room, so the boss was happy.

It was fun. 'Little David was small, but, oh my,' " she sang, a little shakily. "Not as small as he looks, actually. Afterward he wasn't like most of them. He wanted me to stay. I could see he really liked me. He was from Detroit, too. We talked about Detroit."

She looked thoughtful, picking up her glass and downing the rest of the whiskey. "It's funny to talk about Detroit when you're someplace else."

"Really? Why would you say that?"

"Well, you know," she said, "you run into these people and you both are like 'Isn't it great? We're not in Detroit!' Even if you're in, maybe, Buffalo."

"What's so great about Buffalo?" Mulheisen asked.

"Nothing," Bonny said. She got up and went to the cabinet for another drink. "Refill?" she asked. "No? Well, it's just that you're always happy that you're not in Detroit, but still there's some kind of feeling, you know . . . some kind of shared emotion. You've both survived Detroit." She drifted back to the couch.

Mulheisen watched her curiously. She seemed to flicker in and out of character, humorous and wry one moment, then somber and apologetic. She was getting tipsy.

"What about this computer business?" he asked.

"What about it? He's a whiz."

"Well, what is it? Does he sell them?"

"He sells them," she said, "but it's more than that. He sets up programs for people. He does pretty well at it."

"Where is his office? What kind of place is it?"

"It's in a little whatayacallum—a terrace? A bunch of offices in a motel kind of building, around a parking lot? There's a dentist and a record shop and a real estate office . . . that kind of thing. It's over on Nine Mile. He's got a secretary and a couple of guys who sell and schlepp things around."

"This secretary," Mulheisen said, "could she be . . ."

"No." Bonny laughed. "Alicia is not *the woman*. This girl is not having an affair with anyone, Mul. She's the sweetest thing imaginable, and really, I suspect she actually runs the business. But she's definitely not Gene's type, and anyway, it's not her voice on the phone."

"If this Alicia runs the business, what does Lande do?"

"Well, I mean she runs the day to day business. Gene does all the important stuff. But other than that he golfs. Don't be so surprised. He's a terrific golfer. He's nuts about it. I bet that's where he is now. At least, I hope so."

Mulheisen glanced out the window. The rain still fell. "In this?" he said. "I didn't know any courses were open yet."

"He has his own course," Bonny said. "It's out your way. Briar Ridge?"

"You mean he owns a course?" Mulheisen was startled. It had never occurred to him that an individual could own a golf course. He couldn't remember any Briar Ridge. "Is it new?"

"Pretty new," Bonny said. "I've only been out there a couple times. I tried to golf but it didn't work. Did you ever try it? It's crazy. I mean, the little ball sits there, perched on that little wooden thing . . . You'd think you could knock it over the edge of the world . . . Gene does! But they give you these clumsy, odd-shaped clubs to hit with . . . It's crazy. Gene can hit it out of sight, though." She was quite clearly proud of his ability.

"Who does he play with?"

"You mean regularly? I don't know, there are a couple of guys. He'll play with anybody. And when he isn't playing, he's working on the course . . . unless he's got a job that Alicia and the guys can't handle. He plays with people he meets out there. He tells me all about it. To hear Gene tell it, none of them knows the first thing about golf. And they cheat!" She smiled sadly then and said, "You may have noticed . . . Gene doesn't have a . . . well, he doesn't really get along with most people very well. He's kind of abrasive, I guess."

Mulheisen didn't rise to this either. "What about his friends?" he asked.

"That's just it," Bonny said; "he doesn't really have any friends. Oh, he talks about this guy—'my buddy,' he says—or another guy—'my pal'—but it's not real. They never come over to dinner . . . They don't call. She calls." She grimaced, then went on, "Maybe he's the kind of guy who doesn't need a lot of friends. But I think he'd like one friend. A man should have friends, shouldn't he?"

"Most people have friends," Mulheisen agreed. He glanced out the window and tried to imagine a lonely Lande out in the cold rain, lugging his bag of clubs through the squishing grass. He suppressed a shudder.

"He likes you," Bonny said.

"Me!"

"Oh, yes. He admires you. He wants to help you. Also, I think he knows about us."

"Bonny, there's nothing to know about us," Mulheisen said.

"He's heard me talk about you. He knows we were . . . well, friends, in high school. And then after you got him out of that awful jail and then we had dinner . . . Mul, it would be wonderful if you could just be . . ." She faltered when she saw Mulheisen's cold expression.

"Let's talk about the calls," Mulheisen said.

Bonny launched into a long tale about the woman. She called at least once a week, usually more often. It had been going on for at least six months. She never even pretended to leave any kind of business message. If Bonny said that Gene wasn't in, she would hang up and then call back every hour until Gene showed up. Then there would be a cryptic conversation—"Yes, no, when?"—and so forth. Then Gene would go out. Not every time, but often. Sometimes he just hung up and made no further comment. If Bonny asked who it was, he would say, "Nobody." They would go on with their evening as if nothing had happened.

Mulheisen wanted to ask if Bonny didn't ever get angry and demand an explanation, but he knew she wouldn't. Not the complaisant, wounded-looking Bonny. This Bonny now, sitting across the room from him with her frank, nearly cynical manner was something new. He wondered if she was this way only with him. He didn't think so—something seemed to have happened to her.

Sometimes lately Gene would be gone all night, she told him. When that happened, he usually came home for breakfast, or it might be in the very early hours, and he would slip quietly into bed with her. She would pretend to be asleep even though she usually laid awake. At any rate, he never said where he'd been, although in the morning he might apologize for not getting home. He acted as if he'd been out on some business matter, though what kind of business kept a man out all night? The computer business wasn't conducted at night.

Mulheisen felt as gloomy as the day. Lande was such a crude, insensitive kind of guy, he thought, he probably didn't even realize that Bonny was in agony.

"He's really a nice man," she said.

Mulheisen was silent.

"I know most people find him . . . difficult," she said. "But except for this . . . this thing with the woman, he's very kind. Really. I have nothing to complain about—he's a good provider." She gestured around her at the nice apartment. "Mostly, it's like we're on a honeymoon. We go out to the show, to dinner . . . Sometimes we take little trips."

"Where to?" Mulheisen asked.

"We went to the Cayman Islands over Christmas. We stayed at a terrific hotel, right on the beach. Of course, part of it was business."

"Business? In the Cayman Islands?"

"Well, we went out to one of the other islands, to look at a site for a golf course. Gene has been thinking about building another course. He loves golf so much and he's gotten to know so much about it from developing Briar Ridge he's thinking of becoming a golf architect. He spent a lot of time talking to bankers down there."

Mulheisen felt unutterably sad. Lande a golf architect? How could a woman be so deluded? he wondered. Even grateful to such a coarse little thug? Was it just that he'd taken her out of the marketplace, as it were? And how could she tolerate his blatant infidelity, his carelessness toward her? What did she get from it? Was Lande some kind of great lover? A piece of ass? He felt he had to help her.

"What can I do, Bonny?"

"Oh, I don't know, Mul. It's just great talking to you, being able to tell somebody about it. There's probably nothing you can do. I just thought . . . since you're a detective . . . maybe you could just find out for me who this woman is, this Germaine. That's all."

Mulheisen felt helpless. "What good would it do?" he asked. "I mean . . . if he wants to stop, he'll stop. What's the use? Do you know anything else about her? Where did you meet her?"

"It was at a party. Gene had these partners in the golf course—he bought them out. So to celebrate he threw a big party out at the club—all catered. It was terrific! She was there. I don't know who she was supposed to be with. She was flirting with Gene. Somebody said she was a singer. She's tall, dark haired, about thirty . . . kind of stacked. I could tell he liked her."

"Can you remember any names? Who was at the party?"

"Well, there were a lot of people, but I'd never met most of them. The partners . . . there was . . . let's see . . . I think one guy's name was Etcheverry, something like that. And a guy named, uh, Frank . . . Frank . . . Oh, I can't remember."

"Can you call anybody?" Mulheisen asked. "I mean, I'd like to help you, but . . . Really, Bonny, it's not the kind of thing I do. I can't investigate people for no reason."

Bonny got up and poured another drink. She sat down again and drank a little of it. Then she said, "I think somebody said she was a friend of Sid Sedlacek's."

Mulheisen digested this in silence for a good long while, then said, "And her name is Germaine?"

Bonny nodded.

Mulheisen watched her. At last he rose, saying, "Find out who else was at the party. Call me."

She followed him to the door and stood by—expectantly, he felt—while he pulled on his raincoat. She handed him his hat and raised her face. He managed a more-or-less casual embrace with a kiss on the cheek.

It was still raining, perhaps harder now.

Nine

At approximately the same moment but half a continent apart, Mulheisen and Joe Service drove to similar establishments. In Detroit, as Bonny had described it, the terrace on Nine Mile Road resembled nothing so much as a motel—a U-shaped single-story brick building that provided space for several shops and parking within the ample arms of the U. The Ninemile Plaza was practically identical with the La Cienega Center in Orange County, but while it was pouring rain in Detroit, in California the sky was milky white with a high overcast, and the air temperature was eighty-three degrees Fahrenheit, thirty degrees Celsius, according to the rotating sign by the Bank of America branch. There were other differences as well: in Detroit, a dentist's office, a vacuum cleaner sales office, and the Polski Pierogi sausage shop; in Orange County, a pet shop, the Golden Samurai martial-arts academy, and a lawn- and tree-grooming service. Each complex boasted a computer shop (Doc Byte in Detroit, Computerama in California), a video-rental shop, and a hobby shop—in Detroit the hobby shop featured model trains; California's counterpart was a toss-up between supplies for amateur painters and beer- and wine-making equipment.

Mulheisen parked his old Checker directly in front of Lande's Doc Byte shop, which was sandwiched between the hobby shop and the dentist. He wondered if the dentist was annoyed by Lande's sign—

perhaps not. It must have made many people smile, as Mulheisen did now, and remember. A sucker for model trains, he couldn't resist going into the hobby shop first. Although he didn't indulge in the hobby, a friend of his had an elaborate layout of Grand Trunk trains that took up most of the friend's basement. What Mulheisen particularly liked was trolley cars. It had something to do with riding the old interurban that ran to Mount Clemens when he was a child. He was delighted to find an HO-gauge model that reminded him greatly of the Detroit, Monroe and Toledo Short Line cars he had seen many, many years ago. It was made in Germany and cost fifty dollars. He bought it, thinking he might convince his buddy, Fred, to add it to the layout. To that end he also bought the requisite track and some streetlights.

It was still pouring, an absolutely miserable day, though not to Mulheisen; he found it quite agreeable somehow. He tossed the bag of models into the car and ducked into Doc Byte. There was a display room with several computers and printers set up on modern-looking desks. One of the terminals was displaying a constantly changing picture—an experimental automobile in various stages of design and from different angles and perspectives, all in striking colors and accompanied by explanatory captions. There was nobody in the shop. Mulheisen looked about until he noticed a window at the back and what appeared to be the office. He peered in. An extremely heavy young woman, twenty-five or so, was industriously scanning listings on a computer terminal. A telephone was clamped between her cheek and her shoulder, and she was talking all the while. She glanced up at Mulheisen and beckoned him toward a door off a small corridor.

He found his way into the office and stood there, dripping, while for another three minutes she conducted an unintelligible conversation. At last she said, "Okeydoke, I'll order it," and hung up. An absurdly tiny head was perched on enormous shoulders. She had no visible neck, and her bosom projected out before her, resting on the desktop. It must have been a struggle for her to see the keyboard on which she typed.

Mulheisen glanced at the name plate on the desk and said, "Miss Bommarito? I'm Sergeant Mulheisen, Detroit police." He held up a laminated plastic identification card for her to read.

Her dark eyes widened, but a look of comprehension flickered across her face, and she said, "I bet it's about that shooting the boss almost saw."

"That's right," Mulheisen said. "Is Mr. Lande in?"

"You gotta be kidding. It's nearly four. Did you have an appointment?" She began to straighten up her desk and heaved herself laboriously to her feet to file various pieces of paper and reshelve some catalogs. She looked to weigh at least 250 pounds on a frame no taller than five feet two. She wore a neat woolen jumper over a silk blouse, and her legs were like tree stumps, tapering to tiny feet in flat-heeled shoes. Her arms seemed to be inflated; they projected out from her roly-poly body, ending in dainty hands that almost twinkled. Her pretty little head peeped out of the gross body like some kind of fairy trying to stay afloat in a vat of flesh. Long, rich black hair cascaded over her shoulders. She seemed to bounce and roll around the cramped office.

"His wife said he might be golfing," Mulheisen said dubiously.

The woman glanced through the window that gave onto the showroom. "In this rain? Well, why in heck not? He's crazy enough for it. But I doubt that even Gene would be out in this. You might get him at the Eastgate Lounge, over on Cadieux. He sometimes goes bowling when it's raining . . . Well, he calls it bowling, but there's a couple guys there who play a little cards in the afternoon. Whoops! Maybe I shun't have said that."

Mulheisen attempted to allay her fears with a grin that had less than an encouraging effect. "When is he in?" he asked, glancing around.

"Oh, he's in and out," the woman said loyally. "Gene's not much for strict office hours, never was. He gets more done than the average guy, but he hates regular hours."

"So . . . business is good, then?"

"Great! We got more'n we can handle."

"Is it just you here, Miss?"

"No, we got a couple of salesmen, but I sent them home an hour ago. Nothing's happening today I can't handle, what with the rain."

"What exactly do you do here?" Mulheisen asked. "I mean, what is the business?"

"Well, as you can see," she said, "we sell computers—everything from lap models to mainframes. Are you into computers, Sergeant?"

"I'm afraid not. But I guess I'll have to get with it sooner or later."

"You can't avoid 'em anymore," she agreed. "But the thing about Doc Byte is we devise systems for customers, mostly small businesses. Anything up to small factories. You see, a dentist's office has different needs from a tool 'n' die. We tailor-make systems."

"Is that what Lande does?"

"Pretty much. He's some kinda genius about it, though he doesn't really know that much about conventional computers." Alicia Bommarito laughed. She was quite charming, with her lovely little face beaming and her long, lustrous veil of hair swirling as she moved about. "I know that sounds weird, but it is weird. What he knows is all the theoretical stuff and how to get machines to do what he wants 'em to, but if it comes to just what any given stock model is all about, you better ask me. Gene'd just confuse you. Salesmen, and even run-of-the-mill programmers are a dime a dozen nowadays. Gene sets up special deals and invents systems. A genius."

"I see," Mulheisen said, and he had a pretty good idea of what she meant. In Detroit it was not uncommon to find, say, a tool-and-die partnership in which one of the partners was the expert machinist, the tinkerer and innovator, and the other was the salesman and office manager. Separately these partners would probably not prosper, but combined they were formidable. Obviously Lande had found a way to dispense with the sales-and-details partner, thanks to a competent manager like Miss Bommarito and perhaps because of the oversupply of young, well-trained computer hands.

Whatever the details were, Mulheisen could see that Lande had at least won the staunch loyalty and support of his office manager. If Alicia Bommarito was as competent as she seemed, she was invaluable. He hoped Lande appreciated her. Idly he wondered what Lande paid someone like her.

"You like this kind of work?" he asked.

She seemed surprised. "Who wouldn't? A boss like Gene! He's never on your butt—pardon my French—and the pay is great. You pretty much make your own hours, and no union dues either. I'm closing up now because of this muck. Course, sometimes you haveta work till eight. But it's great."

She unplugged the coffee maker and rinsed the utensils, setting them to dry on paper towels. All the while she chatted informationally about the constantly changing computer trade. Mulheisen lounged about, hands in pockets, nodding and asking a few questions from time to time. At one point he casually opened a door off the overcrowded office and looked into a small room that appeared to be a kind of warehouse. It was stacked with large cardboard boxes on which were emblazoned the logos of various well-known electronics firms.

"This must be shipping and receiving, eh?" he called over his shoulder to Miss Bommarito.

She stopped her bustling and looked at him disapprovingly. "I don't think you should be poking around like that," she said. "Don't you need a search warrant or something?"

"What for?" Mulheisen asked. He switched on a light and wandered about the chilly room. "You aren't hiding anything, are you?" She stood in the doorway while he glanced at the work counter with its bills of lading on clipboards, a telephone, a couple of utility knives, and various items of packing equipment—tape, twine, labels. He peered at a pile of cartons on a pallet, all of them with electronics logos and shipping labels that read Corporate Banque, Ltd., 129 Belsize, George Town, Grand Cayman Island.

Miss Bommarito stood by the light switch. "You'll have to leave now, Sergeant. I'm closing up."

"You sell computers to the Cayman Islands even?"

Miss Bommarito flicked off the light, and Mulheisen shrugged past her into the office. She hit the rest of the lights and allowed him to hold a tent-size trench coat while she stuffed her thighlike arms into it. She shooed him to the door.

There were few cars left in the parking lot. Mulheisen peered out at the now-drilling rain and said, "Can I give you a lift, Miss?"

"I'm parked out back. Is there any message for Gene?"

"No, I just had to check out this witness report. Thanks a lot. You've been very helpful."

"Witness report," she sniffed, "Gene didn't even see the shooting."

"Well, we have to check it out. Thanks."

Mulheisen dashed to his car and clambered in. Before he could start the car, he saw that the lights had gone out in Doc Byte. He pulled out onto Nine Mile Road and then turned down the next side street and parked. Sure enough, a few minutes later a brand-new Corvette slunk out of the alley behind the complex and turned toward Nine Mile. Miss Bommarito wore a broad-brimmed hat, and Mulheisen almost didn't recognize her behind the fogged windows. One would never have suspected that an eighth of a ton of flesh was hidden in the low-slung interior of that gleaming red car.

Mulheisen reckoned the cost of that car at thirty thousand dollars or more. Alicia Bommarito must be paid more than most office help, he thought. He wished he'd seen her getting into the Vette; that must have been a feat.

Joe Service parked his rented Tempo in the La Cienega Center parking lot and swaggered into the air-conditioned offices of Hello Central, an answering service, relishing the agreeable chill on his bare arms. He wore a golf shirt and slacks. He removed his dark glasses as a young woman came through the doorway at the back of the office. She was Asian, with long black hair, about twenty-two.

Joe flashed a friendly grin and said, "Hi, I'm just shopping for an answering service."

"Oh, great," the woman said, smiling back. "Is this a personal or a commercial service?"

"Well, both. I'm self-employed."

"Oh, right." The woman slid a tablet of forms along the counter and picked up a ballpoint pen to take down the essential information. "Name?"

"Humann. With two ens. Joe Humann."

"Humann?" She wrinkled her little nose with amusement. "That's neat. What do you do, Mr. Humann?"

"I'm a consultant."

"Uh-hunh. What kind of consulting?"

"It's like locations," Joe said, getting into the spirit of things.

"Locations? Like movie locations? Really? Great!"

"Yes. I'm on the road a lot, naturally, and I don't really need an office, see. Well, I have a kind of office in my house—I live in Malibu. But the answering machine is getting like wiped out. It just can't handle the volume anymore. So I figured I need something more, like, professional. Do you answer the phone as if it was my office or something?"

"Sure. What's your company name?"

"Well, I don't really have a name. I mean, I like use my own name. But maybe I should have a real business name."

"Oh, sure," she said, "that'd be more professional. See, then I—or one of the other girls, whoever's on duty—could say, like, 'Good morning, Humann Enterprises,' or whatever. Actually, that's kind of cute."

"Hey, I like it," Joe said cheerfully. "But how about Humann Resources?"

The woman laughed. "That's great!"

"You don't think it's too corny?" Joe asked. He slipped the sunglasses back on so he could look the woman over. She was attractive, athletic looking, with a slim build. He thought she might be Japanese, but not wholly. He was delighted with her easy manner.

"I don't think it's corny," she said. "It's kind of an informal business, isn't it? I didn't even know there was such a business, but I guess there'd have to be, wouldn't there?"

"It's essential," Joe assured her. "Location means a lot in how a film looks. You know directors these days—everything's got to look just right. If he's got mountains in the script, you can bet he's got an idea what those mountains look like, right? So I find the right mountains."

"Oh, right. Or a house."

"Or a house, or an office building. Usually I can find everything I want right here in the LA area, which is why they like to hire me. But I go all over the country. Out of the country, too, and not just to Mexico. Europe, Asia . . . I was the guy who first found Vietnam in Guatemala, for instance, for *Saigon Saga*."

"*Saigon Saga*? With Corey James? Gol, I loved that! Well, it was kinda violent, . . . but Corey James! Do you go on location? . . . Gol, what am I saying? But, I mean, . . . while they're shooting?"

"Sometimes, but I don't usually hang around much once they've started shooting. I did get to know Martin Shell pretty well, on *Saigon*."

"Neat! He's so great!"

"A great actor," Joe solemnly agreed. "But the point is, Miss . . . uh, what, uh . . ."

"Gisela," she said promptly. "Jizzy, actually. Jizzy Kazaka."

"Mmm, pretty name. Yours?"

"Of course! You goof!"

They laughed together.

"Well, it could be a stage name," Joe said.

"Oh sure," she joshed back, "like I'm a giant star or something. But no, really . . . everybody calls me Jizzy."

"Everybody? Your husband, too?"

"Hey, it's like my mom, my dad, my brother . . . it was like some kind of joke at first, right? My gram, she's Jewish, used to call me Jizzelika or something. I think it's Yiddish or something, you know? And then the rest of the family made it even shorter."

"You're Jewish? I thought you were, maybe, Japanese."

"Both," she said, "and don't say anything that involves the word *princess*."

"Never crossed my mind," Joe said. "So, what are you, the manager, Jizzy?"

"Me? Are you kidding? Gina's the boss. She doesn't own it, though. We're like a chain. She's not in today, though."

"Do you think I could look at your operation, Jizzy?" Joe lifted the hinged section of the counter and stepped through.

The woman looked alarmed momentarily, but then she said, "I guess so. What was it you wanted to see? There's just Martie and Donna on the board right now."

"I'm always interested in locations, Jizzy," Joe said. "Who knows? One of these times I'll have to find an answering service for Cindy Williams." There was a wall immediately behind the counter, painted pink with a couple of doors in it. Service opened one door and peeked inside. There were a half dozen telephone consoles, only two of which were being used at the moment, by two women wearing head-sets. A computer terminal was built into each console, presumably so that the operators could call up, and/or enter data for, their customers.

Joe closed the door and turned back to Jizzy Kazaka. She was a doll, he thought, getting the full view. "Very interesting," he said. He eased Jizzy's tension by stepping back behind the counter.

"One thing I'm concerned about, Jiz," he said, leaning on the counter, "is security."

Miss Kazaka leaned on the counter. She was almost Joe's height, and their heads were fairly close. "Like what?" she said. "We're very security conscious here."

"I can see that. But one of my biggest headaches is these directors—every one of them likes to think I'm working strictly for him, or her. I notice on my machine they never call without saying first thing, 'Where are you?' And that, of course, is exactly what I don't want them to know." He laughed. "I mean, say Steven calls and I'm in Thailand for, oh, Sly. Not only do I not want Steven to know I'm doing Sly's new flick, but I don't even want him to know that I'm not in town."

"Oh, right. No prob. We tell them whatever you say."

"Jizzy, some of these guys—Bob Redford is one—can get anything out of anybody. If Bob calls and you're on the board and he says, 'Where's Joe, anyway?' I mean, it's not so easy to tell Bob you don't know. It's Bob Redford! Have you ever talked to Bob?"

Miss Kazaka was lost in wonder. "Ah, no. I talked to Robin Williams once."

"Jiz, Robin's a sweetheart, I love him. But he's always jiving. He's no problem. Bobby is a whole 'nother show. What Bobby wants Bobby gets."

Miss Kazaka looked Joe straight in the sunglasses very seriously and said, "Bob, er, Robert Redford is old. Anyway, we wouldn't tell anyone anything you said not to."

Joe Service had a feeling she meant what she said, but he summoned up a righteous tone to say, "Let me give you fair warning, Jizzy, Bobby's not all that old. I've seen him charm the pants off plenty girls younger than you."

She arched a heavy black eyebrow and said, "Not mine."

"I hope not. So, you run the board sometimes?"

"When Gina's here."

"This is twenty-four hours, right?"

"Around the clock."

"How many people do you have on at night?"

"Usually three, until ten; then one or two the rest of the night."

"What happens when there's a call at night? Some of my clients call from Europe or Asia or Australia. They don't care what time it is here. How do you answer?"

"You mean after normal business hours? Any way you want. For instance, if you want, we can just give the number and say, 'Can I help you?' Then, when they ask for you, we say, 'Mr. Humann's office is closed now. May I take a message?' "

"I guess that'd be all right." Joe looked thoughtful for a moment, then smiled and said, "You working tonight?"

"No," she said innocently.

"Well then, let's have dinner." He grinned.

Caught off guard, she laughed outright. "That is soo sneaky!"

"I know. I'm terrible. But I'm overcome. Also, I'm just in town for the night. I'm outta here tomorrow—Brazil. That beach house of mine is too big and lonely. What do you say?"

"Serious?"

"Of course! What time do you get off?"

"Not till six."

"I'll pick you up."

"Not here," she said. "Actually, I've got kind of a date."

"Oh, well, . . . I understand."

"But I think . . . I mean . . . what did you have in mind?"

"I know what you're thinking," Service said with a rueful grin. "You're thinking I'm trying to drag you out to the beach, et cetera, et cetera. I'm not that kind of guy, Jiz. Well, I am that kind of guy, come to think of it. But I'm not in that much of a hurry. We're young, right? We got lots of time to get better acquainted. How 'bout I pick you up at your place and we can catch dinner at Radio Ranch and then . . . let's see . . . Hey! Ronny Howard's having a party tonight. We could cruise that, and if it's too boring, we could maybe catch Sal at the Comedy Shop, or something. OK?"

Fifteen minutes later Service was talking to Detroit. "I need a beach house, in Malibu, just for the night. Got anything along those lines?"

It was a huge place and right on the beach. Service spent an hour removing photographs of a man and his family and other items that might give the lie to his enterprise. He locked them all in one of the kids' bedrooms. The bikes and trikes and that sort of stuff he locked in the garage. He pushed the husband's clothes back in the closet and hung up his own stuff from his bag and set out some shaving gear in the bath off the master bedroom, after removing the wife's cosmetics.

Jizzy Kazaka didn't complain when Joe suggested they have dinner at the beach—he'd cook. She loved the lobster ravioli he made with the help of the fancy pasta machine. The sauce was Joe's speciality, a *beurre manié* with zinfandel and finely chopped shallots.

It was too bad Ronny Howard had called off his party—he had to go out of town, Joe explained. They listened to music, strolled the beach, and came back to make a fire in the fireplace—it was chilly by the sea. Joe fixed a couple of vodka tonics and then suggested they do a line of coke.

"No way," Jizzy said. She looked at him rather sharply.

Joe looked grateful. "Thanks, Jizzy. I hate the stuff myself, but anymore people seem to expect it. I'm glad you don't."

For the next fifteen minutes they smugly described to one another how loathesome dope was. They agreed, however, that marijuana was a different matter. Two joints and a couple more vodka tonics brought Joe to the launching pad. He suggested they go into the Jacuzzi.

Jizzy demurred with a sad look. "I mean, I'd kinda like to, Joe, . . . I really like you a lot, but . . . I just can't."

Joe looked down at her, frowning but nodding in agreement. "All right. It's all right. I can dig it. Hey," he looked up with a laugh, "everybody strikes out once in a while. But I respect your attitude. I really do."

Jizzy seemed pleased, and they got back into a conversation about women and sexual harassment. Finally she said, "Oh, darn! It's two. I've gotta get going."

"What's the hurry? The fire's still going. Let's have another drink. No? Another joint?"

Jizzy refused. "I have to be at work in about six hours."

Joe slumped back on the couch, his chin on his chest.

"What's wrong, Joe?"

"Nothing." He got up and said with a sigh, "All right, I'll take you home."

"Joe? You're not mad?"

He stared down at her. She was beautiful, he had decided several hours ago, with her shiny black hair, a heart-shaped face, and precise pink lips. He liked her a lot.

"Yes," he said, "I am mad . . . mad with desire. But don't take that seriously." He smiled reassuringly. "Can we go out on the deck . . . just for a minute? Here, put on my sweater." He tugged the blue cashmere sweater over his head and helped her pull it on.

The sea was only a hundred yards away, rolling in as passively as a lake, under a quarter moon. The surf glimmered with an unconvincing luminosity.

He took her by the arms and kissed her gently. He knew that was all she would permit. Her lips were cool and noncommittal but soft. He looked down into her dark eyes, catching the glint of the moon. A chilling breeze encouraged their warm embrace.

"I lied to you," he said.

Jizzy shivered. "Can we go back in?"

Inside she asked, "Lied?" She sat with her legs tucked under her, on the hearth rug, the blazing fireplace flickering behind her.

"I'm not a location scout," Joe said. He tossed down the last of his drink. "I'm a federal agent."

Jizzy was shocked. "Is this your house?"

"No," Joe admitted candidly. "I borrowed it. Don't ask me the details. I can't tell you."

Jizzy stood up. She looked like a child in the oversized sweater. "Are you a narc?"

Joe shook his head impatiently. "It's another service, one you haven't ever heard about—very few people have. I feel stupid about this . . . I meant to keep it . . . aw, crap! Jizzy, I want you to know that I really like you."

She stared up at him from the flagstones of the fireplace. "I believe you, and I'm glad, Joe. I'd hate to think . . ." She tossed her long black hair out of her eyes. "What is it you want?"

Joe sat for a long moment, staring into his empty glass. Finally he looked up and said, "Jizzy, this is a miserable business I'm in . . . Occasionally, we have to involve people who . . . but it doesn't concern you. It's not about you. Forget it."

"Joe, what is it? Tell me."

He looked glum, sighed, and finally, with resolution, said, "All right. I have to get into the answering service."

Jizzy sighed. "I was afraid it was something like that. So, you weren't really interested in me?"

"Jizzy! Don't believe that. The problem is I do care about you. I had lots of other plans for getting in there, but then I met you, and, . . . well, I couldn't resist asking you out here."

She sat down next to him on the couch, and they each thought about the evening. At last she said, "Well, it was nice. I don't hold it against you. Thanks for being honest anyway."

Joe looked at her sadly. "Jizzy, I really do like you. Look, let's forget all this crap. Forget I came in there today. Couldn't we just . . . I mean, let's do something crazy."

"Tonight?"

"Sure. How about we drive down to Del Mar and watch the sun come up, and then we'll go play the horses."

"I have to go to work!"

"Forget work," Joe said. "Call in sick for once." He fell to his knees before her, seizing her arms above the elbows and looking into her eyes. "I can get this stuff some other way. Be a little crazy with me . . . just this once!" And then they kissed again, a real kiss this time.

"What is it you're looking for?" she asked after a while.

"Forget it," Joe said. "I've got a million resources. I don't need it. The important thing is I found you. Tomorrow the races, then one of those little seafood restaurants around Oceanside."

"Joe," she said after another long kiss, "what are you looking for?"

Joe sighed and sat back on his heels, squatting before her. He looked at her face for a long time, then said, "You ever talk to your grandmother much?"

"My grandmother? What—"

"She ever say anything about . . . Nazis?"

Jizzy stared at him. "What about Nazis?"

Joe shrugged. "There's a guy. A camp official . . . he got out in the confusion after the war. We think he's a client of Hello Central. I think you have a client named Hal Good?"

"Mr. Good? Yes . . . I remember him. Why?"

"The name is Gutekleist actually," Joe said, "Good is an alias."

"Mr. Good? A Nazi?"

"I need his next number, Jizzy."

Ten

"**H**ey, who's this prick?" Tupman asked. He and his four companions were standing near the elevator in the basement parking lot of his apartment building.

The prick was a person in a bulky tanker jacket and jeans and a woolen ski mask covering his face. He had just stepped out of the shadows when the Tupman party reached the elevator. The five men peered at the strange figure, who was fumbling with something that had a long string, or perhaps a leather strap, attached to it. One of Tupman's two burly bodyguards suddenly realized that the strap was attached to the barrel of an automatic pistol.

"That's a gun!" he shouted. He almost got his own pistol out, but a half-second late can be eternally late.

The masked man had finally got the strap unraveled so that it was draped from the barrel of the .45 to his left fist, which he held tightly against his left thigh. When his arm was fully extended, making the tether tight, the gunner squeezed the trigger. The .45 began a raucous coughing roar, bucking and fighting against the tether. The gun swung through a limited arc. It had an extralong clip, and in very short order it was empty. The slugs ripped through the little group of men by the elevator, knocking them flying in a spray of blood and screams. All the men went down, tumbled in a pile of bloody cashmere and tweed overcoats. The ejected cartridge cases continued to ring and ding off the concrete floor of the parking garage in the deafening silence.

Halfway into the firing of the clip, the rapid back-and-forth movement of the barrel housing had caused the leather restraint to slip free. The pistol had begun to climb wildly, sending half the bullets up the walls and, finally, deflecting off the concrete ceiling.

The shooter stared at the leash unbelievingly and then threw it down. In a panic he hastily ejected the clip and flung it aside. Anxiously he fumbled out another clip and jammed it home. Some of the victims were groaning and writhing. One man had clambered on hands and knees toward the elevator call button. The gunner stepped forward, and holding the pistol with both hands, squeezed off another bellowing roll of thunder, spraying the sprawled bodies and ending with a fortuitous shot that caught the man at the call button.

The gunner inserted a third clip, and this time he stepped among the bodies, treading on some of them, squeezing the trigger spasmodically, turning the gun on one or another of the victims as he saw them move, their bodies jumping on the concrete and bullets ricocheting dangerously in a spray of chips when a shot missed. When that clip, too, was exhausted, the killer stared down at the pile, blinking rapidly through the eyeholes of the mask, chest heaving wildly, gasping noisily. He squeezed the trigger spasmodically, but nothing happened, and he finally grew aware of this. He turned and ran to the exit.

The mesh gate that served as the garage door had automatically descended and locked when Tupman's car entered the garage, an eventuality the killer had evidently overlooked. He craned his neck frantically, then jammed the pistol into a jacket pocket. He knelt and grasped the mesh with his bare hands, heaving upward mightily. It lifted a quarter inch, but that was all. The cold metal cut into the palms of his hands painfully.

"God*damn!*" he roared in frustration and panic, looking about wildly. Nobody had come as yet—it was four o'clock in the morning—but it could only be a matter of seconds before a guard of some kind, a night watchman, a passing motorist—anybody!—would come to investigate the horrendous volley of gunfire that had been unleashed.

"Stop it," the killer said aloud, fighting for calm. He stood and walked over to the man who had been driving the Mercedes and rolled him over. The body turned without difficulty. The killer fished out the man's wallet and calmly but quickly found the plastic card that would open the gate. He took the wallet with him and inserted the card into the locking device. The mesh slid obediently upward. When it was halfway up the killer ducked under it and walked swiftly away. He had gone some thirty feet before he stopped and returned to take the plastic card, smeared with bloody fingerprints, out of the machine and stuff it into his pocket. Something caught his eye. He ran across the bloodied concrete and snatched up the two empty ammo clips. The gate had closed again, of course, when the card was removed. The killer swore and got out the card again, inserted it, and then withdrew it. The gate descended behind him as the killer walked calmly away.

   A bunch of cops stood around in the cavernous garage. In the early morning it was as cold as the seventh level of hell. Mulheisen recognized a young detective who had started out in the Ninth but was now downtown. "Who is it, Kip?" he asked.

   "Hi, Mul. How ya doin'? Didn't you know? It's Tupman, and is he frosted." He grinned like a cheerleader and pointed to the sprawl of dead men. Then he caught Mulheisen's grimace and said, almost apologetically, "Well, he won't be missed." He stepped aside as Laddy McClain hove up.

   "Sorry to get you out of bed, Mul," McClain said in a tone that belied the statement, "but I thought you'd want to see this, being as you're still on the Big Sid case. This could be related."

   "Technically, I'm on Sid," Mulheisen conceded, "but nontechnically and in every other way there isn't any Big Sid case. Oh, Jimmy's running down a lead in Iowa, but that isn't looking too promising."

   "Well, you might get something out of this. Anyway, you asked for Big Sid, and it's yours, . . . and so is this." McClain was friendly, but he was making a point. "If you want any help, my boys will be glad to, you know. C'm'ere." He led Mulheisen over to the carnage.

   Marty Tupman had been a thirty-two-year-old white male, until about an hour earlier. Then he had become a pasty blob of inert matter that couldn't do any of the things that differentiate an animate mass of cells from an inanimate one. Tupman's cells were in a different state at the moment, in transition toward some other form. Frosty Tupman had never been attractive in life and now looked awful. He was wearing a blue cashmere overcoat that had been pierced by at least three heavy-caliber bullets that had blown out the back side of the splendid garment. He had a doltish expression on his flabby face, his eyes staring, though now clouded, and his mouth hanging open.

He half-lay on a younger white man, also in a nice coat, tweed, that had been ruined by a single shot. Against the wall, by the elevator, another young man, this one black, stretched an arm toward a call button that he'd never reach. His face was flattened against the fake brick effect of the concrete. Blood congealed in a very large puddle underneath him.

A fourth man lay on his back a few feet away from the others but sharing the great lake of blood. He was young and black and, like the others, wore a fine overcoat. His coat and jacket were open, and there were bloody smudges of hands and fingers on his white shirt. A pistol was visible in a shoulder holster.

There were footslip smears in the pool of stiff blood, and the reversed logo ƎᴷIИ was clearly visible on two of the footprints leading toward the open mesh gate of the garage. The Crime Squad had erected protective barriers and done a lot of chalking and posting of temporary signs to protect the crime scene. Lights were set up and cameras still flashed. A man with a video camera was directing another officer with a portable rack of lights.

A Crime Squad technician brought a curious item over to Mulheisen: a long leather strap, bloodied and dirtied, with a loop on one end. He dangled it from a pencil, like a dead snake.

"What's this?" Mulheisen asked. The technician had no opinion. He suggested that it might be some kind of dog leash; perhaps it had been lying there, innocently lost, when the killing had begun. Mulheisen told him to bag it and log it.

"There was another guy," McClain said, "still ticking. They took him to Grace. The guys said he didn't look like he'd make it there. You wanta go look at him?"

Mulheisen surveyed the remaining corpses with a calm eye. "Not yet," he said. "How many shots do you figure were fired here? Fifty?

Not that many? Let's say thirty." He wandered around, examining the bodies and the pockmarks made by bullets in the concrete. "You think maybe it was a team?" he said to McClain. "What I want to know," he added, "is why you think this is related to the killing of Big Sid."

"Tupman was a pal of Sid's," McClain said. "Andy tells me they may have been into this coke rip-off together."

"Yanh," Mulheisen conceded, "but they sent a lone guy to get Sid and Mickey, who was probably just in the way, but would they send the same guy to get Tupman and . . ."—he gestured at the sprawled bodies—"all these guys? The artist who cooled Sid was a Rembrandt compared to this. He used a .22-caliber brush. Whoever stilled these lives . . . I don't know, they were more the Jackson Pollock type. Maybe it was only one guy, but he didn't have the same attitude." He gestured at the bloody footprints. "That looks like one guy, but maybe he was the only one who approached the bodies." He shook his head, "It's not the same at all, Mac."

"Well, Mul . . . one guy, two guys, a dozen guys. So what?" McClain asked.

"Well, if it's one guy," Mulheisen said, "even if he's got a tommy gun, he's standing here facing five guys, all of whom he has to expect are armed . . . and he's going to take on the whole crew? He got lucky, obviously, but that isn't the way they work, Mac. They send ten guys to take out five. You know that. Also, they know their ground better than this. They know how many there will be. Good, the guy we think took out Sid, he knew he only had to deal with Sid and Mickey, and he was perfectly set up. Waiting by the gate." He thought for a moment, then conceded, "Well, this is almost the same deal . . . But I'll tell you this much, whoever did it was lucky to get out of here alive."

"Let's go talk to the survivor, Mul," McClain said, "if he's still with us. He might be able to say something."

Mulheisen gazed around at the garish lights, the crumpled bodies, the lake of blood. It might be an abattoir, a medieval torture dungeon, or a Nazi execution cellar—not an inappropriate site for the business done here. "Maybe the medical examiner can make them speak," he said.

On the way to Grace Hospital, McClain briefed Mulheisen. "Two of the guys with Tupman were lawyers. The other two were Frosty's heat. One of them almost got his gun out. It looks like the killers took one guy's wallet . . . don't know why. It obviously wasn't robbery. Tupman was carrying a wad."

"Petty theft but not grand larceny," Mulheisen said wryly. "What's that old Beatles song . . . 'She could steal, but she could not rob.' " He half-sang the line. "I suppose he took it so we wouldn't have it."

McClain said, "So you think it was one guy."

"I don't know," Mulheisen replied. "But I don't think it was the same guy. One new guy, or a handful."

"Group art," McClain said, "by the Three Stooges."

Mulheisen pictured those manic dopes with buckets and white-wash brushes, and he smiled. They were riding in a cruiser, behind a uniformed driver and McClain's assistant, Joe Greene. McClain said, "The guy they hauled away was one of the lawyers. Name is Benesh. He had about an ounce of cocaine on him."

"Is this Benesh a mob lawyer?"

"I never heard of him," McClain said. "You?"

Mulheisen hadn't heard of him either. "And Tupman had a lot of cash on him? A buy?"

"Could be. Benesh looked kind of straight to me, a regular yuppie. A client, maybe."

"Any other witnesses?" Mulheisen asked. He drew out a cigar but didn't light it. He had an idea that the hospital people would object, and they were almost there. He put it back in the leather case.

"No, as usual," McClain said complacently. "The guard was in the lobby upstairs. The driver must have let them into the parking garage with an ID card—which is missing. Probably with the stolen wallet. The door would have closed automatically behind them. The shooter was either waiting or had ducked in behind them as they drove through."

"And the guard didn't hear anything?"

McClain snorted. "The guys picked up eighteen .45-caliber empties. Say there were twenty or more shots fired down in that echo chamber, . . . and Rentacop didn't hear a thing. He had a radio going."

"Loud enough to drown out shots at that time of night?"

McClain looked disgusted. "He had on a headset. He said he didn't, but it was lying on the desk next to the radio, plugged in. He's just a kid, twenty years old. Works part-time for Pape Protection. That's the way they do things these days."

Benesh lay on an operating table, festooned with wires and tubes and surrounded by blinking electronics. An intensely bearded young man in a white smock and the blue turban of a Sikh raised his hands fatalistically when Mulheisen asked if it was all right to talk to the patient. "I cannot be optimistic that he will be capable of responding, but I see that you are determined. Do what you must."

Mulheisen bent close to the patient and said, "Benesh. Benesh." The patient's eyes struggled open. Mulheisen looked into the dullness of those eyes and felt he was looking into the beyond. "Benesh," he said, "did you see the killer?"

The dry lips moved. A whisper: "Smaw."

Some more? Or it might be *small*, Mulheisen thought. "Small?" he asked.

Benesh nodded minutely. "Short," he breathed. "Mas'. Gun strap."

"Mask? Don't nod, just blink." The man blinked. "One man?" Mulheisen held up a single finger. "Or two?"

No blink.

"Guns? Trap?" Mulheisen asked.

No blink. He wouldn't be blinking anymore.

Mulheisen, McClain, and Greene stood looking at Benesh, three monumental mourners. They shrugged in unison and left.

It was dawn and spitting rain, just getting started apparently, like a water pistol before a steady stream is brought on. The three detectives walked from John R Street to Woodward, to My Brother's Bar. It was just opening. The bartender didn't recognize them, but he had a sense of who they were. He brought out a fresh pot of coffee from the brew machine and set up a shot of whiskey before each cup.

"I know you been having probs out in the precinct," McClain said, pouring the shot into the coffee itself. "I mean, with Dennis and Buck and witnesses walking. Maybe this'll break things open and lower the heat."

That wasn't the way Mulheisen saw it, but he didn't argue. The way he saw it somebody was going to have to do a lot of explaining eventually, and he hoped it wasn't himself. He shook out a cigar and lighted up. It tasted good, and he didn't mind that both McClain and Greene mooched one off him. And the shot of whiskey and the fresh coffee made things begin to look a little better.

"Let's see," he said, "we've got five dead men, including a dead witness who says, 'Small, short, mask, guns, trap.' Or, maybe it was 'Make it short, ask me, I'm gonna crap out.' "

Greene laughed out loud. "You forgot the deaf, dumb, 'n' blind security guard, Mul," he said.

Mulheisen nodded sagely, drawing in the delicious smoke of the H. Upmann. "What else is there?"

"Lotsa .45 casings," McClain said.

"Yeah, what about that?" Mulheisen asked. "That suggests a guy firing a couple of Colt Commanders, one in each hand. Can he really fire off that many rounds quickly enough to keep the heavies from getting off at least a couple shots in return?" He shook his head in disbelief.

Greene had a theory. "If you modify the shear, you can fire the whole clip in one pull," he said. "Kind of hard to hang onto the sucker, but at least you're not toting around a tommy gun, which is kind of hard to conceal. Also, you could use extralong clips, which could carry maybe fifteen shots per. The danger, in this situation, is that a round might misfire, or it won't have enough of a load to fully cock the gun. Then you've got to manually eject the load. As far as we could see, this didn't happen."

"But how do you keep it from climbing?" Mulheisen wanted to know. "If you make it into a squirt gun, doesn't it just keep climbing?" He was trying to remember firing the .45 pistol in the air force. He had a vague recollection of horrendous noise and a bucking, barely controllable weapon.

"I saw a guy on the range once," Greene said. "Had a kind of leash, or strap, attached to the barrel. He wound it around his other fist and held it clamped against his hip. Worked pretty good."

"Gun strap!" McClain and Mulheisen said it in unison, remembering the leather strap. They laughed and for a moment thought they were on to something, but then they realized that it put them no further forward, except, as Mulheisen noted, the killer was likely a gunsmith, or perhaps a gun freak. "It was probably Dennis the Menace," Mulheisen joked, thinking of the first gun afficionado who came to mind. He marveled again at the audacity, if not plain foolishness, of a killer (assuming it was just one man) who would go into an extremely dangerous confrontation with men who he must have known would be armed, equipped with such a questionable apparatus.

Gun evidence wasn't always helpful in this sort of crime, Mulheisen knew. The trouble with trying to track a killer through the guns he used was that there were so many guns out there. Of course, if and when he was caught, and if the weapons were found, they could be excellent evidence in a trial.

"What did you tell the press?" he asked McClain.

"Gangland slaying," McClain said.

Mulheisen smiled. "How much consideration did you give to coke king carnage?"

"That's good," McClain said, "but what about coke kings croaked?"

"Crack kings croaked," corrected Greene. They laughed.

Then they sighed. Mulheisen expressed it for all of them: "I don't see the mob sending Baby Face Nelson after a coke dealer, especially with these yuppie lawyers present. A competitor maybe?"

"They like Uzis," Greene said. "They like mobility . . . drive by and spray. They don't . . . it's just not . . ." He waved a hand in frustration.

"Not their style?" Mulheisen asked. "I wonder. Sometimes I think we give these creeps too much credit for knowing what they're doing. And the mob is the same. Too many blood relatives on the payroll. You have one or two bright boys who are trying to hold together a billion-dollar business with the assistance of a bunch of cousins who tend to be brainless, bloodthirsty loons, all of whom are walking around with more armament than a World War II rifle platoon. The fact that the yuppie lawyers were present wouldn't bother most of them. It doesn't mean anything to them. Look at it this way: say Carmine or the Fat Man is sitting around at dinner and someone brings up Tupman's name. Carmine says, 'Tupman is getting to be a pain in the ass. Life would sure be easier if someone just blew him away.' So one of the young studs is there, listening, and he . . ." Mulheisen let it die.

McClain and Greene nodded in agreement, but Mulheisen was thinking of someone else, who had said words pretty much along those same lines. Nanh, he told himself, that's too silly. Forget it.

They drank their coffee and McClain said, "So? What d'you think, Mul?"

Mulheisen said, "A short man in a mask with some kind of gun on a strap shot down five guys in an underground garage. But he didn't take Tupman's money or steal the coke, so he probably wasn't a rival dope dealer or some kid looking to rip off Tupman. He had enough sense to take the plastic card that would let him out of the garage. And now, off to work, gentlemen."

They drank up, got the car, and drove back to Tupman's apartment. Jimmy Marshall was waiting. He and Mulheisen went up with the others to Tupman's rooms. There were several detectives and specialists from other departments carefully taking the place apart. Mulheisen talked to Horton from Central Vice, Geiger from Narcotics, and Andy Deane from Racket-Conspiracy. They wandered about, hands in pockets, talking to the men who were doing the dismantling, and comparing notes. The dismantlers were bagging and labeling nearly everything, notebooks, phone books, letters, anything with writing on it. Mulheisen looked at it all before it disappeared, but nothing seemed to lead to anything that rang a bell. Tupman's private phone book would yield something, maybe plenty, to Geiger and Deane, but to Mulheisen it was just numbers with anonymous letters preceding them, Tupman's little code. Someone would work out whose numbers these were, of course, and Mulheisen would get a printout, so the code was pointless.

Mulheisen and Jimmy joined Andy at Tupman's bar, where they sampled his bourbon and gossiped. The popular theory was that Tupman had so many enemies that they had probably formed a committee for extinction and hired a mad-dog killer from someplace very far away, like Canada. Mulheisen finally nodded to Jimmy and they slipped away

"Where to, Mul?" Jimmy asked.

"My car's here," Mulheisen said. "I'm meeting Andy Deane at headquarters. Did you get anywhere on that Iowa connection?"

Jimmy had found three names, with addresses, of men who had booked through to Detroit from Cedar Rapids, Iowa, via Chicago. Only one of them was from Iowa City, and he had paid cash. A check with the police there revealed that the name was not known, nor was the address. Mulheisen agreed with Jimmy that this seemed promising. Neither of them had any idea how large a population was served by the Cedar Rapids airport, but as Jimmy put it, "It's Iowa, isn't it? Farm country. Maybe a clerk at the airline counter would recognize this guy and could put another name to the picture."

"The trouble is, whose photo do we have? Harold Good—the killer? Or is it the late Harold Good—the suicide?" They came out of the building into the rain, and Mulheisen waved Jimmy into his car. He started it up and got the heater going. "It's probably worth going to Iowa," Mulheisen said. "It's the best lead we have. But we need to know about that picture. I'll tell you what. Get a list of the guys who went down to court with Good, and show them the picture. One of them might recognize the photo. If it works there, it may work in Iowa."

He paused. "I've screwed up, Jimmy. I should never have let Good get away from us, but maybe you can find him. This thing here," he gestured through the foggy, rain-streaked window at the parking garage, "it may be related, but it almost certainly wasn't Good who did it. Still, we might get a lead out of it. I'm going to start over on Sid and do it right."

He considered for a moment telling Jimmy about his contact with Bonny and Gene Lande, but decided against it. The whole thing seemed so preposterous, especially Lande's offer to do Mulheisen a favor and the mention of Tupman. Obviously no one does you a favor by killing a casually mentioned nemesis. The problem was Gene Lande was such a flaky guy—a short, flaky guy, at that. And he was already connected with the Sid Sedlacek killing, though in a way that seemed merely coincidental, even irrelevant.

Another problem was Bonny. Mulheisen was conscious of ambiguous feelings toward her. Much of it had to do with their shared experiences in high school, but there was something else. He was attracted to her still and felt an irritating and irrational sense of responsibility toward her. It was the sort of thing she had always done. She came on so helpless and so vulnerable that he couldn't repress an unwilling desire to look after her, to see that she wasn't hurt by a rough, uncaring world. At the same time he resented the urge, aware that her problems had nothing to do with him. They were of her own making. She was a grown woman who presumably could look after herself. Now she wanted him to find out who her husband was seeing, as a favor. It was ridiculous. Mulheisen couldn't mention it to Jimmy. But he would damn well check out Lande further.

"The time you screw up," he told Jimmy, "is when you get complacent and think you know everything. Everybody screws up, Jimmy. Remember that. The trick is to realize it and start fixing the screwup. You go on back to the precinct and start making arrangements to go to Iowa. I'll be back there as quick as I can."

Andy Deane, as usual, had anticipated Mulheisen's questions. The minute he'd heard about Tupman, he'd begun calling his contacts. The initial reports were vague and uncertain, Andy said, but he expected to see his main fish later that day. He didn't invite Mulheisen to come along, and Mulheisen didn't suggest it. A man's sources, especially deep sources like this one, were like fish that dwelt in the Mariana Trench—if you brought them to the surface, they would explode, and you were left with a gooey, unrecognizable mess. Only in extreme cases when it couldn't be helped, were they brought out into the light. This wasn't such a situation. Not yet, anyway.

But Andy had been improving his earlier theories in light of the latest developments. He noted first of all that a slime bag like Frosty Tupman is always killable. "I never heard of a kindly dope dealer, but Frosty was in a league—hell, a species, a genus—by himself. The least vicious of these guys are merely indifferent to the rest of humanity, Mul, but Frosty apparently enjoyed his victims' sufferings. One of my little fish told me that Frosty once made a girl eat one of his turds in exchange for a bit of heroin—and then he didn't give her the smack. Now I don't know if that is just a fish's imagination—I never had the stomach to inquire further—but I was impressed by the way the fish emphasized that the girl didn't score the smack. The fish didn't emphasize the turd part, just the lack of result. True or not, you get an idea of the esteem Frosty Tupman had won in junkie hearts. Maybe I'm gullible, but I think it's true."

Andy had never struck Mulheisen as gullible.

"A creep like Frosty, Mul, lives either by making himself indispensable—through some singular talent, like a willingness to kill anything—or because there aren't any really viable alternatives to his services. In the long run, of course, Tupman had to go down. Guys like him never get old. He defiled too many, stabbed too many backs, kissed too much ass, and generally lined up potential assassins as if he were conducting auditions. I don't know who did it, but except for the heat it throws, mainly because of the yuppie lawyers, the killer has probably made himself a lot of friends in the community. Maybe my lantern fish can throw some light on the subject."

"What about Sid and the money?" Mulheisen asked. "Was Tupman involved?"

"He could have been," Andy said, "and the money is still missing. There's always money missing with these guys, of course. The accounting is so irregular. But this is really a lot of money. Ten, maybe twenty million. It has attracted attention."

"Sid had a girlfriend," Mulheisen said.

"Yeah. Germaine Kouras. What about her?"

"Well, what do you think, Andy? Is she involved in this?"

Deane looked surprised. "Well, Mul, you must have talked to her. What do you think? She's a girlfriend. These guys don't usually involve their girlfriends in their business, especially if they've got something special and irregular going down. I mean, they just don't do it."

"Well, what do you think about her, though?" Mulheisen asked. He was reluctant to confess to Andy that he had never talked to the woman.

"She's interesting," Andy said. "Crazy, I think. Not a very good singer, but she's awfully pretty, and she has a certain flair. Well, you know what I mean." He smiled. "I like her, but I wouldn't touch her with a ten-foot pole, even if she weren't a mobster's girlfriend . . . ex-girlfriend."

"Of course," Mulheisen said. "Say, you ever hear of a guy named Etcheverry, might have been an associate of Big Sid's, or of Tupman's?"

"Etcheverry. No . . . There's a Ray Echeverria, hangs out with Billy Conover. What about him?"

"Nothing. I just heard his name somewhere. He's a dope dealer, this guy?"

"Yeah," Deane said, "or at least we think he is. We've never been able to make anything on him. He's more of a money man, I think, but the money is dope money. He's a little weird, kind of a skinny guy, tall, wears dark glasses day and night. I get the impression he thinks he's some kind of Latin lover."

"Ah. Well. By the way, I don't have my notes on the Kouras woman with me. You wouldn't happen to have her address, where she works?"

Eleven

Mulheisen took a long drag on his cigar and exhaled slowly. Jimmy Marshall had just delivered one of those hateful "good news–bad news" tales: a man named Malfitan had been found; Germaine Kouras had flown. Mulheisen decided to see Malfitan first. They showed him five eight-by-ten glossy photos, including their blown-up picture of Harold Good, and the good-news portion of the tale started to fade.

Malfitan shook his head. "Ain't none of these. This Fogarty, he looked more like Ben Franklin, you dig?" Yes, he had ridden downtown in the wagon with Fogarty and had seen him at night court. He then gave a new, and this time fairly accurate, description of the real Fogarty.

Mulheisen took Jimmy aside and pointed out that according to the docket, both Fogarty and Malfitan had been represented by the same lawyer, one Milton Hyman. Malfitan was not the sort of man to employ an attorney. A quick call to Hyman revealed that, indeed, Malfitan's defense and fine had been paid by the person who purported to be Fogarty. Hyman agreed to come over to the precinct and look at their photo. It took him less than two seconds to put his finger on the photo of Harold Good.

Malfitan was brought back into the interrogation room. Mulheisen had sent out for cheeseburgers and a chocolate malted. The man fell on the food like a grizzly bear. The detective watched in silence, smoking a cigar placidly. When Malfitan had licked his lips and sucked his teeth to his satisfaction and then looked back at Mulheisen expectantly, the latter said, "We now know that one of these men in these photos posed as Henry J. Fogarty. I'm not asking you if you know his real name, because I can't imagine that he would have told you. But I would like you to simply tell me no if the picture I indicate is not the man you saw as Fogarty." With that it took five seconds for Malfitan to preserve his code, such as it was, by denying that four of the pictures were Fogarty. The remaining picture was the one Hyman had picked. So that was a step forward.

Germaine Kouras, however, was the genuine bad news. Not only had she gone, but she had told everybody, including her agent and the manager of the club where she worked, that she was leaving the country, possibly for good. She had given up her apartment. A friend said that Germaine had told her she was getting married and she and her husband were going to live in South America, but she'd left no forwarding address nor even the name of the country she was supposedly going to.

All this was determined by early afternoon. Mulheisen was dead tired, almost depressed (not genuinely depressed; he wasn't giving in to that), and it was still raining. At about three o'clock he received a call from Geiger of Narcotics. One of his people had run off a check of the numbers in Frosty Tupman's phone book, using the phone company's listings by number. Geiger wanted to know if any of the names would be useful. Among them, not surprisingly, were numbers for Sid Sedlacek and other well-known mob figures, including Ray Echeverria. There were also dozens of unfamiliar names, which Geiger and other investigators were now checking out. One was of especial interest to Mulheisen: Eugene Lande—two numbers, home and office. Also listed, in the same location, was a number for the Briar Ridge Golf and Country Club.

Mulheisen hung up and dialed the number for Briar Ridge. He was told by a male voice that Mr. Lande was on the course. The man said he expected Lande in the clubhouse in about an hour or so.

It was decided that Jimmy should go to Iowa. He immediately set about getting the authorizations and lining up a liaison with the Iowa police. Since he'd been working with the airlines already, and since he'd soon be out at the airport, he would make inquiries about when Germaine Kouras had departed and for where.

Mulheisen found the golf course after some difficulty. It was on what he remembered from his childhood as a dirt road that led to farms in the low hills. He'd been taken to the area as early as the first grade, on a field trip to see cows and chickens and, he recalled, a number of enormous and frightening turkeys. Now it was a well-established residential suburb, with paved streets bearing near-farcical names: Bryyerwoode Lane, Calico Circle, Chalkcreek Way. Such names were a silly conceit, borrowed from the presumed glamour of Grosse Pointe and similar older suburbs, where streets were often named Fairbairns or Collie Fields. The developers had turned their backs on the French origins of Detroit (to say nothing of Grosse Pointe itself), on names like Piquette and Saint Aubin and Joseph Campau, which, after all, were simply the family names of the farmers who had settled there in the early eighteenth century.

The golf course had been sculpted out of pasture that bordered a small muddy creek below a bluff that ran along the roadside. Mulheisen thought the stream used to be called Petty Creek (or Petit, perhaps), but signs indicated it was now called Clabber Creek. He wasn't a golfer, but it looked like an interesting bit of real estate. The clubhouse, however, was a simple, low clapboard building painted white, with a couple of pointless cupolas surmounted by cast-iron weather cocks. Not especially prepossessing, which was unusual, he thought. Developers tended to spend on the clubhouse. He had expected something with a lot of glass and timber, perhaps fieldstone, and an enormous fireplace chimney and perhaps a red tile roof. The developer must have run short on cash.

Lande's Cadillac, with its DOCBYTE vanity plate, was the only car in the lot, except for a small Toyota pickup with BRIAR RIDGE GOLF AND COUNTRY CLUB painted around an amusing coat of arms that featured a golf club and a tennis racket crossed on a shield, along with a setter and a spaniel rampant.

The rain had declined to a mist, and it was growing dark. Mulheisen strolled out onto a sodden cedar-plank deck overlooking the first tee. To his left an empty, leaf-filled swimming pool separated the fenced-in tennis courts from the parking lot. The course fell away into the mist. Mulheisen could make out some barren willows and alder that evidently lined Clabber Creek, and a few evergreens that dotted the fairway. Lande was due in shortly. Soon it would be too dark to play, if one could imagine anyone playing in this dreadful weather at all. The temperature was hardly above forty-five, and the ground underfoot was not just damp but positively swampy.

From a distance Mulheisen heard the muffled whump, whump, whump of a shotgun, barely audible in the heavy, soaking atmosphere. A pair of ducks in tight jet formation whizzed up out of the gloom and, seeing the dimly lighted windows of the clubhouse, flared out like F-15 fighters and climbed up into the overcast. Mulheisen was amused.

He peered through the plate glass windows of the clubhouse. A faint glimmer suggested that the barroom was open. He let himself into the broad dining area, its tables stacked with chairs, and saw a young man in a sweater sitting behind the bar at the back, glumly sipping a darkish drink and fiddling with a pencil. There was a crossword book open on the bar in front of him. He watched as Mulheisen came across the floor, which was covered with a green indoor-outdoor carpet.

"I'm looking for Gene," Mulheisen said.

"Still out there." The young man nodded toward the gloom.

"How long has he been out there?"

"Couple three hours," the fellow said. He had streaky blond hair and was handsome despite his morose expression.

"By himself?"

The man nodded. "Who else is crazy enough to play on a day like this? He'll be in pretty quick . . . I hope."

Mulheisen gestured toward the bottles of whiskey on the back bar. "You open?"

The man shrugged. "Why not?"

Mulheisen ordered a large Jameson and took it over to the window. He pulled down a chair and set it where he could look out into the murk—perhaps a hundred feet, anyway. He clipped and lighted up a Partagas Lonsdale. It was not, he knew, the kind of atmosphere that most people would find heartening or pleasant, but he found it most agreeable. It was a tremendous relief from the pressures of the day.

Rather like being in Ontario. After a while he walked back out onto the sheltered deck and gazed off into the dying light with a pleased sigh.

The mist occasionally thickened into a drizzle, then thinned again. The trees were bare, except for the few firs, and he saw that they were not monochromatic but actually a variety of colors. Some were glistening black, others gray, yet others a pale yellow or beige, and down near the creek some low brush was a vivid red. The mist swept softly across the rolling fairway, which was already covered with a thick, dark green turf that would soon need mowing. Wild birds, not city sparrows, hurled themselves off the bluff and sailed down onto the course, where they dove headlong into the thicket that lined the creek. He thought they might be jays, or even kingfishers—his mother would know.

The shotgun bumped a couple more times, and the birds raced about, and then he could hear the rain pattering gently, the trees dripping, and the creek gurgling. There was the sound of a distant city somewhere. He took a great and pleasurable breath and went back inside.

It was OK with him if Lande didn't come in for an hour. It was a fine thing to do nothing for a while, just to sit and draw on an aromatic brown cigar and sip good whiskey while gazing out onto a dripping vista with lights starting to wink on in distant houses.

After a while he called for another drink, and the young man brought the bottle to the table. "You gonna wait for Gene?" he asked.

"I am."

"Fine." The fellow set the bottle on the table and said, "Tell him I had to split, OK?"

Mulheisen was astonished. "You mean you're just going to leave?"

"Why not?"

"Well, what do I owe you for the whiskey?"

"Settle with Gene." And with that he walked out, snatching a windbreaker off a rack on the way. A moment later Mulheisen heard the engine of the pickup start and then a spurt of gravel as it drove away.

"Amazing," Mulheisen said out loud. He refilled his glass and sat back, puffing on the cigar. "My own club." He waved the cigar grandly, taking in all he surveyed.

Forty minutes later Lande stomped across the deck, lugging a bagful of golf clubs. He set the clubs on a sheltered rack and entered the barroom. Mulheisen hadn't seen him approach. Evidently he had come off the back nine, which ended at a green on the opposite side of the clubhouse. Under the hood of a parka he wore a tweed golfer's cap, which he took off and slapped against the glistening nylon of his rain suit. He began to unzip and strip off the fancy blue and red rain outfit.

"Hey! Mul!" he cried out. "What the hell are you doing here?" He didn't wait for an answer. "Where's Eric?"

"He had a date," Mulheisen said, rising and lifting his glass in a kind of toast. He gestured at the whiskey bottle. "He said it was on your tab."

"Lazy fart," Lande said. "Ah, screw 'im. Go ahead. Help yourself."

He tossed his dripping rain gear onto a table and clomped over to the bar in his spiked shoes to fetch a glass. He returned, poured some whiskey into the glass, and drank it. ⁻

"Ah. Jeez, that's great! I needed that." He wiped his bristling mustache and poured another, fuller dollop and poured more into Mulheisen's glass. He dragged down a chair, turned it back to front, and sat down with his arms draped over the back. His pale green slacks were spotted with damp and wrinkled, and his black cashmere sweater was matted. Mulheisen thought he'd like to be able to wreck a great sweater like that.

"Whew!" Lande looked weary and drawn, but his cheeks were ruddy. "It ain't a great day for gawf, Mul, but I had a few good shots. I hit a three wood you wouldn't believe."

Mulheisen cocked his head with interest. "Can you actually play in these conditions?"

"This ain't nothin'," Lande declared. "You ever play in Scotland? I have. I played the Old Course, at Saint Andrews. Hell, I remember once at Carnoustie it was like playing in a hurricane! Those guys, those Scotsmen, they don't give a rat's ass—they play in any kinda weather. You don't gawf? No? I kinda figgered you belonged to Grosse Pointe, or one a them clubs. No? Not that much of a course, actually. This is better."

"I heard shots," Mulheisen said.

"Kids," Lande said. "They poke around down the crick and jump-shoot the ducks. Say," he pointed at Mulheisen's cigar, "you got another one a them?"

"No," Mulheisen lied.

"That's all right," Lande said. He fished out a pack of cigarettes and lighted up. "So. What're ya doin' here?" He suddenly looked alarmed. "It ain't Bonny? Nothin's wrong is there?"

"Bonny? No. Why?"

Lande looked relieved. "Nothin'. Oh, she ain't been feelin' too good lately. It's nothin'. So what brings you out here?"

"I went by your office yesterday," Mulheisen said. "Miss Bommarito said you spent a lot of time out here."

"Yanh, she thinks I'm nuts," Lande said. "Well, yer here. How come?"

"I was just checking out some information on the Sedlacek case," Mulheisen said, "and the Tupman shooting." He watched Lande closely.

Lande sipped his whiskey calmly and gazed back. "Tupman," he said with a snort of contempt. "That piece a shit. Good riddance." He drew on his cigarette. "Kind of a long way to come to ask about nothin', ain't it?"

"It's on my way home, as a matter of fact," Mulheisen said.

"Oh, yeah." Lande nodded. "I guess I knew that . . . You 'n' Bonny, you went to St. Clair Flats High, or something so that figgers. So whataya wanta know?"

Mulheisen looked around at the empty room and said, "What I want to know is what kind of club is this? How come the kid went home and left me here with the bar open?"

"Whatayou, thinkin' of robbin' the joint? There ain't nothin' to rob but a few bottles a booze."

"It's unusual, wouldn't you say? Rather an exclusive club. Just you."

"Oh, I got a few other members," Lande said. "Me 'n' a couple other guys bought it, ya know. This developer built it, about twenny years ago now. He had a cash-flow problem and wanted to unload. I was already a member, so I bought it. It's all legit. You could look it up."

"I never knew anybody who actually owned his own golf course," Mulheisen said. "Do you run it as a business?"

"Sure, but it ain't actually a going concern at the moment. No problem for me, though. These other assholes," Lande said savagely, "they didn't give a rat fuck for the joint. I hada cut them out fin'ly. I haveta do just about everythin' out here. If it wasn't for me, this place'd be a dump. A gawf course is a kinda black hole for money, you know. But it happens I know quite a little bit about gawf courses. I made a study of it, see? I know a lot when you come down to it. And I gotta couple a good kids in here. They do what I tell 'em, and they know their shit. One of 'em even graduated from a gawf-management school down in Arizona. Well, this kid Eric—you met 'im—he can't find his ass with both hands when it comes to business, but you oughta see his swing." He shook his head, gazing off at the course, now nearly lost in darkness. "Yanh, the little shit can swing that club. You realize that kid qualified for the Open? He never made the cut, but jeez—just to play in the Open! I damn near qualified once." He looked wistful.

"Was one of your partners Ray Echeverria?" Mulheisen asked.

"Yeah. Why?" Lande seemed wary.

"How did you meet Echeverria?"

"He was a member here. We both was. When the developer got into a mess, me 'n' Ray and a coupla others, we bought him out. No crime in that, is it?"

"What are you so huffy about?" Mulheisen asked. "Do you have other dealings with Echeverria?"

"I hardly know the guy. He never even comes around anymore. Well, he was a lousy gawfer. Said he was a fifteen handicap, but I never seen him break ninety. Now that's just stupid. Most guys, if they cheat on their handicap, it's in the other direction. But not Ray, . . . he'd rather lose a few bucks and have you think he just wasn't playing to his handicap. Dope."

"Where were you this morning, between four and six?" Mulheisen asked.

"Me?" Lande recoiled. "This morning? You serious? Where the hell you think? Home in bed."

"Really?"

"Sure, whataya think? I played a little cards earlier. At the East-gate. You could check. Then I bullshitted for a while, with the guys, and went home." He watched Mulheisen truculently. "What is this, any-ways?"

Mulheisen said, "I suppose you have some witnesses?"

Lande mentioned a couple of names, and Mulheisen got out his notebook to jot them down. "And you left when?"

"I don't know. I di'nt check my watch. It musta been, oh, three, four A.M. After that, you can ast Bonny, which I guess you prob'ly already did. Am I right?"

Mulheisen looked at the man—feisty, self-important, and abrasive. After a moment he said, "How is it you know Frosty Tupman?"

"Who says I know Tupman?" Lande looked belligerent but on his guard.

Mulheisen considered for a moment, then said, "You don't have to answer my questions. You have the right . . ."

"What the hell is this?" Lande said, rising. "You readin' me my rights? I know my rights. You wanta ast me somethin', just go ahead. I ain't got nothin' to hide."

Mulheisen nodded. "OK. You know your rights. We have evidence that you are acquainted with Tupman."

Lande poured out another shot of whiskey for himself and Mulheisen. "I don't know Tupman," he said.

"Tupman had three phone numbers listed for you in his personal phone book."

"So what? I can't help that. Maybe he wanted to buy a computer, or maybe he wanted to join the club. That's not illegal, is it? Is that all you got? Jeez, fuckin' cops!"

Mulheisen said, "You mentioned his name the other night when we were having dinner."

"I mentioned his name? I thought you did."

Mulheisen couldn't remember if he had mentioned Tupman first or if it had been Lande. He shrugged. "How about Sid Sedlacek? Did you know him? Or his girlfriend, Germaine Kouras?"

"I mighta met Sedlacek sometime," Lande conceded, then he

brightened. "Yeah, that's right! This chick Germaine, she sings at the Blue Moon sometimes, right? I used to go there, once in a while. I thought she was great. I met her, and I think she introduced me to Big Sid. I di'nt think nothin' of it. Anybody can meet a singer and her boyfriend, can't they?"

Mulheisen sighed. This wasn't going well. He asked, "Did you ever have a relationship with Miss Kouras?"

"Are you kidding?" Lande was frankly surprised. "Hey, I gotta wife who's a helluva lot better looking than that broad. I shou'n't haveta tell you that."

This last was said in a way that insinuated a great deal. Mulheisen replied, "You must get a charge out of being obnoxious."

Lande looked pleased. "Gotchoo, eh? You dig them tits, don'tcha? Hey! Fifty million guys whacked off on that centerfold. Join the crowd."

Mulheisen leapt to his feet, his face red. "You are an asshole!"

"So? Who ain't?" Lande had risen. He looked up at Mulheisen pugnaciously. "You knew her when, din't djou? You prob'ly saw them tits in the flesh! D'jou fuck her?"

Mulheisen came close to smashing Lande in the face. The man, with his outthrust jaw, seemed to be inviting a blow. Mulheisen forced himself to a casualness he didn't feel. He looked down at the cigar in his hand. He had almost crumpled it. He took a tentative drag and sat down.

But Lande wouldn't let it go. "I knew it," he crowed. "You fucked her. And you'd still like to shag her. Well, go ahead." He abruptly lapsed into a peculiar mood and slumped back onto his chair. "That's prob'ly why you went over there yesterday. She ast you to come over, din't she?"

Mulheisen shook his head, mystified. "What's wrong with you, Lande? You seem to care for Bonny, but you say things like that!"

Lande looked up dully. "You wouldn't know. You don't know nothin'. Bonny digs you," he said.

Something in his tone unsettled Mulheisen. "Are you nuts?" he said. "Wait a minute. What do you mean, 'I don't know anything'?"

"You went to see her yesterday," Lande said. "You din't notice nothing? Nanh, why would you? You on'y had one thing on yer mind. Bonny's sick, you big prick."

Mulheisen was stunned. "Sick?"

"Yanh. Sick. She's got cancer. Terminal." Lande's face had turned bitter.

For Mulheisen the entire world turned grotesque and bilious. "This better not be some kind of joke," he rasped. He ground the cigar into the ashtray violently.

"It ain't no joke," Lande said. "She got a tumor in her womb bigger'n a can'aloupe."

Mulheisen stared, mouth open. Lande looked at the floor.

"How long have you known this?" Mulheisen asked.

Lande looked away, his face mottled with anger, the foolish mustache bristling, his eyes small and watery. "'Bout a month," he said, "maybe a little longer. The docs said it prob'ly wasn't much, at first. They fin'ly tol' us the troot just the other day." His face suddenly crumpled. "Ah, shit," he said. He gulped down the whiskey angrily and uttered a slight gasp. When he looked at Mulheisen again, he said gruffly, "Ya don't see a wooman like that . . ." he stumbled, ". . . off-ten."

The two men sat in silence for a long time, occasionally glancing at one another, then away. The light outside had failed. The light inside was weak, emanating from the bar.

"You ever been in love?" Lande asked after a while.

"Ah . . . well," Mulheisen said softly, "I guess so."

"I never been in love," Lande said, musing. He looked at the rain-streaked windows. "I thought it was some kinda joke . . . you know, like in the movies or somethin'. I din't know what it was at first. I jus' felt like . . . you know . . . everythin' you do is for the broad." He cleared his throat. "It's . . . diff'runt. I din't know you could wanta do things for another person . . . for her, I mean. Yer allus doin' something for the other person, see? An' you like doin' it. Ever'thin' I do is for Bonny."

Mulheisen picked up the bottle of whiskey and poured them both a stiff drink. He drank from his glass and said, "How do you know it's sure? They're wrong about these things a lot. They have all kinds of therapy. I have a friend, he's a doctor, he could—"

"She seen enough doctors," Lande said bitterly. "She has to go in tomorrow."

"Tomorrow? For what?"

"Surgery—whataya think, stupid?"

Mulheisen couldn't believe it. "I just talked to her. She didn't say a word."

"To-fuckin'-morrow."

Mulheisen said, "Well, if they're going to operate, they must think there is a chance."

"There ain't a chance. The doc talks about surgery, then radiation . . . There ain't no chance." He drank some whiskey and said, "It ain't fair, Mul. There's all kinda assholes in this world, and they just go laughin' along." He rubbed his mustache reflectively. "They won't laugh. They ain't gonna laugh."

"What do you mean?" Mulheisen asked.

"I don't mean nothin'," Lande said, looking up calmly. "She ain't gonna . . . Somebody's gotta pay, Mul. Some a these pricks, they weren't too good to her—"

"Lande," Mulheisen said, "don't talk like this. Whatever is happening to Bonny, it isn't anybody's fault. It happens."

"Oh yeah? Whatayou know about it? She got kicked around pretty good. A wooman like that!"

"What are you talking about? Who kicked her around?"

"None a yer bidness. Whatayou care, anyhow? Oh, sure, you got the hots for her, yer an old pal 'n' all . . . but didjou ever think that just because a wooman's beautiful, it might nota been a bed a roses? Guys hittin' on her alla time, guys promisin' shit, and then when she won't go out on the street for 'em, they start bangin' on her."

Mulheisen had an image of how this might be, as Lande said, and it was a little shocking, particularly since it had a plausible ring. "Well, you took her away from all that, didn't you? You were her knight in shining armor?"

Lande cocked his head, not displeased with this image. "Yeah, you could say that." Then his face knotted. "But it ain't over. They still come around. I ain't mentionin' no names, but I know who it is. Anyways, they can't hurt her now. Now it's this . . . this goddamn shit that you can't do nothin' about. She don't deserve this."

"Nobody deserves cancer," Mulheisen said. "Things happen to good people, we don't know why. It just happens. You can't hold other people responsible. That's naive, silly."

"You think it's silly? What the fuck do you know?"

"That's crazy," Mulheisen said wearily. He had to leave, to get away from this awful little man.

"How come you don't like me?" Lande asked suddenly. "You think I'm some kinda jerk. Yer the jerk. You got the hots for my old lady. I don't mind that. You knew her first. She digs you. But I got a lot goin' for me, you know that? I'm drivin' a fuckin' Cadillac, and yer pushin' some kinda weird taxi or somethin'. You ain't shit, Mulheisen. I'm a inventor! D'jou know that?"

"What?" Mulheisen almost laughed. "What did you ever invent?"

"A lotta things," Lande said. "I invented a new gawf bag."

Mulheisen laughed. "A new golf bag? What the hell is that?"

Lande jumped up and ran outside, dragging his golf bag back in. "See this?" He demonstrated how the bag had a kind of built-in tripod, evidently activated by the handle. "I invented that," he said triumphantly. "It keeps the bag standing up. But when I showed it to the bag manufacturers, they laughed at me, and then they ripped me off. Now some asshole's making a million bucks oudda it! And I invented it!"

"So what?" Mulheisen said.

"So what? They screwed me, that's what! I invented a car jack, it inflates offa tire, or a air bottle. They ripped that off, too. But there's a buncha shit they couldn't rip off. I'm gettin' royalties right now on a buncha machines that I couldn't even explain to a dumb shit like you. Ford and GM bought machines offa me. I invent computer systems. I figgered out a way to use old glass for all kindsa stuff."

"All right, you're a genius," Mulheisen said. "Why don't you go home? If Bonny has to go to the hospital tomorrow, she needs you."

"Yeah, I'm goin' home. No point in sittin' here talkin' to a dumb ass like you. Who don't understan' nothin'. Yer s'poseta be a big detective, but it looks like you don't know shit."

Mulheisen could hear something in Lande's voice, but he couldn't discern what it was. "What am I supposed to understand?"

"Nothin'. I tell you somethin', and you sit there like a fuckin' turd."

Mulheisen drained the whiskey from his glass. He was a little drunk. "You know, Lande, you're one of the most tiresome bastards I've ever met."

Lande seemed to take that as an accolade. "Thanks, Mul. Say, why don't you come over to the house with me? Bonny could fix us something."

Mulheisen looked at him with awe. "Bonny could fix us something? Isn't she sick? What's the matter with you? Why aren't you home looking after her?"

"I'm lookin' out for Bonny, don't worry 'bout that. I just want her to be happy. Whatever she wants."

"I don't think you know what she wants," Mulheisen said.

Lande scoffed. "Yer the wise guy, tell me what she wants."

"For reasons I can't fathom," Mulheisen said, "she wants you."

The little man just gazed at him, his eyes glittering. Finally he said softly, his voice choking, "You . . . ah . . . you . . . that's a very kind thing to say." He turned away to hide his emotion but soon turned back with his customary sarcasm. "That's the kind of guy Bonny said you was. Just a big ol' soft-ass pussy."

Mulheisen sighed. "Yeah, I'm the well-known softhearted cop. But," his voice hardened, "there's another side to me." He stood up. "Don't forget it." And he walked out into the rain. It felt better on his face than he could have imagined, very refreshing after the colloquy in the clubhouse. It was simple and honest, wet and cold.

Lande followed after turning out the lights and locking the door. "Hey, wait up, Mul! Why'ncha come over, cheer up Bonny? We could pick up something on the way."

"Go home," Mulheisen said, "I am."

"Wait up!" Lande crunched across the gravel in his golf shoes and opened the door of the Cadillac. He sat down in the driver's seat and shucked off his soggy golf shoes, then slipped on a pair of wing tips. "We could go to Fazio's," he said, "pick up some stuff and take it home. Bonny'd love to see ya."

Mulheisen looked down at the eager, pleading face and uttered a short laugh. "You're too much, Lande. Go home!"

Lande looked up at him uncertainly, then laughed. "Yeah, yer right. Bonny says I don't know when to quit. That's my big failin'. I push too hard." He tied his laces and stood up. "Hey, thanks for everythin', man." He stuck out his hand, and as soon as Mulheisen unthinkingly took it, he knew the grip would be fierce. Lande's hand was powerful, and of course he couldn't resist cranking on a larger man's. Mulheisen attempted to resist at first, just to avoid the crush, then he angrily wrenched his hand free.

"Hey, sorry man! Don't know my own strinth," Lande said. "But seriously, I 'preciate you talkin' to me like this, man-to-man. A lotta guys don't, you know? It helps. We oughta get together more off-ten. Whataya say? I think we could be pals. Hey, I could teach ya gawf. I'm a helluva teacher. I'm a scratch gawfer, ya know. I even beat Eric . . . once in a while."

"I've got to go," Mulheisen said. And all the way home he thought of the things he should have asked Lande but hadn't. He was still screwing up, he thought.

Twelve

Amtrak's Zephyr pulled into Mount Pleasant, Iowa, at 8:40 A.M., right on time. Joe Service had been awakened in good time by Mr. Alonzo Johnson, who knocked softly on the door of suite A/B. He had risen and bathed and shaved, and Mr. Johnson had brought him a bottle of champagne, nicely chilled, along with a carafe of coffee. Joe was grateful. Three days earlier he had ridden into Oakland from Los Angeles on the Coast Starlight, and it had not been fun. That train had been overcrowded with noisy people. There had been a long wait at the dining car, and there were no vacant seats in the lounge. The Zephyr was a much better ride. For one thing he'd spent the night in San Francisco, a city he liked, and he'd been able to provision himself properly. He had boarded the Zephyr with one bag and a newly purchased canvas carryall filled with fresh sourdough French bread, various cheeses, several bottles of wine and Perrier water, and a plastic sack full of fresh fish.

After establishing himself in the suite, Joe had slipped down to the galley and conferred with the chef. This was a large black man named Walker who at first was not inclined to listen to Joe. But Joe pressed a significant amount of cash into his hand, as well as the bag, filled with sea bass.

"It's the morning catch," Joe explained. "I bought it right off the boat. Now I understand you are serving sole for dinner, and I know from experience that it is very good, but I just had this yen for sea bass.

There's plenty for you, if you like that sort of thing . . ." There was enough for the whole galley crew, in fact.

"That's all right, bro," Chef Walker said. "I grill it with my own special sauce, kind of a Cajun sauce that I learned in New Iberia. Just let the maître d' know when you come in."

Next Joe had gone to Mr. Johnson, a very pleasant gentleman, and placed fifty dollars in his hand, along with six bottles of French champagne and six bottles of California chardonnay. Joe explained to him that he needed at least two bottles of the champagne daily, before breakfast and with lunch. There was also the Havarti and the Cheshire, a Brie and a Wensleydale, all of which needed to be refrigerated. He would nibble on them en route, along with a bunch each of red and green grapes, a melon, and some oranges. Alonzo Johnson cheerfully agreed to place all of these provisions in the cooler and to bring them to him as required.

Joe went up to the lounge for the run up to Suisun Bay and the Sacramento River. He enjoyed the cormorants and herons flying up as the train ran smoothly and swiftly past the mothball fleet of World War II warships. The train was not overcrowded, and Joe reveled in the peculiar, smug sensation that he always felt when a two- or three-day train journey commenced.

Later they began to climb up into the Sierras, and Joe relaxed in his spacious suite with magazines and an excellent caper novel by Donald Westlake. He detrained for a minute at Truckee, relishing the mountain air and ogling a party of attractive women on the main street, a young sultry blonde and her eagle-eyed mother and a strapping six-foot blonde with her slim and sexy mother. There was no time to pursue adventure. He reboarded and dined on Chef Walker's splendid version of bass, with garlic and onions and a hot, spicy wine sauce. The sauce was really too much for the bass, he thought, but it was good. He drank a bottle of the chardonnay.

The Rockies were great the next day, especially the stretch through the Glenwood canyon and then the run through the Moffat Tunnel before they thundered down into Denver. But he spent most of his time in his suite, cleaning guns and joyfully reflecting on his successful liaison with Jizzy. She had shown him more than the expected forwarding telephone number for Hal Good. There was an actual street address in Iowa City. Joe could hardly believe it. Surely this couldn't be Good's home address? Well, he would check it out, but it seemed awfully lax for a presumably competent professional hit man.

As for Jizzy . . . well, Jizzy had been superb. He would remember her fondly for days, even weeks. Maybe some day, when he had amassed enough capital and could live on his investments and give up this goofy life, he would give her a ring and they could get together.

On the morning of the third day, in Mount Pleasant, Joe apologized to Mr. Johnson for leaving the suite in such disorder. There was a bottle each of champagne and chardonnay left, and he commended them to Alonzo, along with another portrait of Ulysses S. Grant.

It was a cool spring day in the farm country. All the snow was gone, but the plowmen were not yet in the wet fields. Joe thought about renting a car, but there was none to rent, a possibility that had not occurred to him. He abandoned the new canvas carryall against the wall of a bar, walked out onto the highway, and stood there with his one remaining bag. Within minutes a stout young farm lad wearing a Simplot cap and driving a splendid four-by-four Jimmy pickup truck with jumbo wheels stopped for him. He wasn't going far, but he got on his CB radio and started calling. Within seconds a trucker northbound on the same highway, just a few miles south of them, responded. The farm lad explained that Joe was going to Iowa City and would be left at milepost 67. "I'll be looking for him, ten-four," the trucker said.

Joe thanked the farmer when he dropped him off and took up his stance next to milepost 67 in the fresh breeze, delighted to be in this excellent and accommodating country. Sure enough, about eight minutes later an enormous semi rig came howling up the line, and as he roared by Joe, he blasted his air horn twice. The wind of his passing nearly knocked Joe down. Crestfallen, he stared after the huge truck as it echoed away up the next hill. Then he laughed. Not ten minutes later a salesman in a new Buick stopped. He was headed for Cedar Rapids, on the other side of Iowa City. He had all his clothes hanging on a rack across the backseat, and Joe had to put his bag under his legs in front. He also had to listen to the salesman's philosophy of life, which seemed largely a condemnation of "niggers, hippies, an' dope-a-dicks." All the while the tape deck screamed out songs by Barbara Mandrell. Still, in less than forty minutes he was in Coralville, a kind of suburb of Iowa City.

Here Joe was able to rent a car, a Ford Escort, and he drove over to Iowa City, where he quickly found Black Street. The street ran up a hill off the Iowa River. The house he was looking for turned out to be a simple white frame house next to a park. There was a driveway on one side, with an unattached garage. In the drive was a four-by-four Blazer. A fifteen-foot fiberglass launch with a huge outboard motor sat on a trailer next to the garage, covered with a blue tailor-made canvas cover. Joe parked the Ford next to the little park and watched a buxom blond woman throw a Frisbee to her even blonder four-year-old girl. Joe got out and leaned against the fender in the pleasant spring sunlight. Inevitably the Frisbee came his way, and Joe picked it up, spinning it back to the woman. Eventually she walked back with the child, a very pretty young girl, and said, "Hi," with a broad smile.

"Hey, are you a student?" Joe asked her.

"No," she said.

"I'm looking for a buddy, from the navy," Joe said. "He gave me his address, but I lost it. He said he lived on Black Street. His name is Hal?"

"Hal?" the woman said. "I don't know any Hal. What does he look like?"

"About my age," Joe said, "kind of slim, a little taller than me. Fair hair?"

"There's a guy sort of like that who lives over there," said the woman, pointing to the white house with the boat. "I don't know his name. He's a cop, I think. Is your friend a cop?"

"A cop? No way. Maybe your husband knows him." Joe walked across the street with the woman to the gate of her little house.

"Husband? I seem to have misplaced my husband," the woman said, sizing up Joe in a frank, amused way. She had a narrow, attractive face with a small, expressive mouth and nice blue eyes. She had a way of standing with a hand on her hip. The little girl squinted up at Joe with the same blue eyes, but with a slightly sidelong look that was endearing.

Joe leaned on the picket fence. "Well, maybe we could have a beer or something." He grinned pleasantly.

"Some other time," the woman said. She nodded at the little girl. "I've got things to do."

"Well, thanks anyway." Joe strolled off to a little shopping plaza a block away and looked up Hal Good in the telephone directory. There was no listing. He returned to the car and drove downtown to the police station, where he asked for a driver's license application. He asked the uniformed woman in the license bureau if Hal was around. She didn't know any Hal. There wasn't any Hal Good on the force. Joe took the application and the driver's manual and left.

He went to a nice older restaurant on Governor Street, not too far from where Hal was supposed to live, and was pleased to discover that the woman from the park was his waitress. She smiled in a friendly way and recommended the ravioli. It was very good, as was the Italian wine. It was a relaxed kind of place, frequented by older students and professors, as far as Joe could tell. It wasn't very busy. The waitress, Rita, chatted with him in a cheerful, mildly flirtatious way, and so he pleasantly passed the time until dark.

He drove back to the park and changed into a dark blue jogging outfit of sweatpants, sweatshirt, and running shoes. Over the sweatshirt he wore a dark windbreaker, and after a moment's reflection he slipped a Smith & Wesson .38 revolver into his pocket. It was the Bodyguard Airweight model, and despite its appellation it was a little heavy, but he had never found anything to recommend a lighter caliber in his line of work, and this gun had a shrouded hammer to prevent snagging in the pocket.

He walked down through the weeds and alder brush until he reached the back of the property he had scouted. There was a heavy wire fence and a doghouse in the backyard but no sign of a dog. He had noticed the doghouse earlier. Where was the dog? In the house? Perhaps Hal had once owned a dog but no longer.

He sat in the bushes for a long time, two hours by his watch, until a convertible came along Black Street and turned into the driveway behind the Blazer. A man got out of the passenger seat, and a woman got out from behind the wheel. The man fitted the Fat Man's admittedly limited description of Hal Good. The woman was very young, perhaps a teenager, with long dark hair, wearing jeans and a man's sport jacket that was too big for her. The man carried a bag of groceries, and the girl, two cartons of Mexican beer in bottles.

There were no welcoming barks from a dog when the couple entered the house. That was good. The lights went on, and through the curtained windows of the kitchen Joe could see the man and the girl, evidently making supper.

Joe sat quietly. After a while, when it was well into the evening, he saw the waitress, Rita, return in a Volkswagen and park across the street. She hauled out the little girl, who seemed to be asleep, and carried her into the darkened house. The lights came on. Joe stood and stretched. All along the quiet street there were lights in the little frame houses. People came out and walked their dogs. Across the street he could see Rita occasionally passing a window. He decided that the applicable epithet for her was *statuesque*. The mild traffic noise of the town ebbed and waxed, ebbed and ebbed some more.

The lights in the house Hal and his girlfriend had entered were still on in the kitchen. He saw the couple standing by the window where the sink must be. Washing up, he thought. Finally lights went on upstairs. There were no more dog walkers. A group of boys who had been tossing a football under the streetlights at the end of the block wandered off.

A man came out onto the porch of a house across the street, two doors from Rita's, and stretched. He lighted a cigarette and crossed over into the park. He walked no more than twenty feet before stopping to urinate, then he walked home. In all this time not more than five cars had come to park on the street, all of their occupants bustling into their houses.

Joe wondered if the girl would leave. He walked around quietly and carefully to ease his boredom and to keep from getting chilled. When the time rolled around to midnight and most of the lights on the street had gone out, he decided that the girl must be spending the night. That complicated things. He went back to his car and changed into his usual pants and shirt and a sweater and drove away. It would have been nice, he thought, to have caught Hal at home in the afternoon, alone.

He went to a bar uptown that was filled with college students. The beer was excellent, and he had a good chance to pick up a lovely girl who seemed to think Joe was a young professor or something, but he kept his senses and took the opportunity to call the Fat Man in Detroit, just to report his progress.

The Fat Man was very excited. "Joe! Where you been? Carmine's about to flip. That crazy Hal blew away five guys last night. Talk about a loose cannon!"

"In Detroit?" Joe was puzzled. The behavior of Hal with the girl, his casual manner, didn't strike Joe as that of a man who had boldly shot down five men less than twenty-four hours before. It was possible, of course, but mystifying. Joe explained that he had found Hal—or at least someone who looked like Hal was supposed to look and was living in the house with the address that Hal had given the answering service. There was a girl at the house, Joe said, but he guessed under the strain of present circumstances he'd just have to go in, girl or no girl.

The Fat Man was all for it. "Don't forget the money, Joe. If you want, I could send a couple a guys down to help you out."

"To help me out? Forget it, Fat."

Of course, Joe thought, as he drove back to Black Street, the Fat Man is uneasy about my getting to the money first. But bring in a couple of his heavies? Joe knew he'd be lucky to get out of the house alive, money or no money, if he had some of Carmine's or Mitch's bozos backing him up. If Hal didn't get him, they sure would. It was a dicey game without them. But then he was delighted to see, as he cruised by Hal's house, that the convertible was gone. Not only that, there was a light shining through the opened drapes of the living room.

OK, Joe said to himself, time for a chat. He parked up on the next street, above the park, and pulled off his sweater. On went the armpit sling and into it the .38. He donned his tweed jacket and jauntily strolled back to Hal's house. On the porch he realized that the light he'd seen was really in the kitchen, not in the front room. He pressed the doorbell and took hold of the heavy storm door. To his surprise it was unlocked.

My, my, he thought, this Hal is careless. He was about to try the front door itself when it swung open and the girl, dressed in nothing more than a man's too-large shirt, said, "Dope! It's open."

Joe slammed her in the chest with a straight-arm, and she fell against the foot of a staircase with a squeal. He was in. He closed the door behind him, the .38 in his hand.

There was little to imagine about the girl as she sprawled before him. Before she could yell, Joe stepped between her legs and clutched her throat.

"Damn it all, anyway," he said regretfully and gestured with the pistol for her to get up. She got to her feet shakily, her eyes and her mouth forming huge O's. He spun her around and jammed her against the door of the hall closet. Her face was mashed against the door, and she whimpered.

"Where's Hal?" Joe demanded.

"Nnngh." She shook her head uncomprehendingly.

She didn't know what Joe was talking about, he saw. He kept her pressed there at arm's length and glanced up the stairs, then danced to his left and peeked into the darkened living room. "It's open," she'd said. Obviously Hal had gone out. For what? More beer?

For an awful moment it occurred to Joe that he was in the wrong house. This was not Hal's house. This was some cop's house, a cop not named Hal. Could this be the cop's girlfriend, or even—pray it wasn't so—the cop's wife? What the hell had made him believe it was Hal's house?

Nothing for it now. He jammed the barrel of the pistol into the base of the girl's skull, her fine black hair flowing around his hand, and reached back to lock the front door.

"Oh-m'god-please-don't-kill-me," she whispered woefully.

"In here," Joe said, dragging her into the living room. He released her, and she sagged to her knees before him in a dark corner, staring up at him. "Who the hell are you?" Joe asked, trying to modulate the anger and tension in his voice.

"Kathy," she whispered. She held her hands before her as if praying.

"Kathy." Joe had gotten command of his voice. "OK. What's your last name, Kathy?"

"Bunse."

"Kathy Bunse. Fine. Who lives here, Kathy?"

"Art. Art, uh . . ." She seemed stymied for a moment, then she remembered and said, "Holbrook."

"Oh," Joe said, sighing. He lowered the pistol until it was pointed at the floor, almost as if he'd relaxed. "Art Holbrook. Are we talking about Art Holbrook the cop?"

She shook her head. "Art's not a cop."

"Good," said Joe. "So, ah, Kathy, . . . where is Art?"

"He went to the little store, for cigarettes and, and beer," she said. She lowered her hands and rested them on her thighs.

"That's good," Joe said. He extended his left hand and helped her up. "Sit down, Kathy. Right over there." He gestured with his gun toward a chair that was in the dark shadow of the room. "Just be quiet and let's wait for Art. OK?"

She scrambled to the chair and sat, pulling the shirt down over her pelvis to hide her crotch. She sat, wide-eyed, and watched as Joe moved back to the entry and stood with his back to the wall, next to the front door, the gun held at waist level now.

Things settled down. There was no sound. Actually there were some sounds . . . a radio, or a phonograph, was playing upstairs. Not very loud. Some kind of mood music, a mindless, vaporous hush of synthesizer and bass. The refrigerator was cycling. The gas furnace was breathing. The girl was breathing rapidly, or was it himself? She took a deep breath finally, and Joe understood that she had regained her courage and was going to talk. He shook his head at her silently. But she only paused before asking, "Are you going to kill him?"

"No," Joe said. "Shut up."

His ears picked up something. Something had happened. A door? No. A car. A car had slowed, then driven by.

Joe stood in the little alcove of the entry for about ten minutes before asking the staring girl, "How far is this little store?"

Before she could answer, a man's upper body appeared at the floor level of the entryway between the living room and the dining room, and his extended arm held a pistol. The head craned for a fatal second, looking for a target.

Joe did not hesitate. He fired three times as rapidly as he could squeeze the trigger, a horrendous flash and crash filling the room. The man managed one wild, evidently convulsive squeeze, and the thin pop of a .22 was lost in the reverberations of the .38. Then he rolled sideways with a groan and lay still. The gun fell from his hand.

This time the girl did scream, and Joe backhanded her as he skipped by. She crumpled into the corner, sobbing, as Joe kicked the fallen pistol away from the outstretched hand and knelt over the man.

He turned the man's head. His eyes were glazing and he gasped. A froth of bubbly blood issued from his mouth. All of Joe's shots had struck the man: one in the upper chest, a lung shot; another in the left shoulder; and a third in the face, tearing away most of the left cheek and left ear and laying bare the maxilla. Blood was spattered up the jamb of the entry and now began to ooze sluggishly from the facial wound.

"Damn, damn, damn," Joe muttered, cursing the man for a stupid son of a bitch. He wheeled to the girl. "Get a towel, anything . . . hurry!"

The girl scrambled up and raced into the kitchen. Joe realized suddenly how idiotic that command had been, and he bolted after her, slipping on the spreading blood. She was halfway through the back door when he caught her. He grabbed her by the hair and hauled her to her butt on the kitchen tiles, kicking the door shut as he did so.

"Aagh!" she screamed, and he had to clutch her throat again to silence her. He stuck the gun in her face and somehow levered her upright. "Get the goddamn towel," he rasped.

They both looked wildly about the kitchen. Then as one they snatched at a dish towel hooked through the refrigerator door handle. Joe let her take it, and they moved swiftly back to the dying man. The girl knelt and tentatively reached for the man's head, but it looked so ruined and painful that she couldn't touch him. She looked up at Joe, weeping, and said, "We've got to get help."

"Nothing can help him now," Joe said flatly. "He's dead."

The man clawed agonizingly at his shirt, ripping the buttons off

and revealing the oozing hole where the most serious blow had hit. His
face looked atrocious, but it was nothing. He'd taken a bad hit in the
lungs, and it must have severed some vital artery or vein. He was
drowning.

He arched his back, and his eyes focused briefly on Joe, bending
over him. "Gol——" he gurgled. He shook his head as if trying to clear
it. Then he lost it.

He relaxed utterly. He didn't die right away. It took a long time.
Perhaps three minutes.

The girl was hysterical, sobbing and lying curled up on the dining
room carpet. Her head was pressed against a heavy carved leg of the
massive dining room table. Joe sat back on his heels and watched them
both. He observed her buttocks. They were round and smooth, but
there was a pimple or some reddish thing on the left cheek. He noticed
the abandoned disposition of Hal's body. Joe cocked his head, listening.
There were no external sounds of doors slamming, of voices, of sirens.
Only the sudden cessation of the furnace's respiration. The refrigerator
had quit cycling. The mindless music still trickled down from upstairs,
now with a deep, hushed, resolving electronic bass. The hair around the
girl's vagina was coarse and clotted with a dried whitish substance. It
caught the kitchen light, which fell across her buttocks and her lover's
ruined face in a yellow swath.

There was a final little burbling rush, then an issue of bright blood
from the man's mouth. His feet twitched. He collapsed into the deep
relaxation of death.

Joe pulled the girl upright and em-
braced her, smoothing her hair with his free hand. She hugged him
desperately, sobbing, until she finally took a huge breath that pressed
her breasts against his chest and he sensed a certain tension take command of her body. She drew away from him. Without a word Joe took
her by the hand and led her up the stairs to the bedroom. He made her
lie down on the bed and covered her with a quilt. She lay there
passively, staring up into the light while Joe moved methodically about
the room, opening drawers, looking.

Finally he sat down on the bed and looked at the girl. She continued to stare at the ceiling. She was indeed a teenager, he saw, not more than eighteen, if that. Her face was deadly calm, though tears leaked from the corners of her eyes.

"Do you want to live, Kathy?" Joe asked in a cool voice.

She nodded, tears staining her cheeks.

"Tell me what you know about Art."

She knew very little. She spoke in a quiet, almost dreamy voice. Art was a lawyer, she said. He'd picked her up at a bar near campus a few days ago. She was a freshman at the University of Iowa. She came from Nebraska. She was going into journalism, she thought. Art came into the bar a lot, she said. Another girl she knew, Merilou, had gone out with him. Merilou had said that Art was rich and cool. He didn't try to feel you up right away, and he took his girlfriends to concerts and good dinners. A real nice guy. The convertible belonged to Art. She had spent the last two nights with him. He wasn't a cop, but she thought he had a lot of cop friends.

While she talked, Joe looked through a wallet he'd found on the dresser. It contained a driver's license for an Arthur H. Holbrook. There was an identification card from the Iowa Bar Association in the same name, along with a card made out to Art Holbrook as an auxiliary deputy sheriff of Johnson County. Joe had no idea what an auxiliary deputy might be. Perhaps it was nothing more than the kind of unofficial status that some law-enforcement groups confer on contributors to the Policemen's Benevolent Fund, or something. On the other hand, it could be a legal deputization, he supposed.

In the closet Joe found a shoe box. The girl fell silent as Joe emptied it of some fifty thousand dollars in old bills. Also in the box were three large plastic pill tubes filled with a white, powdery substance. Joe assumed this was cocaine, possibly heroin. He had never used either substance, but he thought he recognized it as cocaine. This would be a hell of a lot of cocaine, he thought. There were also two handsome briefcases in the closet, both of them containing .22-caliber Smith & Wesson marksman's pistols and ammunition. Joe set the shoe box and the briefcases on the dresser.

"Get up, Kathy," he said quietly.

She stood there, shivering with fright, her hands clenched at her groin. She was spattered with blood, and her hair was tangled, but she was a pretty girl even as she blubbered and her features were blurred by weeping and terror.

"Take the shirt off, Kathy."

Trembling, she slowly unbuttoned the shirt and let it fall about her heels. She looked at him hopelessly.

"Get dressed," Joe said, gesturing at her clothes, which were scattered about the bed.

She quickly pulled on the panties and jeans and a colorful sweatshirt that had two gaudy toucans emblazoned on it. She didn't bother with the brassiere. While she slipped on her running shoes, Joe quietly explained that he had to lock her in the closet for a little while, but that if she kept quiet and didn't try anything foolish, he wouldn't harm her, and someone would come in an hour or so to let her out. Joe would be in the house for at least another hour, he told her, "cleaning up."

She thanked him for not hurting her, and she went docilely into the closet after Joe had carefully searched it. He handed her a pillow and a blanket from the bed and closed the door. He jammed a chair under the doorknob. Then he went downstairs.

Joe looked at the dead man with casual interest. He had not wanted to kill, or even hurt, the man, but then he had to admit he had entered the man's house with a loaded pistol. What should he have expected? Still, there was no way he was going to confront Hal Good without a pistol in hand. He was determined, nonetheless, to feel no remorse, nor to allow himself to be affected at all—at least for now. Perhaps later, when he was sitting somewhere in security—he envisioned suite A/B of Amtrak's Zephyr—he could afford to reflect and expose himself to the emotional consequences of killing this man. He reckoned he would do that, but not now.

He didn't move the body, or even touch it, but peered at the face, distorted as it was. Joe didn't recognize him and didn't expect to. There wasn't anything to see. Just an ordinary-looking guy who had somehow got into a business that had made him a lot of money and had no doubt brought a good deal of excitement into his life, which was now prematurely ended.

For the next hour Joe carefully searched the house and turned up only one thing of additional interest. A telephone book with the number of the California answering service, next to which was written *Hal Good*. A little reminder. Another number, in Chicago, had the name Carl Stevens written by it. There were also numbers in Detroit, New York, Miami, and other large American cities. Often names were written out clearly, with addresses, such as "Sid, 3716 Fairlawn, Detroit," or "Lande, 29970 Kelly Rd., Apt. 1, Detroit," or "Tupman, 4200 Conner Towers," and so on. It was amazing. Joe didn't like to take the book—it could be damning evidence if he were stopped—but he felt he had to, to show the Fat Man. And it might be worth something.

He considered doing a deep search—tearing up floors, dismantling the furnace and the heating ducts—but he had a feeling that if there was more money to be found, it wouldn't be much. Certainly not millions. There might be additional interesting information, but it wasn't worth the time it would take. Hal—or Art, as Joe was beginning to think of him—was supposed to be a professional, but Joe was leaning toward the view that he had been more lucky than anything else. He hadn't really covered his tracks very well, and he wasn't as careful as a working hitter should be. How had the man ever gotten into the business? Through a client he had defended, perhaps? It was a mystery. His obscure life-style had helped tremendously, and if he had a good liaison with the police, as it seemed, that, too, would be helpful. But Joe didn't see Art lasting much longer, whatever happened.

Anyway, the job was done. Joe had found his man, if not the money. He didn't want anything else here. The fifty thousand in the shoe box was owed him, he figured, for past services and for overfulfilling the contract on Hal. Not that he would mention the money to the Fat Man. It was of no use to Hal, that was for sure, and it obviously wasn't the skim that the Fat Man wanted. He decided to leave the two pistols, as well as the similar pistol that Hal had tried to use on him. They weren't his kind of artillery, and heaven only knew what crime scenes they had once adorned.

A light flickered through the darkened living room and caught Joe for a second. A horn tooted. Joe froze. The living room had two large picture windows in it, and the drapes were open. Joe darted to the edge of the window and caught a glimpse of the lights of a police squad car as it continued down Black Street. He realized it was just an ordinary patrol. Obviously some pals of Art Holbrook. They would have seen the upstairs light on and would, perhaps, have suspected what Art was up to. He glanced at his watch. It was barely two o'clock. He was surprised. He felt as if he had been in the house for hours.

Could the patrol have seen him standing in the dark room? Nah, he told himself. But it was time to move.

What to do with Kathy? She was a wonderful witness. She could definitely identify him—if he were ever brought before her (he had no police record, no photos or fingerprints on file). It would be a shame to kill a pretty, innocent girl like Kathy. But a sensible, careful man like Joe—unlike Art—had to think about such things. He sighed. This job was not unbounded fun. It struck him all of a sudden how convenient it would be if Kathy would just go blind. Of course, she could be blinded . . . Nah. Too stupid for words. Hell, when you considered it, damn-near everybody in Iowa City had seen him, including the woman across the street, Rita. He'd even been to the cop shop, asking after Hal Good. Should he go across the street and murder Rita and her wise-looking daughter? Should he kill the lady cop in the license bureau? Maybe he should kill everyone in Iowa City and track down that goddamn racist salesman who had given him a ride to Coralville and kill that son of a bitch, for sure. He laughed out loud. No, no, there was no need. They'd never make him. He was sure of it. But they were sure as hell going to have a terrific mystery on their hands for a while. They'd never begin to solve it. But, he thought sadly, he would never be able to come back to Iowa City. Such a pretty little town.

He got a can of Coke out of the refrigerator and took it upstairs to Kathy. She cowered when he opened the door, but she quickly realized he was just being thoughtful. "Hey, I'm taking off now, babe. You be cool, OK? I'll give the cops a ring in about a half hour, and they'll be by to let you out."

He gathered up the shoe box and let himself out the back way. He walked into the park and stopped for a minute to urinate. There were some noises in the underbrush, a scuffling of old leaves, and he was startled to see two enormous, fat opossums rummaging about. They looked like overgrown rats but seemed oblivious to him. He zipped up, noticing that a light was still on in Rita's house, upstairs. Maybe she was reading in bed, or maybe the kid had to have a night-light.

Just then a squad car drove up rather quickly from Governor Street and pulled to the curb in front of Art Holbrook's house. Joe backed into the shadows of the trees and watched as a slender, black man in plain clothes got out and, accompanied by a uniformed policeman, approached the front door. It would take only a glance through the unshaded window to see the late Art Holbrook, Joe knew.

He walked to his car and drove calmly away. He had noticed Merilou's phone number in Art's book, and he'd planned to call her and tell her to help her friend Kathy, but now the police had forestalled that kindly gesture. Joe was disappointed.

Hours later he dropped the car at Midway Airport in Chicago and took a bus downtown, where he booked a roomette on the Amtrak to Detroit.

Thirteen

"**C**adillac Communications Con-
sultants," said a pleasant female voice. Mulheisen asked for Helen
Sedlacek and was asked to give his name, then politely put on hold
while Simon and Garfunkel sang a few bars until the voice returned to
say, "I'm sorry, but Miss Sedlacek is on another line. Would you care
to hold?"

Mulheisen grudgingly agreed to hold, and he listened to a few
more bars of "Mrs. Robinson" before noticing that another light on his
phone had lighted up. He put Sedlacek on hold and punched the
operator's button. "A Miss Sedlacek for you," he was told. Mulheisen
punched the second button. "Miss Sedlacek?" he said.

"About time, Mulheisen," a woman's voice said sharply. "Listen.
What have you been doing about my father's murder? You know, we're
citizens, too. My mother is distraught. She can't sleep, she can't eat,
she—"

"Miss Sedlacek, we're doing all we can. I'm work—"

"Oh, sure," she cut in, "you're busting your butt to solve the
mystery, only there is no damn mystery. My father was shot down by
one of Carmine's goons, and you damn well know it. I know it. The
whole world knows it!"

"Do you have some evidence that I don't, Miss Sedlacek?"

"If I did, you'd never know it. You've never even questioned me,
except for a few minutes at the house."

"As a matter of fact, I was just calling you to make an appointment," Mulheisen said.

"Sure," said the basic Detroit cynical voice.

"Your secretary has me on hold this minute."

The phone made a noise and Simon and Garfunkel sang, "DiMaggioooo," and then Helen Sedlacek was back. "Sorry," she said without seeming at all sorry. "What did you want?"

"I told you—an interview." Mulheisen laughed. "Now tell me, do you have any information about Carmine?"

There was a measure of silence, then: "What if I did?"

"If you do, it's your duty to come forward and inform the police."

"And get blown away myself?"

Mulheisen laughed again. He didn't really sound amused this time. But after a moment he said, "All right. If you have something, I want to know it. If you just *know* that Carmine is behind this, then I'm not going to waste my time."

"I might."

"You might. Should we meet? Are you staying at your fa—
. . . er, mother's?"

"Don't come there, for heaven's sake. And not the office, either. Mmmm."

They bickered for a few minutes over a suitable restaurant before settling on Tom's Oyster Bar, out on Mack Avenue.

After they'd disentangled their phone lines, Mulheisen sat and stared at a list of witnesses and others who had been hauled in on the night of Big Sid's murder. He wasn't really looking at it; he was thinking of Helen Sedlacek, trying to remember exactly what she looked like. He unconsciously rubbed his chest, where she had punched him. Then Jimmy Marshall called from Iowa City.

"Well, we're a little further along, Mul. The girl has given us an Identikit picture of the hired killer. We took a lot of latents. We ransacked the house. Found some coke, some guns—.22's. Holbrook was an expert shot, a marksman—he belonged to a local gun club and used the firing range regularly. I'm beginning to get a pretty clear picture of him."

Mulheisen was fascinated by Jimmy's account. "Could this guy really have been a professional killer?"

"I'm sure of it, Mul. Pretty unusual, but there it is. He was in private law practice—mostly deeds and wills, that sort of thing—but he was a cop buff, and he liked to hang out with them. They welcomed him as a kind of house lawyer. He did a lot for the guys for free. Used to ride around in the squad cars, got invited to the picnics. Hell, when I showed them the picture, they said right away, 'Art!' "

"What about the girl?" Mulheisen wanted to know.

"She's all right, a little shaken, but she said the killer was—get this—'a real gentleman'! He was very cool, Mul. He just sat and waited till Holbrook showed up, then blasted him. The way the girl puts it, though, is that he didn't mean to kill Holbrook, just talk to him. She says Holbrook snuck in with a gun and was going to blast the killer, but he beat him to it. Now this is a little puzzling, Mul. I mean, she just got out of bed with this Holbrook, and now she's taking the killer's side. Is this the Stockholm syndrome?" Jimmy was referring to a syndrome in which hostages come to identify with their captor and speak well of him, or even assist him.

Mulheisen was skeptical. "Maybe he was nice to her," he said, "and maybe Art Holbrook was not so nice. Also, it may have been just as she said."

On the way to Tom's Oyster Bar, Mulheisen stopped at Bon Secours Hospital in Grosse Pointe. Bonny was out of surgery but not receiving visitors. Lande was presumably with her, but Mulheisen didn't inquire. He left some flowers and went on.

Helen Sedlacek was more attractive than Mulheisen had remembered. She was small, but her head looked large. It was her hair, a black cloud streaked with silver. He hadn't noticed the silver streaks before—they were very dramatic. Her face was pale, with a straight mouth and very strong, dark brows. She wore a dark gray suit with wide, padded shoulders. They stood in the sawdust at the bar and sipped ice-cold Polish vodka. Miss Sedlacek declined the oysters—"I never eat oysters when I'm more than five hundred miles from the ocean," she said.

"What does a communications consultant do?" Mulheisen asked.

"I find out why people don't talk to each other at work and why they hate their bosses. Mostly, it has to do with parking."

"Parking?" Mulheisen sniffed at the oysters. They smelled good, but Helen's seafood theory was too plausible.

"Who has a parking spot and where it is in relation to the office," she said. "I do this for many small firms in Detroit."

"There must be more to it than that," Mulheisen said.

"Of course, but people tend not to tell the consultant about nepotism, love affairs, harassment, jealousy, and inadequate pay—at least not initially. They prefer to complain about minor things. Eventually it all comes out. Then I have to decide how to pitch it to the boss, who is paying my bill. He doesn't want to hear that he shouldn't be feeling the girls up or promoting his nephew over more qualified people. There's a world of resentment in most workplaces. I have to let him know, subtly and painlessly, that he's an asshole, that the women who work for him don't love him but loathe him, that he's a fool, and if he doesn't watch out, he's going to be indicted."

"Nice world," Mulheisen said. They agreed to move to a quieter spot, away from the hubbub. They found a reasonably secluded booth.

"I've been unfair to you, Sergeant," Helen Sedlacek said. "I suppose you're doing your best. I have one little item that may help."

"Let's hear it."

"I'm afraid it isn't very much . . . It's not really clear in my mind. That evening, when I heard the car crash into the fence, I ran to the window. I saw the car in the fence, and I saw Papa's car. I saw a man near the car, on his hands and knees, moving. What I wonder is could it have been Mickey? Or was it the killer?"

"On his hands and knees? It couldn't have been Egan. He was dead. There was no indication that he had moved after being shot. The medical examiner would have found gravel or dirt on his hands I think, and he didn't mention it. Where did the crawling man go?" Mulheisen asked.

"I didn't see. Mama ran in and I went to her. Then Roman came in."

144

Mulheisen considered this. "Are you sure you didn't see the kid in the wrecked car? He was getting out of his car. Maybe you saw him and unconsciously transferred him mentally to your father's car."

Helen Sedlacek thought about this and nodded. "Yes, it's possible. I must have seen Mickey, but if he wasn't moving . . . Gee, I don't know. I didn't think it was Mickey at the time. I didn't really think anything. It was only later it seemed to me it might have been the killer."

"I've had a problem with this myself," Mulheisen said, "trying to get it clear in my mind. I decided the killer was not in the car. Why? All the evidence indicates that no shots were fired in the car, although if the killer had been riding with your father and Mickey, it would have been the simplest and smartest thing to do the shooting before anybody got out. But Mickey was out, and your father was fifty feet away. This strongly argues a killer standing on the sidewalk or nearby, waiting. He must have known the car would have to stop at the locked gate and Egan would get out. The only thing I can think, from what you are saying, is that the killer shot Mickey in the chest first, mortally wounding him but not necessarily stopping him from crawling, and then finished him off with two shots to the eyes after he shot your father . . ."

Mulheisen's voice trailed off. The woman was gazing at him with a look of appalled distress. "Sorry," he said.

She shook her head, her heavy hair surging about. "No, no, it's all right. I have to think about it. I have to see it." She ducked her head, letting her hair hang like a curtain before her, but she soon looked up. "I guess it was Mickey I saw. I just didn't think so. I guess when I turned away, to hug Mama, I missed the killer."

Mulheisen nodded. "Have you ever heard of a man named Hal Good?" he asked.

She brightened with interest. "Hal? Yes. I met him. Papa brought him to the house a few times."

"Recently?"

"Yes. He seemed like a nice guy, not like most of them. Friendly. Ordinary. Good looking, too. He flirted a little. Papa gave me the sign."

She raised an eyebrow, shaking her head slightly. "I knew what that meant forget it. Why? What about him?"

"Let's get out of here," Mulheisen said.

They left the bar and began to walk along Mack Avenue. It was raining again, not much more than a mist. "What about Hal?" she demanded after a half block. A steady hiss of traffic flowed along the wide street. The streetlights had already come on.

"I'm fairly certain that Hal Good killed your father and Mickey Egan," Mulheisen said. "He was picked up in the area that night, but he managed to get away. He was found dead yesterday, in Iowa City. He'd been hit in his own house."

"Christ," Helen muttered, striding along with her hands deep in the pockets of an expensive trench coat. She looked up into the mist, then shook her head. "So he was the one?"

"I'm pretty convinced," Mulheisen said.

"So I guess I'm supposed to be pleased," she said. "You solved the mystery. Papa can rest easy!"

"Well . . ."

She shook her head, moisture flying from her hair. "It doesn't work that way." Her voice was tight and angry.

Mulheisen sighed. "I thought you'd be . . . well, not pleased exactly, but a little more at ease."

"It doesn't solve anything," she said. They reached the end of the block and paused, looking around. She turned to the right, and they began to walk along a residential street. "I have my obligations," she said.

"Obligations?" Mulheisen asked. "What obligations? We found the killer. He's dead."

"You wouldn't understand."

"It's not easy," he admitted. "But then, I'm a cop. Every society seems to find it necessary to have police. It's not a new thing. I imagine they even have police in Yugoslavia, or whatever they're calling it these days, and people are not expected to go out and take an eye for an eye."

"Things are very eye-for-an-eye in Serbia these days," she said, "but this isn't Serbia. There's more to it."

Mulheisen hesitated, then said, "The word is that Sid was about to leave town."

"Papa? No, no," she said. "What do you mean?" She stopped on the sidewalk before a little frame house with a wire fence. The lights were on, and a kid's gaudy skateboard lay on its side next to the concrete porch.

Mulheisen looked down at her anguished white face. "We have very good indications that Sid was planning to emigrate to South America. With Germaine Kouras."

"No," she said vehemently. "He would never leave Mama. You didn't know him. My father might keep a whore like that, but he would never leave Mama. I know my father, Mul. He was not exactly a pillar of respectability, but he was a man who deeply respected my mother. He loved her . . . and me. There was no hint that he was running out on us. It's slander. He was a man of honor. He was betrayed. Probably by that slut."

They walked on. "What do you know about Germaine Kouras?" Mulheisen asked.

"She's a whore," Helen said simply. "Papa was a man. That's the way men are. He liked a pretty girl. She's pretty, I guess. A Greek," she said with contempt. "Younger than me. She's not even a good singer."

"Apparently she's left town," Mulheisen said. They turned a corner and walked on in the rain, which had gotten heavier now.

"Of course," Helen said. "Carmine sent her away. She betrayed Papa, and Carmine sent her into hiding . . . or killed her. I hope he didn't kill her."

Mulheisen looked at her inquisitively. "I've tried not to entertain that possibility."

"I'll kill her," she said.

"Oh, hell," Mulheisen replied.

"Oh, yes," she said calmly. "Not right away, but eventually. I'll find her and kill her. The slut. It has nothing to do with you. But Carmine, . . . Carmine has to pay."

"Oh, stop it," Mulheisen said. "I'm sick of you people. You think you can just kill people. It doesn't work that way. Maybe back when you were in tribes or something . . . Anyway, it's not so easy. These people are obviously pretty dangerous. What are you, a hired consultant? Give me a break."

"You know nothing!" Her eyes flashed, and she shook her wealth of black hair stormily, striding on.

"Your father and his associates," Mulheisen said sarcastically, "seem to think that their business only concerns them, and they'll take care of it when things go wrong. But that's not what happens. Other people get involved, like this Hal Good. Or sometimes people just get blown away because they're in the line of fire—like those young lawyers slumming with Tupman. And now you come on with this Old World vendetta crap. Grow up."

"I knew you wouldn't understand," she said. "Everybody knows better than to talk to a cop."

"That's the problem around here," Mulheisen said. "Everybody thinks he knows better than the cops, that he—or she—can do better than the cops. But believe me, Helen, that's weak thinking. It's just foolish cynicism. It plays well in Detroit because we all like to believe we're tough, we've been through the mill, we've seen it all, we can take it and dish it out. It's just ignorance."

The woman shrugged, striding on. "OK. You're right, of course. I'm not a Sicilian like Carmine, after all. I was born here. I went to school here. But I loved my papa. You didn't love him. I know what a Serb has to do. I was Papa's only child. I wasn't his son, but a daughter can do what a son would have done. It isn't enough for me to hear that Hal Good is dead. It doesn't satisfy here." She pounded her fist against her breast.

Mulheisen glanced at her, fascinated. What a difference, he thought, between this woman and Bonny. But they both seemed to be ready to kill Germaine Kouras. He shook his head.

"What?" Helen Sedlacek demanded, observing his quizzical expression.

Mulheisen was thinking of a note his mother had left on the refrigerator door a couple of days earlier. A developer was proceeding with a trailer-court project down the road from them, despite bitter complaints from the neighbors and environmentalists. The note had read: "Mul—the bastard is going ahead with it. Meeting at 7:30. Bring grenades."

"Nothing," he said. "I was just thinking how bloody-minded women can be."

"You're too soft, Mulheisen," she responded. "It isn't just all testosterone, you know."

"Do you know a man named Eugene Lande?" he asked.

"Lande? Sure. Smart little prick," she said. She laughed. "He designed my computer system and installed it. Cheap, too. Great guy. Why?"

Mulheisen was amazed. Lande—a great guy? Was there something he didn't know? "How did you happen to hire Lande?"

"I don't know. Somebody suggested him. His bid was a lot lower than anybody else's."

"You never knew him before?"

"No. He's a real screwball, come to think of it."

They had returned to Tom's Oyster Bar. Helen stuck out her hand and shook his firmly. She looked up at him resolutely. "You're a well-meaning man, Mul," she said. "Thanks for finding out about this Hall Good. I appreciate it. I really do. It goes a long way toward making it better." She actually patted him on the shoulder, then turned away with a simple "Thanks again."

Fourteen

" . . . **B**ring grenades."

Cora Mulheisen was outraged. The little maple-lined road on which they lived was being raped. A developer had bought the estate of the late Sarah Goldkette, a lifelong neighbor of the Mulheisens', from her grandchildren, who had lived in California and/or Arizona most of their adult lives. The developer was said to have paid "a cool million" for the forty-acre property, which was located about a quarter mile up the road from the Mulheisens. The old Goldkette farmhouse would be torn down and replaced with a convenience store and lots for a hundred mobile homes. Outrage!

The Mulheisen home was itself an old farmhouse. A man from Ohio had built it in 1892, thinking that his sweetheart would soon join him; but she died, and after a few years another farmer, named Jabez Cooke, a black man from Ontario who had been employed by the Ohio man, bought the property and built a small cabin near the river. Cooke built a good-size barn, which still stood, and a few smaller buildings—a henhouse, a toolshed, an outhouse, and so on—which were long gone. Grampaw Cooke raised onions and other garden crops and kept a few cows and chickens and pigs. He had never lived in the main house. He had been a lifelong bachelor, reputed to be a great fisherman and a trapper of muskrats. In 1921 Mulheisen's father, then an engineer but eventually the water commissioner, bought the property, granted Grampaw Cooke a lifetime lease, and had the old farmhouse renovated to accommodate himself and his wife. Grampaw Cooke lived in the cabin by the river until he died, in 1934. Mulheisen had not, of course, known the old man, but the cabin survived until 1962, when it was swept into the St. Clair River during a great spring flood caused by an enormous ice jam.

Grampaw Cooke was a legendary figure to Mulheisen. In his lonely but otherwise quite happy childhood he had often lingered in the cabin, imagining himself to be a runaway slave, very bold and adventurous, a famous hunter and trapper and all-around outdoorsman. The cabin became his bunk, as he called it, and it was variously situated on the Arctic Circle, the Missouri River, the upper Amazon, and even the Congo—regardless of season, for the season was dictated by young Mul's reading. Thus, it mattered not if a frozen Saint Clair River could only rarely be transformed into the great gray-green greasy Limpopo, all set about with fever trees.

Mulheisen still possessed a few old artifacts that had belonged to Jabez Cooke—a couple of rusted traps, an old cracked cane pole that had been made in Mobile, Alabama. They were in the attic now, next to the pile of goods that included the picture of Bonny Wheeler.

There were now Detroiters in the six farmhouses that lined the opposite side of the half-mile-long road, all of which had been converted into more-or-less gentrified country homes, nominally preserving the familiar style of the midwestern farmhouse—two storied, with wide front porches and sash windows—but lately sporting such California modifications as carports, crank-open windows, sliding glass doors that opened onto redwood decks in backyards that featured hot tubs and even swimming pools. Though Cora Mulheisen laughed derisively at these innovations, she had not denounced outright this relatively benign form of domestic evolution. But mobile homes!

All forty acres of Mulheisen property fronted on the Saint Clair River, now controlled by the federal government and maintained as part of a national wetlands system. Somehow the Goldkette property had not been included in the same scheme. Cora Mulheisen felt it should have been and that the proposed mobile home development had a suspect waste-disposal system. She was not opposed, in principle, to the introduction of lower-income housing to the area, but she did loathe mobile homes—instant aluminum slums, she called them—and she reckoned that the potential traffic and the impact of that many people on a fragile ecosystem would be disastrous. She was particularly suspicious of the notion that one hundred mobile homes could adequately dispose of their domestic waste through the developer's system without contaminating the river and the wetlands project and, inevitably, the lake below. Current zoning laws did not prohibit the development. Indeed, there was federal money involved—a different agency, of course. Cora Mulheisen's plan was to pit the agencies against one another, in the hope that the wetlands project would win.

This was going to be a bitter fight. There were community meetings, picket lines, letters to be written to the editors of newspapers, to congressmen, to environmental groups. Mulheisen felt he should support his mother in this, but he couldn't find the time or energy. She had plenty of both, however.

Jimmy Marshall was not sympathetic to Cora Mulheisen's crusade, although Mulheisen tried to convert him with the environmentalist views he had acquired from his mother. The way Jimmy saw it, a rich old white woman was trying to stop poor folks from moving into an area where they could give their kids access to the river and the great outdoors.

When Mulheisen told him his mother was working to get the wetlands designated the Jabez Cooke National Wetlands Reserve, Jimmy riposted, "First and last nigger in those parts." But privately he knew that Mulheisen and his mother had no animus against black people, nor against poor people of any race. They just hated to lose their isolation, and they hated the developer, who had no altruistic notions of providing homes for the poor. If regulations permitted it, the developer would build a high rise or some other yuppie-oriented development.

The fact was Detroit was moving out. It had always been doing so. In Mulheisen's eyes it should never have been situated where it was in the first place. Militarily it must have made sense to control the straits, but the native peoples had never seen any reason to live in this low, marshy area. When they occasionally met at the straits, it was always on an island—Belle Isle, Peach Island, Harsen's Island—or on the higher Canadian side, which was more healthful. Only commerce-minded Euro-Americans could seriously contemplate building a settlement there. After the village burned down in 1805, it would have been a good time to abandon the site. But, alas, along came Judge Augustus B. Woodward with his mind full of L'Enfant's plan for Washington—another city, like St. Petersburg, built on a swamp (visionaries are perhaps by nature swamp drainers, cloacally obsessed)—and it was used for Detroit.

Still, it was mainly social issues—racism, mainly—that prompted the population shift beginning in the mid-twentieth century.

Mulheisen himself was gloomily contemplating a reverse migration, back into town. Not right away, of course, no matter what happened with the development. He would wait until his mother died. She was seventy-nine, but a vigorous woman. She looked good for another twenty years, or more.

Mulheisen was expressing some of these thoughts at dinner, at the Marshalls'. Jimmy and Yvonne had purchased a house in the Chandler Park area, just off Outer Drive. It was their dream house, a well-built brick home with three bedrooms and a fenced yard in the back. To their horror they had recently discovered that drug pushers were operating practically on their corner. Their eight-year-old son, Kirby, was scared. Kids in his school had been caught with crack and even pistols. Yvonne had promptly enrolled him in a Catholic school. Then she had organized a neighborhood watch group, mothers and fathers patrolling the streets at night and warning off the pushers. But lately the pushers had become more insolent, threatening the neighborhood patrols with guns, occasionally slashing the tires of the cars of the more active parents, even shooting at houses.

Mulheisen had arrived with a bottle of wine. He and Yvonne Marshall greeted each other politely. She was a large, striking woman who tended to dress in gorgeous African gowns. She had a master's degree in social science, and Mulheisen was frankly intimidated by her. She seemed to be accusing him of something. Tonight she was wearing a wildly patterned robe with a lot of red and orange to it, along with several necklaces of colored beads and one of silver with many dangling, obscure shapes attached. Her hair was pulled back severely and then allowed to explode behind her head in a great black and silver bush. Her earrings were immense, silver bangles in intricate shapes that clamped as she moved.

The children were attractive—the girl, Tanza (short for Tanzania, where Yvonne had been a Peace Corps volunteer), who was six, and Kirby, who seemed very bright, an impression underscored by his heavy, black-rimmed glasses. Mulheisen had brought Tanza a picture book by Ezra Jack Keats, which was well received, and Kirby a box of baseball cards, in which the boy politely feigned interest. They were presented to Mulheisen in their pajamas. Tanza surprised him by throwing her arms about his neck and kissing him on the cheek. "Goodnight, Fang!" she cried with a giggle. Then Kirby gravely shook his hand and said, "Thank you and good night, sir." As they went up to bed, Mulheisen overheard Kirby admonishing his sister. "You dope!" he said, "that's not his real name."

Dinner, as always with Yvonne, consisted of a curious mixture of strange grains—dark rice, barley, oats, or perhaps it was ground garbanzo beans—and chopped vegetables—green peppers and onions and carrots—along with tiny fragments of grayish meat that could have been anything but was probably goat or lamb. Mulheisen could never quite figure it out. It didn't taste bad, but it didn't taste good enough for him to overcome his suspicions. There was the inevitable yellowish paste (more garbanzo beans?) with a strident flavoring that he just couldn't be enthusiastic about—neither sweet nor sour, hot nor bland, just strong. One was supposed to dip into this with a piece of flat, tasteless bread and then dip the whole thing into a lurid, streaky liquid that reminded Mulheisen of transmission fluid. It was very hot. All of it was presumably Tanzanian cuisine, though perhaps not. Mulheisen gulped the wine, as did Jimmy, but Yvonne did not.

Afterward, drinking coffee in the living room, Yvonne impatiently brushed aside Mulheisen's arguments about the threatened development in Saint Clair Flats. "You just don't realize how most people have to live, Mul," she said. "I don't just mean in the rest of the world, but right here. We are fighting for our lives here, and for our children's lives."

"Oh, now, honey—" Jimmy began, but she cut him short.

"It is nothing less," she insisted. "If I was a young African-American boy growing up in Detroit, I would be scared to death. You know my cousin June—she lives in Highland Park?—her neighbor's boy was shot two weeks ago. He was just walking home from school, and some other boys were driving by, and they shot him. He's all right, but he could have been killed. And do you know what it was? They thought he was some other boy who wore the same kind of jacket and was in a rival drug posse, or whatever they call it."

Mulheisen didn't know what to say. He knew it happened. He had investigated similar cases, although it wasn't his usual area of responsibility. There were task forces assigned to such crimes, but since he was unofficially the chief detective in the precinct, many of the cases came his way, at least initially. It was a tremendous problem, an overwhelming problem, and he couldn't see any clear way out of it.

"It's not just a crime problem," he said. "It isn't just a matter of busting the pushers, breaking up the drug trade—although that has to be done—but it's unemployment, bad schools . . ." He started to recite the all-too-familiar litany but stopped. What was the use? The whole society seemed in peril, on the verge of anarchy. Still, as daunting as it seemed, he wasn't ready to give up. It was his city, after all. He felt that his job, and Jimmy's, were important; if he could just do it, that would contribute to a solution. He wasn't going to take on all the city's problems, however.

Yvonne snorted contemptuously. "Well, something's going to happen, I can tell you that. This reminds me of '67. There'll be riots again, you know. But," she drew herself up, "this time we aren't going to fall back on the same old sorry half-assed patch up of the good-ol'-boy system. This time we're going to figure out what has to be done, and we'll do it! If the whole bunch of you folks have to go."

"If you mean white folks," Mulheisen said, "most of us have already gone."

"Yeah. You ran to the suburbs and left us here to clean up your shit."

"Jesus, hon," Jimmy said.

Yvonne turned on him. "Hell, he ain't my boss. But you're right, Mul. Most of you did go, but you didn't let go of the money and the power. Or am I supposed to believe that you turned it over to us, and we trashed it?"

"No, I don't mean that," Mulheisen replied. "It's not as if somebody just said one day, 'OK, we got what we wanted, now it's your turn.' It happened over a long period of time. You know that. Those who could get out, got out. Maybe they were racists, maybe the real estate scammers scared them out, but maybe they were just ordinary folks who thought they'd like to bring up their kids in a better environment. Maybe you'd like to get out, too."

"You got that right," she responded. "Maybe I could move to that trailer court in Saint Clair Flats. But you know they aren't taking applications from people like me."

Mulheisen shook his head wearily. "It's a government-funded project," he said; "I suppose they'd have to take you. But let's face it, Yvonne—you don't want to live in any trailer court, especially not out in the suburbs. You're an urban woman. Hell, you should be out there with Ma, fighting these sleazy developers. It doesn't do any good to junk up another place for the benefit of the poor. Are they going to love it? I doubt they will for long."

Surprised to find that Yvonne did not rebut this statement, he was encouraged to go on. "There is a reason, presumably, that all these people are here." He waved his hand vaguely at the city beyond the walls of the pleasant living room. "Maybe it was never a good reason—industry, with all that that implies—but for a long time nobody paid much attention. Everybody seemed to like it . . . jobs, prosperity. But somewhere along the line—the sixties? earlier?—they started not liking it. The problems were always there—racism, crime, poverty, you name it—but they used to seem manageable. Or at least approachable. Now . . . I don't know."

The three of them sat in silence for a moment, each recollecting a time, perhaps not too distant, when Detroit had seemed a much better place. Of course, they'd all been younger, more enthusiastic, more optimistic. Perhaps most generations have this feeling, but somehow it seemed more pressing these days.

"Just about every city in the country has problems like Detroit's, to some extent," Mulheisen said. "You know, Detroit has had longer to deal with these problems. No doubt I'm just a fool, but I suspect that if anyone in the country comes up with any answers to these problems, it'll probably be in Detroit."

"You are a fool," Yvonne said.

"So, what's your answer?" Mulheisen asked, annoyed.

"I'm thinking I might get me a gun," she snapped back. "Anymore of these punks come into this neighborhood, I'm just liable to blow them away."

"Whoa!" Jimmy cried.

"No, no," Mulheisen pleaded. "You can't think like that. That doesn't get us anywhere."

Yvonne laughed, sitting back triumphantly in her easy chair. "Look at you two! My, oh my. Mama say she gon' get her a gun, and two big ol' mens—both of whom are packing—say 'Whoa!' "

"Actually, Yvonne has a different idea," Jimmy said, sitting forward. "Tell him, hon."

Her idea was simple, perhaps simplistic. She was one of the organizers of a group that was planning to push for a new form of urban government, one that would not just oversee the city of Detroit but would embrace all the outlying suburbs and towns.

"You white folks have run out on Detroit," she said, "but you still need it, to make money out of it. We'll have something called the Greater Detroit Urban Zone. Reorganize all the services, realign the taxes, and cut through all this bull crap of all these little towns that ring the city—Warren, Harper Woods, the Grosse Pointes (why in hell should there be five Grosse Pointes?), Royal Oak, Ferndale, Hamtramck, Center Line (Center Line!) . . . Why there's dozens of them. Already the police have so much bureaucratic red tape to get through when someone robs a store on Eight Mile Road—it's just crazy. The zone will take in Wayne County, Oakland County, Washtenaw . . . and we'll have a CEO instead of a mayor, . . . a zone commission instead of a city council . . ."

She went on for a considerable time, quite excited and exhilarated. Mulheisen listened, fascinated but skeptical. Schemes of this sort had been bandied about for decades. She was right, of course; the present system was insane and part of the problem itself. It would have to change, and it was in transition now, but Yvonne was working for radical, abrupt change—go to bed in Royal Oak and wake up in the *zone.* And finally, it appeared that Yvonne herself was planning to be the CEO.

When at last Yvonne tore herself away to prepare for her next day's classes (she taught at Macomb County Community College), the two men went down to the basement, to Jimmy's den. This was a room that the previous owner had partitioned off from the conventional part of the basement (washer, drier, clothesline, laundry tubs, hot-water heater, furnace, heating ducts) but had never really finished. Jimmy had paneled the walls with sheets of pressed composition board that was patterned to look like expensive wood—rosewood, perhaps, or something more exotic. It did look like wood, except for a much too slick, plastic finish. He had a thick carpet on the floor, and he'd furnished the room with an old, but passable couch and a couple of easy chairs. The lighting was recessed into an acoustic-tiled ceiling. It was almost cozy, except for an ineradicable dampness and a certain faint odor of detergents.

Jimmy kept his computer down here, on a desk in one corner, but the main feature of the room was an elaborate stereo system and floor-to-ceiling racks of jazz recordings, mostly old LP's but now more and more CD's. He was a complete jazz buff, one of his most attractive traits in Mulheisen's eyes. Jimmy liked just about any kind of jazz, but particularly the small groups that had flourished throughout and after the swing era, groups that were led by Benny Carter and Coleman Hawkins and Chu Berry—the powerful, smooth, and fluent players who could break your heart with the blues or a ballad and then swing you silly. He also possessed a clarinet, on which he sporadically practiced, and he could play a pretty decent low-register imitation of Benny Carter on "Just a Mood."

Jimmy corresponded with several jazz record shops across the country, and now he eagerly put on a recently obtained recording of some forgotten armed forces "Jubilee" broadcasts from the forties, featuring singers like Savannah Churchill and Helen Humes with the Carter band and others. Mulheisen would normally have been delighted with this record, but he was distracted and troubled, not just by Yvonne's extended rap, but by the cumulative effect of an investigation gone sour and, probably more important, although he was not yet openly admitting it, the news of Bonny's illness. He also longed for a cigar, but that was not something that could be seriously contemplated in Yvonne Marshall's house, even in her husband's basement den.

The fact was Mulheisen was very close to depression, a state he greatly feared. From early youth he had fought depression, not frequently, but memorably. In his adult life he'd had at least two episodes of profound depression. They were devastating. He had learned from experience that alcohol was not a good idea in this premonitory state; he surprised Jimmy by refusing a drink from a carefully sequestered bottle of Jameson whiskey.

"Jimmy," he said, "I told you before that I'd screwed up this investigation. Well, it's gone even further than I told you then."

"What do you mean, Mul?" Jimmy was alarmed. Mulheisen didn't look well. He had grown accustomed to his mentor's occasional withdrawals into distraction and uncommunicative rumination, but this seemed more serious. "Are you all right?"

"I'm OK," Mulheisen said, "but I've got to get this straightened out. It's Lande. There is starting to be just a lot of little things popping up that seem to point to a connection between Lande and the Sedlacck killing and the Tupman killing." And with that he began to pour out the whole business—Lande's name in Tupman's book, his acquaintance with Germaine Kouras, his strange offer at the dinner party, Bonny's mention of a woman named Germaine—all of it, including Mulheisen's own connection with Bonny.

"The thing is, Jimmy, every time I get around Bonny and Lande, I seem to get kind of confused. I can't focus on what I'm supposed to be doing. It's as if my judgment were clouded or something . . . I can't put a finger on it. I mean to ask certain questions, push for answers, but I don't. I get distracted. I'm sure it has something to do with Bonny. I think I can work through it, but I need your help. I should have confided in you from the start, but I didn't, and then it was easier to just keep it to myself. Under the circumstances, I'd just as soon keep it between us—after all, it may be nothing, and if certain people got the idea that I coddled this Lande because of an interest in his wife . . . well, it'll just complicate things."

Jimmy understood completely. In fact, he hastened to assure Mulheisen that he was probably making too much of it. He was confident, he said, that the personal side of it needn't be revealed. "The fact is, Mul, any other detective would simply have written Lande out of the picture long before this. But you've kept at it, I guess because you must have unconsciously suspected something. There's nothing wrong with that."

"You don't think so?" Mulheisen felt relieved. He felt much better. "Why don't you put on that old Artie Shaw record," he suggested, "the one with 'Summit Ridge Drive'?" This piece never failed to cheer Mulheisen up.

"You realize, Mul," Jimmy said when the mood had lightened sufficiently, "that we really don't have a ghost of a fart on Lande? What's really bugging you about this guy . . . I mean, apart from Bonny?"

Mulheisen thought about it for a moment. "There's a couple of things," he said finally. "There's the money. Every time I talk to someone, the amount has grown . . . a couple million, five, ten . . . soon it'll be fifty. Then I saw some boxes at Lande's shop, computer equipment presumably, labeled for the Cayman Islands. I didn't think anything of it, but then there's this stuff about Big Sid maybe going to South America, possibly with a stop en route. Now the Kouras woman has split, also for the south. And then there's Lande babbling something at that dinner about how money isn't just a fifty-dollar bill. Frankly, I don't know what he meant by it, but I took his point—nowadays it isn't really necessary to ever actually see money, in currency, as long as the crucial people and—probably most important—the machines are convinced it exists."

"Sort of like that Wettling case," Jimmy said, referring to a murder case Mulheisen had got drawn into through a now-retired partner, a strange character named Grootka. Wettling, a bank official who had been an auditor, had invaded his bank's computer system with his own program, which made minute withdrawals and deposits in the customers' accounts at whirlwind speed, an essentially undetectable act that provided a more-or-less constant balance of thousands of dollars in an account to which Wettling had routine access. The account was never enormous, but it was like a magical pitcher—no matter how much you poured out, it remained full.

"I hadn't thought of that," Mulheisen said, "and I guess that isn't really what I have in mind, but the idea is similar. I really don't have any notion of how it would apply here. It probably doesn't. The trouble is Lande. He's supposed to be a computer genius, but when you talk to him, it's hard to believe it. Well, you saw him. He's rough, crude . . . he hardly seems literate. But evidently he's done very well for himself." He told Jimmy about the golf course.

"If he's rebuilding a golf course, some kind of development project," Jimmy pointed out, "that would be an ideal way to make money disappear."

"Washing money?" Mulheisen was skeptical. "This is sort of washing money in reverse. Presumably Sid and Tupman, and maybe others, were skimming extensively, collecting actual cash that now has to be got out of the country so that whoever has inherited Sid and Tupman's scam can make use of it in South America. It's bound to be complicated. It seems almost easier just to smuggle the damned cash out of the country."

"No," said Jimmy, "it's really not that difficult with computers. I've been working on programming, and it's amazing what you can do if you just take the trouble to devise a program."

"If they're washing money, we have to go to the feds," Mulheisen pointed out. They both knew what that meant—inevitably the case would be taken out of their hands. And like all local cops they had no confidence whatever in the federal agencies' ability to accomplish anything without totally screwing it up.

Jimmy came up with an interesting thought: "How do we know that the mob hasn't already found the money?"

"Andy Deane assures me that the word is still out on the street. Anybody who can come up with a lead to the money can make big bucks from the bosses. And, they say, Carmine seems to be throwing a lot of weight around. Andy hasn't seen it—nobody is filing a complaint—but apparently people are being roughed up. They want answers."

"Which I guess is why they blasted Tupman," Jimmy said.

Mulheisen shook his head. "No, there's something weird about that. Nobody tossed Tupman's apartment, you notice. If the mob thought Tupman had something to tell them, wouldn't they have shaken the place down? And I still don't buy the idea of sending a single hit man to take down five guys. No, it doesn't compute, as you would say."

They talked for a little while longer and mutually admired Jimmy's treasured recording of "Down the Road a Piece" by Freddie Slack—Jimmy never played the actual recording anymore, just a well-filtered and cleaned tape (he used videotape rather than the common cassette stuff—it seemed to offer more possibilities). And Mulheisen went home feeling infinitely better, the dark beast at least temporarily at bay.

Fifteen

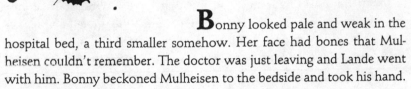

Bonny looked pale and weak in the hospital bed, a third smaller somehow. Her face had bones that Mulheisen couldn't remember. The doctor was just leaving and Lande went with him. Bonny beckoned Mulheisen to the bedside and took his hand.

"How have you been, Mul?"

"Me? I'm fine. How are you doing?"

"I guess I'm doing as well as expected," she said, "but I feel wrecked."

"You look pretty good," he lied. Actually, he was appalled. It hadn't been long since he'd seen her, and although he hadn't known she was ill and thus had not been looking for signs of illness, now she looked radically changed. It didn't seem possible.

"How's our investigation going?" she asked.

Mulheisen sighed. "Not too good, I'm afraid. I can't find Germaine Kouras. She seems to have flown the country."

"Well, that's good news."

"I think she's flown, Bonny; I don't know it. The airlines have no record of her leaving. Of course, she might have left under another name, but if she was actually leaving the country, as she told everybody she was, she'd have had to use her passport. She could have flown to, say, Miami, and then used her passport, but I really don't have the facilities to check that extensively."

Bonny frowned. "As long as she's gone, that's good enough for me," she said. "Why are you so concerned?"

"There's more to it, Bonny. We think she was involved in some kind of scam with Sid Sedlacek." He pulled up a chair and sat down next to the bed. "Bonny, . . . I have to know . . . how much do you and Lande know about Sid and Carmine?"

She gazed at him for a long moment, then said, "Forget Germaine, Mul. She's not important." She looked away, at the rain on the window, then said, "I've always loved you, Mul."

"Bonny, . . . don't."

"I always thought you were just terrific, even when you were a skinny kid. You weren't a big jock or anything, like Jack Street and those guys, or the class president, . . . but you were just this terrific guy. Everybody knew it. You weren't even a brain." She uttered a whispery little flutter that was a kind of laugh, and she patted his hand. "Oh, you were smart enough, Mul. But the point was everybody in the school respected you, even the teachers. You had character."

Mulheisen was embarrassed. He shook his head.

"I know you never loved me," she said. "You liked me, though, didn't you?"

"Oh, yes, I liked you."

"I knew you did. Maybe you lusted after me. But I think sometimes that you're one of the few people who have any idea who I am. That's a kind of love, I think. Now don't . . . oh, come on, don't get so damn embarrassed."

Mulheisen's eyes blurred. "Oh yeah," he said, in a husky voice, "I like you, Bonny. I always liked you, more than you know."

He held her slender little hand, which gripped his passionately. She had to close her eyes, and her face became tight, but after a moment it relaxed, and she looked at him and managed a wan smile. "Love is very different from like, Mul. Like has reasons and logic, . . . it makes sense."

Mulheisen nodded agreement, but Bonny stared at him until he dropped his eyes. The whispery flutter of her laugh made him look up. She said, "Maybe you're stupid after all."

Stung, Mulheisen looked at her indignantly.

". . . As the rest of them—men, I mean," she said, modifying the accusation. "Maybe men can't help being stupid. Maybe it's a trade-off in evolution for being larger and stronger, more powerful . . ." She glanced away at the gray skies outside her window, the black, wet limbs of a tree on which there were tiny leaf buds. Half a dozen miserable starlings hunched along the branches, their beaks startlingly yellow against their bedraggled feathers. Suddenly they all flew. "This has been the wettest spring," she said. "I wish . . ." Her eyes filled with tears. She blinked and one ran down her cheek. Mulheisen wiped it away.

"Birds learned how to fly," she said, speculatively. "That was a very great trick, learning to fly. But they ended up with tiny brains and hollow bones." She glanced slyly at Mulheisen. "You're pretty smart, Mul, but you can't overcome gender stupidity."

Mulheisen decided to take this jocularly. "At least I don't have hollow bones. Anyway, if women are so smart, how come they marry men?"

Bonny's face darkened instantly, and she snapped, "You know nothing!"

Mulheisen was mortified by his gaffe, and he immediately tried to mollify her with assurances that he was just kidding. She impatiently pulled her hand free from his. Then Lande returned, evidently from conferring with the doctor.

Lande was quite changed. He was friendly and cheerful. "Well, the doc says it looks pretty good," he told both of them. "Doc says you'll be up in no time, Bon. Looks like they got it all. A coupla weeks of therapy, and you'll be good as new."

"That's great," Mulheisen said. He hoped it was true. Lande seemed to believe it.

Lande nodded and said, "Yup, looks like they got it in time. Boy, the things they can do these days!" He turned to Mulheisen. "So, . . . how's the cop business, Mul? Say, don't Bon look great?"

"She looks fine," Mulheisen agreed, but Bonny had turned her head away and was staring out the window. It was raining again. Mulheisen gestured with his head toward the door, and Lande nodded. "I've got to run, Bonny," Mulheisen said. "I'll try to stop in later." She smiled and he left.

Lande caught up with him in the lounge. The cheerful look had entirely vanished.

"No hope," Mulheisen said, not even questioning, and Lande only nodded, chewing on a thumbnail.

"They want to do chemo," Lande said. "But what's the point? Maybe she gets to stick around a few more weeks."

"How long otherwise?" Mulheisen asked. His heart felt like it was bursting. He couldn't breathe very well. He had to sit down.

Lande stared at him, stricken. Perhaps he had only just now let himself look the horror in its face. "A month," he said, in disbelief.

"A month! But, my god, man, . . . they only just . . ."

"It's too far gone." Lande could barely utter the words.

"A month?" Mulheisen couldn't believe it either.

"Maybe less."

Mulheisen struggled to his feet. He felt panicky. He had to get out of there.

"Mul, don't go," Lande pleaded. "I gotta talk to you. I gotta talk to somebody."

"I've got things to do," Mulheisen said brusquely. "I've got a murder . . . Hell, I've got a dozen murder cases. And a couple of them have your little footprints all around them."

"Mine? I don't know what you're talking about," Lande said, shaking his head. "Listen. Forget that shit. This is more important. I don't have nobody to talk to about this . . . I . . . and you're . . . well, you're my on'y frien'."

This was a sobering thought for Mulheisen. He looked down at Lande, with his bristly mustache and watery eyes. He had to fight an urge to laugh, to inform this absurd little creep once and for all that he wasn't his friend, . . . that he chose his own friends with great care and he would never, never, choose to be a friend to any little crack-brained schemer and . . . and . . . He bared his long teeth in the semblance of a smile. Then it became a real smile, and he clapped the man on the shoulder. "Later, Gene. Later. I really have to run."

*   *   *

"Jim," Mulheisen said, "I want a look at that shipment in Lande's back room."

"What makes you think it'd still be there?" Marshall wanted to know.

"If it's just an ordinary shipment, it'll probably be gone," Mulheisen said, "but if it's something illicit, I'm thinking that Lande will want to take care of it himself, and lately his hands have been full."

"Something illicit," Marshall said. "Like money?"

"Like a lot of money. Stashed in, say, computer terminals or whatchacallum . . ."

"Drives? Stashed in the drives of computers?"

"Well, they're just boxes aren't they? Plastic boxes that are pretty heavy anyway and not easily opened. I think it would be a rare customs agent who decided to pry open a lot of computers."

Jimmy nodded. "So what do we do? I hate to say this Mul, but no judge is going to give you a search warrant on that information. Do you want to just run out there and take a look, see if they're still in the back room?"

"No. Miss Bommarito will certainly tell Lande, and it could scare him off. There's really not much to it, Jim. All I need is a quick look. The boxes are either there or they aren't. But listen, Jim, I'm the one who screwed this detail up. It's not your problem. Believe me, if you want to steer clear of this, just say so."

Marshall laughed. "Don't be silly, Mul. You know I'm with you. What do they say, 'In for a dollar, in for a dime.' What do you think? Is this a job for the telephone company or Detroit Edison?"

Mulheisen considered. "Computer people are always nervous about their power supply, aren't they? Better make it Detroit Edison."

An hour and a half later a Detroit Edison van pulled into the parking lot at Nine Mile Plaza, home of Doc Byte and other fine businesses. Jimmy Marshall, in overalls, started at the first shop, inquiring about the report of a drop in line voltage, and he continued around the U even after he had been into the back room at Doc Byte. He was happy to report to Mulheisen that a full pallet of cartons was still there, all with shipping labels for Grand Cayman Island.

"What do you think, Mul? Should we go back tonight and have a peek?"

"What?" Mulheisen was shocked. "Certainly not. If we don't have sufficient grounds for a warrant, we have no business there. No, . . . if it's what we think it is, . . . it'll sit. We ought to keep an eye on the place, though. It'd be too much to ask for a stakeout, but get the word out to the blue men and the cruisers and the detective staff—if anyone's in the neighborhood, just take a swing by there. Tell them to check the alley. They can call me anytime if anything's going on. I'll be spending a lot of time at Bon Secours, . . . which is where Lande will be, too."

"**A** lot of things are clear to me now, Mul," Bonny said later that evening. She looked a little better, actually, a little more color in the face, a little stronger. Evidently she'd had a discussion with the doctor about chemotherapy, and Mulheisen suspected that she had learned all she needed to know about her chances. He sat by the bed, holding her hand. Every little once in a while she squeezed it.

"Nothing is worth anything but love," she said. "I know it sounds trite, but I can't find any other words. There's a lot to say—too much—but no way to say it. The pain . . . it makes it hard to focus at times, but I have things to say."

"Don't worry about it," Mulheisen said.

"This is not a worry, Mul—it's important." She stared into his face for a long moment, and then she smiled. "Well, you know what I'm talking about. You always knew, I guess."

Mulheisen had no idea what she was talking about.

"I'm worried about Gene. He doesn't have anyone but me, and I'm . . ."

"Hush," Mulheisen said.

"No, I won't hush. It's all right. I can deal with it, . . . though it makes me so sad." Her eyes glittered. "I would have thought I'd have longer. It's so . . . disappointing. What an inadequate word," she said, as if to herself. "But Gene, . . . who will look after Gene? He's so stupid sometimes."

Warily Mulheisen remarked, "He's only a man."

"Oh, don't be so sensitive," Bonny said. "I'm sorry, I shouldn't have jumped on you about that. I don't think you're stupid, not really . . . well, not like most men, anyway. Oh, now I've done it again."

She raised his hand to her lips and kissed it. Her lips were dry as paper. Mulheisen let her do it, even helped her, but he couldn't help wondering where Lande was.

"Gene's gone out to get something to eat," she said. She released his hand and resumed the conversation with "Well, he is stupid, at times. And he's in trouble."

"What kind of trouble?"

"I don't know exactly. I'm not sure I should tell you if I knew. He sure wouldn't want me to."

"Gene is a big boy," Mulheisen said; "he can take care of himself."

"Most of the time," she agreed. "But this time . . . he's in something deep. It has something to do with Sid, of course."

"So, he did know Sid," Mulheisen said.

Bonny made a feint at shrugging, but it must have hurt. After a moment she said, "Not all that well . . . not that I ever knew about. But I think he had some kind of deal with Sid."

"What kind of deal, Bonny?"

"Sid was going to bankroll a golf resort, in the islands, and Gene was to be a partner. Gene was setting it up. Well, that was the deal, as far as I knew. It was all legit, above board. Except there was something else to it, and that's what I don't know. If I'd known, I could have . . ."

"What? Oh, you mean you wouldn't have thought it had something to do with Germaine Kouras."

"Well, that, of course. I don't know why I was so blind. I ought to have known that Gene wasn't the kind of guy to fool around. It was just jealousy. I heard that voice, . . . and she was so secretive, so . . . well, she sounded like one of those women. I feel so foolish, Mul. But when you told me that she'd gone and that she was involved in some scam . . . I mean, I knew right away that my early suspicions were just . . . foolish. But, if I'd known that Gene's deal with Sid was . . . well, complicated, I could have helped."

Mulheisen couldn't figure this out. "How could you have helped, Bonny?"

"Well, I knew Sid. For years. Sid was always very . . . what would you say?" she frowned, trying to think of a word. "Flirty. Friendly, but always on the make. I don't know if Sid ever talked to a woman, other than his mother or his daughter, who he wasn't at least casually trying to make it with. He liked me. We . . . we had a little thing, years ago."

Oh, dear, Mulheisen thought. "Did Gene know about this?"

"I suppose so." She closed her eyes for a long moment. "It wasn't anything. It was over long before I met Gene. It wouldn't have bothered him."

"Is that where Gene went that night, the night Sid was hit?"

Bonny's eyes closed again. She looked tired now, but patient. "Mul, please don't think that Gene was concerned about something that went on between me and Sid, that ended before we even met . . . not that it was ever anything much anyway. But, yes, I think it was Germaine who called him that afternoon and shortly afterward Gene went out, I guess on business, probably with Sid." She looked at him wearily, as if to say, Are you satisfied, stupid?

"Not to get rosemary, then?"

"As a matter of fact," she said, "as he was going out the door, he asked, 'Need anything from the store?' And I said, 'Rosemary.' "

Mulheisen sat there for a long time, watching her rest. A nurse came by to give her some medication. Lande still didn't return. Mulheisen held Bonny's hand. They didn't talk much, but at one point she said, "Isn't it odd that I should be in love with two such different men? You and Gene? Once upon a time I would have refused to believe it was possible to love two men at once."

Mulheisen felt torn by this little confession. One part of him rejoiced to think that Bonny loved him, but to be linked in such an intimate way with Gene Lande . . . !

"But it's a lucky thing," she went on, "now that I'm . . ." She gestured helplessly at her body.

Mulheisen was puzzled and his face betrayed it.

"Oh, I know I've already asked too much of you," Bonny said, "and you've been so good to us, but I have to ask you to help. If I were able, if I were healthy, I'd just go to Carmine . . ."

"Carmine! Don't tell me you and Carmine—"

"Well, of course," Bonny said; "I've known Carmine for years. We never had any great relationship, but . . . I know what he likes. He likes to be stroked. Naturally, you have to be prepared to go all the way if you start stroking him, but it wouldn't come to that. I don't think. Anyway, that's out of the question now."

Mulheisen stared at this woman wonderingly. He thought he had known something about her. Clearly he knew nothing. She lay there dying but plotting how to save her goofy husband. He didn't think he could put anything past her.

Bonny opened her eyes. "I'd kill for Gene if I could, if it would help. You have to help me, Mul." The eyes fell shut, then flicked open almost immediately. "Don't take him away from me, Mul."

"I'm not taking him away, Bonny," he protested. "I have to question him, but—"

"No. He stays with me. Promise me." She was tense, trying to sit up in the bed, and he was alarmed for her, but she resisted his attempts to calm her, fixing him with her eyes.

"I . . . ah . . ." He spread his hands helplessly. Then he sighed and nodded. "Yeah. All right. I promise."

Bonny relaxed and smiled. "I knew you would help, Mul. You love me. I love you . . . and Gene."

"But, Bonny, you have to help me, too. I can't do this in the dark. You've got to find out what he was up to."

"Don't worry," she said, calming him, patting his hand. "I'll take care of this. Relax. You worry too much, Mul. You have to take better care of yourself. Anyway, I already saw Carmine. He wouldn't tell me what it was all about, but I got him to promise to leave Gene out of it."

"What? When did you do this?" Mulheisen was amazed.

"Oh, a while back. I just called him up and went in to see him. I told him all Gene had going with Sid was the golf resort. He bought it. He even kissed me—a friendly kiss—as I left."

Mulheisen stared at her. She had drifted off. He wasn't sure what to make of this last statement. Had she just dreamed it? Was it something that had happened years ago?

Not long after Lande returned, sucking his teeth and saying with false cheer, "Hey, babe! I'm back. Shift break! Oops, she asleep?" He dropped his voice to a whisper. "Thanks for lookin' after my girl, Mul! Ain't she great? She looks great, don't she?"

Sixteen

$\mathbf{A}$t nine-thirty in the morning a long, deep-brown Cadillac rolled sedately down a side street on Detroit's East Side. It had tinted windows so that gawkers couldn't look inside, and it cruised so carefully because there were cars parked on both sides of the street, leaving only a single lane for traffic. It wasn't a very nice neighborhood, although it had once been respectable. The houses were large, four-plexes, some of them substantial brick homes with large porches upstairs and down. But now they were in poor repair, the miniature yards stamped bare of grass, the wrought iron fences bent or flattened, gates hanging awry if not absent, and plywood nailed over many of the large window frames.

About midway down this block, which was nearly an eighth of a mile long, there was a factory where potato chips and allied products were made. This wasn't unusual; there are many such industrial enclaves in Detroit, left over from an earlier period, when zoning laws didn't always keep pace with the city's development. The original factory had been built in the twenties, when this was still an outskirt of the city, and then the housing had flooded in around it. That factory had made machine tools. Krispee Chips was a fairly modern plant, having replaced the original structure with a long, low building whose construction had necessitated the destruction of some of the surrounding houses. The Krispee Chips Company had purchased several of the houses on either side and refurbished them, so that they now stood in marked contrast to their neighbors, and fenced in the whole complex with a high cyclone fence that had angled barriers on the top with strands of barbed wire. The houses were ostensibly used for additional office space, but the neighbors knew that there were also many people living there, mostly young men who spoke a foreign language and liked to kick a soccer ball around the little recreation yard.

The front gate to the complex was manned by uniformed guards who wore side arms, and you could see shotguns in a rack inside the little gatehouse. This morning the guard waved the deep-brown limousine through with a kind of salute, and it pulled up by the canopied side door of the factory offices. A burly man hopped out on the passenger side and opened the back door. A small, slender man got out and walked briskly through a door that was held open for him by another armed guard. He passed through the carpeted outer offices, with their array of pastel-colored desks and video-display terminals, at each one of which sat a pretty young woman. He greeted some of the women by name and with a smile and a wave of his hand, and each one smiled gaily back and called him boss. At his secretary's office he stopped briefly to say, "Get me Mitch in New York." Then he disappeared through the door and into his inner sanctum.

This was a large office with thick carpeting and a half dozen very colorful and dramatic paintings on the walls. There was a striking man-size metal sculpture in one corner, of a ratlike creature wearing a fedora and a loose suit jacket, beneath which was slung a double-barreled shotgun. The rat-man had an eerie grin, at once lewd, humorous, and malicious. The boss smiled involuntarily when he saw it. But then his smile faded, and he snatched up the warbling telephone and settled himself primly in a large teak and fabric chair behind the enormous desk.

"Mitch? Carmine. I'm getting nowhere. Yes? I had a man on it, but evidently he didn't find out anything." Silence. Then, "Joe Service. Yeah, I know he's supposed to be good, but he wasn't good this time. So I need a few guys. As many as you think we'll need. We're going to just have to go out and beat the bushes." A dry laugh. "Let me know how many you can send and how we'll meet. Talk to you."

He hung up and punched a button. "Candy, doll, get me Fat." He

puttered about the desk for a minute and then snatched up the telephone when it warbled.

"Fat? Did you take care of what's his name, Service? He did, eh?
Well that's too bad. He knows how these things . . . Fat, don't take his
part . . . He knows . . . He has to learn. Sure, he's good, they're all good
. . . until they don't deliver. You don't deliver, you don't collect, Fat. No
more screwups. This whole thing is one long screwup. I won't have it.
No, no, no, listen to me. Let the bastard bitch. He's made plenty off me.
Once in awhile he has to take the dirty end of the stick." He paused,
listened for a long moment, then said, "No. He's a wise ass. I put up
with it in the past because he got the job done and he was amusing, but
after a while, Fat, you get tired of his snotty remarks. If he won't listen
to reason, then . . ." There was a pregnant pause, and he continued.
"That's right, Fat. Nobody lives forever. All right, that's settled. Now
listen—I've just been talking to Mitch. He's sending over some heat. It's
time to quit playing patty-cake. Maybe one or two of them can take care
of Mr. Service while they're at it. I'll let you know when I hear from
Mitch."

He replaced the receiver and sat at his desk for a long moment,
looking about him. He caught the metallic eye of the rat-man, aimed
right at him. He wondered how the sculptor had done that. The eyes
were so weird. There was no eye there, really, just built-up ridges with
a hole in the center, but they seemed to glow, sometimes red, sometimes yellow. It was something that came of burning the metal, he
supposed. He liked the pin-striped pants and the narrow shoes and,
especially, the writhing tail and the way the rat-man held the shotgun
out, almost shyly, as if offering you a little death.

Carmine smiled at the sculpture and stood up. He smoothed his
silk suit jacket and pants, then looked at his small, soft hands, excel-
lently manicured. They weren't in the least soiled, but he felt a vague
need to wash them. He walked across the office and opened the door
to his luxurious bath and lavatory and stopped cold.

Joe Service was sitting on Carmine's expensive Swedish commode,
fully dressed, pointing a revolver that had a large, ugly protuberance on
the barrel.

Carmine started to slam the door, but Joe was there like a panther, his hand holding the door open. "Come on in, Carmine," he said, gesturing with the pistol. He closed the door behind them. The room was large with a carpeted floor and a tiled alcove that the putative bather approached via three polished teak steps that led to a teak deck in which was sunk a seven-foot-long oval tub that was made out of some kind of marblelike black substance with gold veins running through it. The bath and shower fixtures were gold, too, or looked like gold, and there was a switch for a device that jetted water into the tub through hidden ports. There was a shower head but no curtain or screen to prevent water from splashing all over. Joe had spent some time that morning trying to figure out just how it worked, but he'd given up.

Joe turned on the water in one of the sinks on the counter, which was also made of the gold-veined black-marble stuff. "Go ahead, wash your hands," he said. He sat down on the uppermost step of the bath alcove and watched while Carmine soaped his hands and rinsed them. They watched each other in the huge mirror. "Clean now?" Joe asked, tossing Carmine a fluffy lilac-colored towel that was warm from hanging on a chrome frame through which hot water ran. "Just leave the water running, Carm."

Carmine dried his hands and tossed the towel onto the floor. Someone would pick it up, Joe realized, and then he knew that someone would also mop up and vacuum up if the shower water splashed too much. The idea was satisfying to him.

"You owe me money," Joe said. "Let's have it."

Carmine laughed. He was a handsome man, about Joe's height though slighter in build and twenty-five years older. He had steel-gray hair and a narrow face.

"Joe, you made a big mistake," Carmine said. His voice was soft but with a slight rasp, like a banana with a welding rod imbedded in it. "You found the man, but it didn't help us."

"So I heard," Joe said. "It sounded to me like the Fat Man wanted to plead my case, but you wouldn't hear it. I guess I did make a mistake, a couple of them." He didn't sound contrite. "Mistake number one: I took another job from you. And I didn't get paid up front, that's number two. But, I'm young, Carmine, and I'm bound to make a few mistakes. I imagine you made some when you were young. If a man's lucky and he's good, he can probably get away with a few screwups—when he's young. But when you get old, like you, Carmine, mistakes start to pile up and–*pow!*–you're gone!" Joe grinned to see Carmine flinch at the plosive word.

"Joe, you don't have a chance," said the banana voice, "especially if you screw up now." Carmine had recovered his poise. "You can run but you can't hide. The old boxer said that—Joe Louis. But everybody knows . . . you can't hide from us. We are everywhere." Carmine smiled.

"That was the old mob," Joe said. "I wonder if it was ever true. Well, it may still be true for most of the guys you deal with, Carmine. It was certainly true for Hal Good. But he had Joe Service on his case. And you don't know where I live, Carm. It's a big country. You could never find me. I'm not Hal, and you won't have me to look for me. But I know where you live, Carmine, and the Fat Man, and all the rest of you miserable pricks. At worst, I figure I'm losing some business, and as it happens, it's the kind of business I can do without. But what the hell, Carm, . . . you want to talk, we can talk. This doesn't have to be the end. Just give me what you owe me, and I'll get out of your hair. And . . . I promise never to bug you again." His smile had the effect of erasing Carmine's.

"You didn't do the job, Joe," Carmine said stubbornly. "I still don't know where the money is, and they're still blowing my guys away out there like it was Beirut or something."

"Hal didn't have your money, Carm, and who knows why they're blowing your boys away? It's not my business. You contracted for me to find Hal Good. I found him. Unfortunately, he and I didn't get a chance to chat—he wouldn't have it any other way. But I had a good look around, and the money wasn't there. While we're on the subject, let me point out to you that the contract was for me to find Hal. I know you planned to pop him, but that would cost you more. I guess you would have called Mitch for that. What does it cost? A hundred? No? Fifty? Maybe an easy shot like Hal would go for a measly twenty-five." Joe shrugged. "As I've always told Fat, I'm not in the fatality line. I'm pro-life, Carm. But I will do it . . . when it seems necessary. Now I have this Hal on my conscience . . ." He shook his head with genuine rue.

"You'll have to pay extra for that. Let's say another fifty. The contract was for a hundred and a half. You gave me an advance—which was really just what you owed me from the last time—so if we figure that soaping Hal is worth another fifty, that's a hundred fifty you still owe. Now, if you can give me that, I'll make like the little dot on the screen when you turn off the TV."

Carmine laughed despite himself. "Can we talk?" he asked.

"Sure. Just move your lips and your tongue," Joe said.

"I mean . . ." Carmine gestured toward his office.

"No. It's better in here," Joe said. "I can run the tap, and it gives us some cover from the bugs."

"My office isn't bugged," Carmine protested.

"You wouldn't know," Joe replied. "Have you had it swept lately? No? Well, as you can see, anybody can get in here. I just walked in here this morning, nothing to it. That's the kind of help you've got, Carm. It's also why I don't want to screw around with you guys anymore. I knew better than to come back to Detroit, and yet maybe it was my soft heart, I let Fat talk me into it. But no more."

"No, wait a minute, Joe, you've got a point. I like what you're saying. We've been getting a little soft. You're right. I need to talk to you. You could help us out. There would be a lot of money in it for you. A lot."

Joe sighed. "Go on. Let's hear what it is this time."

"This is how we got screwed up in the first place," Carmine said, "with Sid. He burned us once, a while back, and we stepped on his fingers, but we took him back into the fold. Then he did the same thing again, which is when we called in Hal, who—before you say anything, Joe—always did good work for us in the past."

"Hal was in it with Sid," Joe said.

Carmine eyed him carefully. "How do you know this?"

Joe fished out the telephone book he'd taken from the Iowa City house. "Hal's," Joe said. "There's lots of numbers for Sid in here—home, office, certain bars, certain women. They were close. It was coke, right? Sid was skimming, or is the word dipping? Scooping? And he was going to take a hike, right? The thing is, Hal was in it, too. Maybe a bunch of others. Tupman, for instance."

"This is interesting," Carmine said. "How do you figure it? Was there anything else?"

"I didn't really apply my mind to it," Joe said. "It's not my business. No, he didn't leave a detailed plan or anything, but there are a lot of interesting little names and numbers in here. I'll throw the book in for free when you pay up."

"Yeah, sure," Carmine say, nodding. "We'll get to that, . . . but why did Hal pop Sid if they were in it together?"

"The minute you gave him the contract you showed you were on to Sid. But were you on to Hal? He couldn't take the chance, he had to take Sid down. And . . . he probably figured if he cooled it, kept his mouth shut, he might still have a chance to cop the skim. Did you recover any of it?"

"Not yet," Carmine said, "but we've got a couple of lines on it. We'll find it."

"I'm sure," Joe said dryly.

"But, Joe, this is a perfect job for you. It's what you do best, right? Hey, why am I fooling around with these local dopes when the best in the world is right here, talking to me? I'll tell you what. You find the skim, find out who all was in on it—you don't have to do any wet work—and you can take half."

"Half of what?"

"We don't know, Joe. That's the problem. Only Sid knew how much it was, though we hear rumors. Say it's a million. It had to be a million because Sid isn't going to leave a sweet setup here, even if he's crazy about some chick, for less than a million. Wouldn't you say?"

Joe thought about it. "Who knows? Who's the chick?"

Carmine gave him a long, sad look. "Forget about the chick, Joe. She ain't in it. We talked to her already, and believe me, she's not part of the problem."

"We are talking about Germaine Kouras?"

Carmine nodded.

"I see," Joe said. "An accident, I guess."

"You could say that."

"Can I talk to her?"

Carmine looked pained. "No, I don't think so, Joe."

"And she wasn't able to enlighten you beforehand? Yeah. Well, it can happen. It happened in Iowa City. But, to get back to the main point . . . How much would you say Sid—and his friends—had access to?"

"That's hard to say, Joe. It depends over what period of time it went on. Let's face it, we didn't notice anything wrong. So he couldn't have been taking a high percentage, but for how long? We don't know."

"Do you think he could have taken two million?"

"Yeah."

"Four million?"

Carmine made a face. "Now, Joe, . . . you're starting to get speculative here—"

"Maybe I'll just take all of it," Joe said.

"All of it? Who the fuck do you think—"

Service pulled the trigger on the pistol, and the mirror behind Carmine shivered and collapsed onto the counter. Carmine leapt away, staring wildly at Joe.

"Are you crazy?" he gasped.

"You were forgetting to be scared," Joe said. He had not moved from the alcove steps. He swiveled slightly and pointed the pistol at Carmine's stomach. "Is it two million? Or is it more?"

"It's more," Carmine said. "Maybe it's four, but we don't know. Honest."

"I'll take fifty percent," Joe said, "with a minimum of a mil. But first I want my hundred fifty. Right now."

"Sure, sure," Carmine said. He gestured toward his office. "I can give it to you right now."

Joe smiled and stood up. "You can turn off the water, Carm." He opened the door and they went into the office. Carmine went to a painting on the wall, a kind of collage of fire engines and numbers and obscure angular shapes, and opened it like a door. He spun the dial of the safe and reached inside.

"Easy," Joe said. He had slipped up behind Carmine and placed the barrel of the silencer against his head. He reached around him and withdrew the neat little .32-caliber automatic and slipped it into his pocket. Then he pulled out several packets of bank notes and let them

fall onto the carpet. He stepped back and said, "Go ahead, C
. . . start counting."

Carmine knelt and began to count. Joe sat on the arm of one o
the teak chairs and watched. Then he studied the sculpture in the corner
for a while, whistling "Spring Is Here" in a whispery way. Carmine's
phone warbled, and without hesitation Joe picked it up. "Yeah," he
rasped, holding the receiver a foot away.

"New York," the secretary's voice said, "Mitch."

"I'm busy, doll," Joe growled. "Tell him I'll call back in a minute."

"Yes, sir."

Carmine gathered the money up and dumped it on the desk, then
collected the remainder from the floor and pushed it back into the safe.
Joe stepped close and stuck the little automatic back into the safe, then
slapped the safe door shut.

While Carmine put the payoff into a large manila envelope, Joe
said, "Do you really think you're clean here?" He waved the pistol
around the walls and ceiling.

"Certainly," Carmine said.

Joe stepped over to the rat-man. It was almost as tall as he. "What
do you call this dude?"

"It doesn't have a name. It's a Jabe."

"A Jabe? What's that?"

"He's some kind of hotshot sculptor," Carmine said. "My wife
got it for me. Don't you like it?"

"It's cute," Joe said, running his hands about the sculpture. "How
much does something like this cost?"

"You could afford it," Carmine said.

Joe slid his hand up the wicked tail and up the inner thigh, feeling
the little bumps of burned steel. There was a hole precisely where the
anus should be. "What kind of realist is this Jabe?" Joe wondered out
loud. He stuck his forefinger into the hole and felt about, then jerked
a tiny little lump of plastic and putty out.

"Hmmm, doesn't look exactly like the sort of thing that would
come out of a rat's ass," Joe said, "but . . ." He carried it over to the
bathroom door and tossed it into the commode. Turning back to Car-

begin to unscrew the silencer from the revolver and said, "So
Carm, who else do you think was in it with Sid?"

Carmine sat back in his chair and rubbed his smoothly shaven
looking at Joe speculatively. "You know, Joe, I believe I have
terestimated you. I apologize. We really ought to discuss business. I
mean the business, you understand?"

Joe sighed. "I don't think so, Carmine. I like my business. I'm a
snoop. I'm curious. And it's fun. Your business—the biz," he said
sarcastically, "doesn't strike me as fun. It's awful. You know what you
should do? You know what I'd do if I was running this awful biz?"

Carmine shook his head.

"I'd shut it down. Especially this crack biz. You know what you've
got? You've got teenagers standing on corners hawking poison. Actually
waving it in the air. Can that be sane, Carm? I mean, think about it.
You're already making a fortune out of numbers. The folks have a
dream, they consult the dream book, they run down to the corner bar
and put a buck or two on a set of numbers that no way in hell might
make them a couple of hundred. Is that a bad thing to do? No, that's
not bad, Carm. That's a service to the community—feeding the dream.
And you've got dozens of these splendid community services—a guy
finds out his wife is screwing Jim Bob, he comes to you for a gun, he
shoots Jim Bob, and his marriage is saved. What a guy you are! Better
than a priest. But selling crack on the corner, Carm, . . . that's just nuts.
Why don't you shut it down? It just gets you into trouble, like with Sid.
Now who do you think was in it with Sid?"

It was Carmine's turn to sigh. "Joe, you're way out of touch. We
don't run the crack. We've managed to get a wedge into it. That's what
Sid was doing for us. But the thing is we saw it the same way you saw
it. We didn't want it. You're right, it isn't the kind of business we ought
to be in. So . . . we let it go. The Colombians, the Bolivians, the
Peruvians, the Panamanians . . . they all jumped right in. We let it
happen." He waved a hand sadly.

"You let them?" Joe asked, incredulous.

Carmine grimaced. "It wasn't my decision, but I went along with
it. It was decided at a higher council."

"You let a bunch of South Americans come in and run a biz like that, on your turf? I don't believe it."

"OK, so we kept a few handles," Carmine said, "but we didn't have the biz. We figured if it started to look good, we could take it back. Better to let these goofy dick heads take the first heat. But," he sighed, "it kind of got away from us. It really took off. It wasn't really organized. It was one of those things, like Prohibition. All my life, Joe, I heard from the old ones about how Prohibition opened up the country. They didn't know what was happening at the time, but they fell into it, for Chrisake. You think Capone and the rest of those crazy Sicilians knew what was going to happen? Don't be silly. But once they saw an opening . . . You gotta hand it to them, Joe, they stepped in and made something out of the opportunities."

Carmine laughed quietly, gazing at his rat-man in the corner. "They were wonderful tough guys, Joe. We're just a bunch of wimps by comparison." He looked up and his chin stiffened. "That's what these Colombians look like, Joe. They fell into it. They were ready, they were tough, and they didn't give a shit. We let them in and they just took it. And once they had it, once they had this street network, well . . . I'm like you, Joe. It looked like hell to me. The kids, the violence!" Carmine's features contorted in disgust. "They don't have any standards. They're a bunch of savages!"

He sat forward suddenly, clasping his hands. "I saw we had screwed up. I decided to take it back, . . . but quietly. So I put Sid into it. I figured somebody was going to get honked here, in the early days. Better it was Sid. You understand?"

Joe nodded. "But Sid went over, is that it?"

"That's the way it looks. Maybe he was playing both sides, I don't know. But we couldn't go on with Sid."

Joe considered all this in silence, then said, "Icing Sid wasn't enough, though. Fat told me you thought Tupman and Conover were in it, but you didn't do the job on Tupman. Who did? The Colombians?"

"They didn't have any reason to as far as I know," Carmine said. "We don't know who did it. Maybe it was them. Conover? Well, he's walking a tight line, but he seems all right. I think you should talk to him. Who else? To be honest, Joe, I don't know. That's why we need you. We had a long, hard talk with Roman Yak, Sid's old hand. We were a little rough, but the Yak held up. Roman wasn't in on it, he didn't know anything. He was just a spear carrier."

"What about this Lande?" Joe asked.

"Lande? What Lande? You mean Gene Lande? What about him?" Carmine seemed genuinely surprised.

"His name is in Hal's book, next to Sid. He even drew a little box around it, like a guy draws when he's talking on the phone . . . He writes the name down, he draws a box, he doodles a star in each corner—"

"This is a chump, a nobody," Carmine said, a disbelieving smile on his face. "You know who he is? He's one of those guys who likes to hang around the edges, you know? He likes to pretend he's a big criminal, public enemy number seventeen or something. He got into trouble with us years ago . . . gambling, or was it a loan? I can't remember. Sid leaned on him, straightened him up. The guy was into electronics, I think. Sid gave him a little business. His wife was an old punch of Sid's. You know Sid—well, you didn't know him that well—but he always had a bunch of ex-girlfriends, and he was the kind of guy he'd try to do something for them. He fixed this chick up with this Lande and Lande began to do a little work for us from time to time. Nothing big or even crooked, really, but he'd do it for next to nothing."

"I think I should talk to him," Joe said.

"I already talked to him. And his old lady." He snorted a laugh. "Hah. She called me up one day, says it's about Sid and her old man. So I tell her to come in, we could talk—I knew her from old times. Soon as she hangs up I send Fat to get this Lande. She comes in here, throwing her tits and ass around, whining about her poor li'l Gene—I had to laugh. Turns out she's scared shitless because Lande had been working on some kind of golf-resort development with Sid, and she was afraid I'd get the wrong idea. I gave her a pat on the ass and a big kiss, just to make sure her lipstick is smeared, and I waltz her out of the office. Lande's out in the office, see, waiting. She doesn't see him, but I make sure that he gets his eyes full. Christ, you should have seen his face when Fat brought him in." Carmine laughed loudly. "He didn't know if he was mad or scared. I threw a good scare into him, and I let him know he couldn't pull any shit. He's nothing."

"Well, I'd better check him out," Joe said.

"Sure, you be the judge. And listen, Joe, I'm serious about the biz. What you say makes sense to me. I think we're on the same wavelength. We've got to overhaul this operation. We've gone stale. Relying too much on muscle, not enough on brains. We've got to take back the street. You could figure very large with us."

Joe shook his head. "No, Carm. I'm too young. To go down, that is. Because that's what I see—you guys are going down." He looked almost sad. "I can't afford to get involved with an outfit like this. A year from now, maybe two . . . you're gone. It's going to go down, Carm, believe me."

Joe picked up the manila envelope and tucked it under his arm. "Thanks for this, Carm. I'll let you know on the other as soon as something comes up."

As soon as he'd left, Carmine buzzed his secretary and said, "Get someone in here to fix the bathroom."

"What's wrong with the bathroom?" she wanted to know.

"Get someone," he snapped. "And get Mitch on the phone."

A minute later the phone warbled. "Mitch," she said. "The plumber's on his way."

"Get a carpenter," Carmine replied. "Hello, Mitch? Hey, put that business on hold. I think I'm onto something. I was just talking to Service, he's got some ideas. But I'm gonna need a hitter before it's all over. Top of the line. Price is no limit. I'll let you know."

Seventeen

Bonny looked dreadful. There was no other way to put it. The course of her disease was so rapid that even the doctors were surprised. Mulheisen and Lande were stunned. Neither had been prepared for this. It was like a stop-action film of an apple rotting. Not only was she markedly changed each day, but it began to seem to the two men that they could see almost hourly changes. The chief doctor, a youngish man, was himself a little shaken, and he did his best to ease the situation for them with explanations. Bonny needed no discussion; she was all too aware of what was happening to her. Obviously the disease had been much further advanced than the original assessment had indicated. It was in the lymph system and out of any prayer of control—the young doctor called it wildfire.

Bonny's skin was frankly yellow now, and ghastly lumps distorted her jaw and cheekbones. Mulheisen quickly learned not to see these hideous distortions in order to actually see her. When he returned to her room from having slept himself or after attending to some business, he was relieved if he found her asleep, as she often was. It made it easier to approach her, to accept what had happened in just the few hours he'd been gone. Painkilling drugs were no longer very effective, and they had begun to provide her with cannabis and hefty "cocktails"—pure grain alcohol in a blend of fruit juices. She was always a little high, if not drunk. And she was curiously cheerful, though often her grotesque face was swept by a visible curtain of pain, reminding Mulheisen of the wind blowing across the reeds that he often watched from his bedroom window, looking toward the river.

He would not have thought that mere physical transformation would make such a difference. It seemed a mockery of his firmly held belief that his affection for Bonny was not simply lust for her body. That body no longer existed and, in any case, had not been the glorious body of youth for some time (though it was undoubtedly still very attractive less than two weeks before).

They often passed hours together, saying nothing. If Lande weren't present, Mulheisen would sit by her bed, holding her listless hand, which was like parchment—there was no warmth in it. She lay there, seemingly oblivious to his presence, eyes shut or staring at the ceiling, occasionally sipping at her cocktail. She was drifting away, her mind focused on some other place. Once in a while she would turn slowly to look at him and, after a moment, would seem to recognize him. She would smile and say, "Why, hello, Mul," which she had already said a half hour before. Sometimes, in clearer moments, she would hold her skeletal hand before her face, as if to shield him from the horror of her deformity.

Mulheisen knew he should be talking to Lande, questioning him about Big Sid and Carmine. But he'd promised Bonny, and she was all that mattered now. Early on she had given him a few tidbits that she'd wormed out of Lande, but they weren't very specific. Sid had asked Gene for some help with a money deal. They were all going to make a lot of money, Gene had told her, and they would go to live in the Bahamas, at the golf resort. They'd lie on the beach all day and drink large, frosty drinks made from exotic fruits. They were still going to do it, Gene would tell her. As soon as she got well enough to travel, they'd get away. There was some kind of miracle cure the doctors "down there" had—the American Medical Association wouldn't let it be used, he told her, because they wouldn't have any business, and the big drug companies were in on it. Bonny didn't pay any attention to any of this, although she told Mulheisen that it would be nice to get away from all the cold and rain.

Mulheisen was spending almost all his time at the hospital, and so was Lande, of course. Mulheisen watched Lande and Bonny. They would all sit together in the little room, occasionally taking a break but really not talking much. Lande talked about "gawf" and his inventions, about plans to build a new golf course somewhere "in the islands." He was going to teach Mulheisen how to golf.

Once in a while Mulheisen would take a few hours to take care of business at the precinct and to catch up on other work, but not for long. He asked Andy Deane to make a serious effort to find Germaine Kouras. Nothing had come up yet, but Andy was now convinced that Kouras had not left the country after all. But nobody had seen her. She'd simply disappeared. The pressure on the street had eased apparently. The muscle stuff, anyway, according to Andy. But somebody was looking—that was the new word—some slick guy from the West was asking a lot of questions.

A couple of times Lande asked Mulheisen if he'd mind staying with Bonny while he took off for an hour or two to "do some business." Mulheisen readily agreed, but before he would let Lande go, he would excuse himself. "I'd better call in and let the precinct know I'll be here for a while . . ."—and Jimmy Marshall would then follow Lande. Jimmy said Lande went to his office and then to the golf course but never spent more than a half hour at each place, and then he would return to the hospital.

One day a young man appeared at the door to Bonny's room, looking for Lande. Mulheisen thought the man looked familiar, but he couldn't place him. The fellow, who did not identify himself, said he was a friend of Lande's and he'd call him later. Mulheisen just nodded and turned back to Bonny, who hadn't noticed the intrusion.

Mulheisen was finding it difficult to focus. His mother, who saw even less of him than usual, sensed that something was amiss, but she was busy with her own struggles with the dastardly developer. Mulheisen didn't notice. Nothing seemed important to him but the struggle going on at Bon Secours Hospital. He was losing somebody whom he had never possessed. He had discovered a love at the moment it was being taken from him.

Lande was grateful for Mulheisen's company. It was annoying to Mulheisen, however, that Lande seemed to believe that Mulheisen's presence was as much on his behalf as on Bonny's. As for Bonny, she was glad they were both there. "My boys," she'd say with a sly smile when she awoke and caught sight of them sitting dully, reading, or quietly talking—almost all the talk coming from Lande, who reminisced about past triumphs or complained about those who had swindled him in some ancient deal. They would immediately race to her side, the first one there seizing hold of the hand that was not enmeshed in tubes and wires. But they were thoughtful of one another, too, bringing sandwiches or magazines or even little nips of whiskey to the one who had stayed while the other took a break.

In this way, almost against his will, Mulheisen began to acquire a certain understanding of Eugene Lande. Day after day the two men sat in the little room, looking at Bonny, who was practically disappearing before their eyes. When she began to be mostly comatose, they listlessly perused magazines (neither of them could bear television, and Bonny couldn't stand its banalities), so inevitably Lande would begin to talk. Naturally he chose his own life as his subject. Mulheisen didn't pay close attention, but snatches of this sotto voce reminiscence seeped through his indifference.

"I don't remember a thing before I was twelve, . . . not a thing, but I been told things . . . My mother was a waitress . . . My dad was a bomber pilot in the Korean War . . . I don't remember my folks . . . I think we lived in Texas for a while . . . Uncle Ernie and Aunt June were my real folks . . . We lived on the East Side. They used to lock me in when they went to meetings . . . I think they were Communists . . . Yeah, they were Communist spies; they went to spy meetings alla time . . . When I first come to Detroit, they put me in that front bedroom, upstairs . . . I was thrilled—you could hear the paperboys goin' up and down the street, yellin' . . . They yelled"—a hoarse whisper— "'preee press pay-per!' . . . kind of a little jag on 'pay-per'—you come up on the last part of it—'pay-per' . . . I thought it was the *Pree Press* for a long time . . . Just sat in the room and listened to the radio and the clock tickin' . . . I took the clock apart about a dozen times, then I started on the radio, but I musta lost a part; I couldn't get it to work . . . Uncle Ernie was pissed, but they never hit me. They were never really mean, but they wouldn't let me out . . . They musta been 'fraid I'd snoop and find their Commie stuff, maybe turn 'em in . . . I wouldn'ta turned 'em in . . . That's the worst thing you can do, in my book, is squeal, to letcher pals down . . . He got me a new radio, but it didn't have the range of the old Philco; it couldn't get New Orleans or Denver . . . They were gone when I come back from the navy . . . They never wrote once . . . I couldn't read very well, but I had some *Popular Mechanics;* I read them a lot . . . School was no good; the big kids allus picked on you . . . I joined the Barons first, but they ratted on me; they left me to get caught by the cops when we hit this one K Mart . . . The Baggies was a nigger gang; they wore baggy pants . . . They let me in; well, they let in a coupla white kids; they were tough . . . The leader was called Hitler; he was a weight lifter, had a body you couldn' believe, . . . but they run off, and I got caught by the cops . . . Well, they were good guys, but they was scared . . . In the navy I was a cook, never left the country, never even left dry land, stationed all the time at Great Lakes, near Chicago . . . I met this guy, Derek, from Detroit, too . . . We come home on leave together, but I didn' have nobody to see; Uncle Ernie and Aunt June were gone, no forwarding address—the Commies sent them under-ground—and the guys from the Baggies were either all in jail or they were in the army, in Vietnam, all over the place . . . Me and Derek hitchhiked out West, but we got separated in Salt Lake City . . . He went into this giant drugstore, to cop some pills, an' after a while I went in to find him, and I guess he must of come out the other door and couldn' find me . . . It was nuts . . . I never went back to the navy; well, I went back, but they give me an early out, . . . but Derek's old man, in Detroit, he run a 'lectronics store; he give me a job . . . Derek never showed up, never saw him again . . . I met Tony Luke, great guy; we did a little you know in 'lectronic parts, nothing heavy . . . Sid, well, Sid was just a good frien', one a my best buddies; he threw a little business my way, took me to Las Vegas, interduced me to Bonny . . . I did his daughter's office computers. She's a brain, very smart broad . . . tough, too; I wouldn't wanta cross her . . . I just picked it up, the 'lectronics . . . I was always real good at that kinda stuff . . . Started gawfin' with Uncle Ernie, it was the on'y thing we ever did together . . . He wasn't a real good gawfer, but he was a good teacher, very strict, made you stand just this way, hold your clubs like this, not like that, like this, 'you little dummy' . . . an' purty soon I could outshoot him an' he quit—" He laughed raucously, waking up Bonny. "Sorry, sorry, hon, there, there, there . . ."

The endless droning half-whispered narrative only began to suggest the intense rage that drove the man, Mulheisen realized. He became interested despite himself and his pledge to Bonny and started to ask an occasional not too pointed question. Thus, he learned that Lande could vaguely remember his mother, as a waitress, but that most of the information about his parents had come from his mother's much older brother and his wife, to whom Lande was sent at age twelve, "just to visit," in Detroit. The mother disappeared. The aunt and uncle were good people, though rather strict. The idea of them as Communist agents seemed to be sheer fantasy, but one that Lande clung to. He did not, in fact, have any secure, first-person memories of his life before age twelve—"Just about a total blank, Mul." He thought he had lived in Cincinnati because he could remember being taken to some Reds games by, he thought, a relatively benign foster "keeper"—he couldn't bring himself to refer to them as parents.

The aunt and uncle were much older than his mother, he thought. Uncle Ernie worked at "the Dodge," and Aunt June was a bookkeeper for a man who owned a small string of garages. It was true that they often went to meetings, and the boy was locked in the house, in his room, but Mulheisen got the impression that maybe it wasn't every night, and maybe it hadn't happened throughout the boy's youth. For one thing, there was the gang period. Obviously, Lande was out running the streets by then. The couple was not otherwise unkind to him. They didn't beat him; they didn't starve him or deprive him of good clothes. They just didn't pay much attention to him, and they clearly didn't love him. Lande appeared to have no feelings for them, pro or con, although it was their name that he used. (Jimmy Marshall's casual research revealed an Ernest and June Lande, formerly of Detroit, now living in retirement in Scottsdale, Arizona.)

School was a different matter. Lande hated school and hated the whole idea of education, still. He had a withering contempt for people who had to be taught things; he himself had just learned everything "by paying attention and finding out." Inevitably he'd been a victim of bullies, and he argued with his teachers. He didn't make friends. A gang recruited him to help them shoplift—he was sent in to cause a diversion while they stole things—and they casually abandoned him when he was caught. This was still a source of bitterness. Lande had longed for and relished his inclusion in these groups, and their callous betrayals still hurt. He was, nonetheless, as Mulheisen could see, attracted to the crime community while simultaneously furious with it.

He left school early and wangled his way into the navy, where once again he got into trouble with authority and was given what he at first called "an early out." Mulheisen asked Jimmy to check it out and discovered the truth—court-martial, stockade time, and a bad-conduct discharge—which he then coaxed Lande into revealing. What was interesting to Mulheisen was that the navy, then mired in Vietnam, had not bothered to send this troublemaker to the war zone but had simply got rid of him with a fairly lenient court-martial.

But evidently he was a talented tinkerer, and the world of electronics fascinated him. He'd done very well in it. But the absolute star of his existence had appeared in his personal heaven when Bonny burst upon his consciousness like a supernova. From all their conversations it had become apparent to Mulheisen that Bonny Wheeler was probably the only real friend he'd ever had. And she was beautiful. A little wounded, too, and grateful for his assistance. He was very proud of her youthful debut as a centerfold girl; it was evidence that the woman who loved him was beloved by the rest of the world. Curiously he had little real jealousy of other men; indeed, he relished the notion that his wife was desired by others, although he frequently expressed conventional macho attitudes—"No guy better fool with Bon—I'd blow 'im away."

All this information was acquired haphazardly, and it took Mulheisen considerable time to digest it, distracted as he was by the center-stage event—Bonny's rapid and shattering decline.

One afternoon while Lande was taking a break, Mulheisen sat at Bonny's bedside, holding her hand. It was not raining for once, but broken clouds rumbled across the sky, intermittently permitting brilliant shafts of sunlight, then darkening everything. Mulheisen was staring at Bonny's ruined face without really seeing it, not thinking about anything at all, when suddenly she gripped his hand tightly.

"What is it?" he asked, aware that something was wrong.

She looked at him, and her sunken eyes lighted up with a glow of alarm. She'd been having trouble speaking because of her distorted palate and jaw, but she struggled to say, "Get Gene. Something is happening."

Mulheisen raced down the corridor and met Lande running toward him. They turned together and ran back. Lande grabbed Bonny's hand, and Mulheisen stood over him as she said, "This is it, boys." She caught Mulheisen's eye. "Look after him," she said.

A few seconds later her eyes became fixed, and Lande dropped his head onto her breast with a sob. Mulheisen didn't see the exact moment when it happened, but after a short time he realized that it was over. He turned away and picked up his raincoat and left the hospital.

Mulheisen drove home, his mind in a dull, cobwebby state. His mother was not there. He changed into jeans and an old sweater and pulled on rubber boots and a windbreaker. He walked out beyond the weathered barn and let himself through an old, sagging gate. Hands in pockets, he followed the old path through the dried reeds, most of which had been flattened by wind and snow, until he came to the edge of the ship channel. He stood there for a long time, staring down toward Lake Saint Clair shimmering in the distance. He barely noticed the red-winged blackbirds or the ducks that flew here and there. A gaggle of coots evidently decided that he was no threat and continued to work along the edge of the channel, their chalky beaks rhythmically projecting forward and then drawing their dumpy charcoal-gray bodies after them. Mulheisen didn't notice. He was struggling to understand what had just happened. He knew that something serious, something profound had occurred, but what? It didn't make sense.

He was suddenly struck by an appalling recollection—at some early point in Bonny's confinement—he couldn't recall the exact moment—she had embarrassed him with a remark about their shared school days. She'd said something to the effect that he'd always had "character." He had let it pass at the time, but now that she was dead, it had come back to haunt him. The fact was a long-repressed sense of guilt had reasserted itself, based on an incident that dated from the very first days of their grade-school careers.

Bonny had just moved to the Saint Clair Flats School District from, he thought, Detroit. He'd been immediately attracted to her, and at the morning recess he had made the incredible social blunder of following her about the playground, teasing her and, finally, holding hands with her. His schoolmates had instantly pounced on this uncharacteristic behavior, and at the noon recess, after he had sat by her in the lunchroom, they had ridiculed him when he came out onto the playground with her. Obviously they had already decided that Bonny was not "in," and they pointed out to him that she had a hole in her sock. It was true. It was quite visible, a little crescent of naked flesh above the heel of her run-down loafer. Mortified and confused, Mulheisen had instantly repudiated his affection for the new girl and had run away with his pals, abandoning her.

After school, lying in the still-sweet old hay in the barn, little Mul moped over the humiliations of the day. He was struck by two things—the quiet, brave way in which Bonny had endured her humiliation, withdrawing to a remote corner of the playground alone, and the fact that he knew exactly what his parents would think of his behavior.

The next day, and on every possible occasion in the years they spent together in public school, Mulheisen defended and promoted Bonny. He encouraged other girls to befriend her; he nominated her for class president in high school; he had even bribed a buddy to ask her to the prom. All of this had seemed necessary because despite the fact that Bonny was very attractive physically, she was never popular with the other kids. This had always been inexplicable to Mulheisen, although he himself never sought any relationship with her more intimate than a kind of casual friendliness. And now he saw that he had spent the rest of his—or her—life regretting and paying for that single act of repudiation on the sixth-grade playground.

The fresh breeze brought tears to his eyes. He blinked and looked about him. Green shoots were emerging between the dried stalks of the reeds. The coots—even he knew they weren't ducks—looked comical as they bobbed and turned, constantly looking for food and picking up shreds of grass for their nests, but Mulheisen didn't register their behavior. Rather, he was appalled by their industry. What was the point of coots in this universe? Why would there be these mindless coots but no Bonny? For that matter, what was the point of himself? Of cops? He could taste the bitterness at the back of his palate. Out on the lake a large ship was angling toward the channel. He drew himself up with a groaning sigh—there sure as hell was no reason for crooks.

Eighteen

The way Billy Conover saw it was a guy might not be some kind of hunk, but if a guy had enough clout (a word he liked—it had a nice solid sound), the hot-looking women had to go to bed with him anyway. So he loved the drug biz. He'd been in the loan biz, and that was all right (he kept a finger in that pie), but it didn't bring the women in, and Billy really dug women. The drug biz brought him women who ordinarily wouldn't have talked to him. The problem, aside from an uncharming personality, was that Billy also liked to eat, which tended to make a chunk out of a hunk. But Billy had never been a hunk anyway. He was about six feet tall and had one of those unfortunate shapes—small head, narrow shoulders, swelling belly, and very wide hips and ass—cruel Sid Sedlacek used to say Billy looked like an ice cream cone that landed on its head.

Lately Billy had fallen in love with Mexican food. He was introduced to it by his friend Ray Echeverria, who although a Basque by origin, had become enamored of Spanish-American cuisine. Billy was particularly fond of seviche. Echeverria took him to a little Mexican place down on Cass Avenue that made a great seviche. Tonight they'd had the seviche and a terrific *chili verde con carne,* in this case pork, washed down with a considerable amount of *cerveza.* At a few minutes after ten Billy and Ray—a wonderfully slim and elegant man in middle age, for all his gourmandizing—had strolled out, arms about two incredibly lush young women and accompanied by a couple of lesser-ranking pals from the biz, all of whom agreed that Casa Pablo's had the greatest seviche in the world.

It was raining, of course. Billy cursed and ordered one of the heavies, a hood named Gus, to go get the car. At that point a little guy in a raincoat passed by, wearing shades, of all things, and a sailor's rain hat. He had his hands in his pockets, and he suddenly turned back and swung up his right hand, through a reach-through pocket, the raincoat swinging open to reveal a gun of some sort. The little man took a stance, bracing himself and holding the top of the gun down with his gloved left hand. It was now clear from the large bore of the barrel that the man was holding a shotgun. He pulled the trigger.

It was a firestorm. Five of the group were standing in a kind of alcove that formed the entrance to Casa Pablo's. In the rolling thunder of the five blasts, Conover was the first to fly. Two tremendous blows struck him in the chest and lifted him off his feet. He struck the girls and Echeverria like a giant bowling ball, and his movement might have saved some of their lives, though not Echeverria's.

The shooter struggled for a moment, extricating his right hand from his raincoat pocket. Gus, who had started to jog down the street after the car, turned back, gun in hand, and got off two shots with a .357 Colt. One of the shots may have hit the shooter, for he seemed to stagger momentarily, but then the left gun came up, and the man stood like a rock, bracing himself with his right hand on the top of the gun while it crashed away and blew Gus into the street. The gunner swiveled and blasted the remaining bodyguard, who had struggled to his hands and knees in the alcove, then emptied the chamber into Billy and Ray.

In the silence that followed, the gunner calmly delved into a pocket and reloaded one of the guns, the other swinging by his side from its leather strap. Then he stepped among the bodies and carefully blew Billy Conover's and Ray Echeverria's heads into indescribable mush with two shots apiece. He then tucked the two dangling guns back into his raincoat and walked quickly down Cass, buttoning the coat as he went.

Afterward a cab driver who had just pulled up when he saw the party leaving the restaurant, hoping for a fare, described the whole process as instantaneous. Bodies had been flattened like ripe wheat in a hailstorm, he said. The killer had used a shotgun, all right, but it looked more like a long pistol. The barrel had been sawed off, as well as the long part of the stock. It must have been an automatic, he said, "'cause the fire poured outta that cannon like shit through a tin horn."

Conover and Echeverria had each received more than a dozen .30-caliber pellets in their chests and twice as many in the head. The pellets had blown up the two men's hearts, but they hadn't the penetrative power of a rifled bullet, and that had saved the lives of the two young women, lying beneath the two men. They had received some serious wounds to their legs, however. Gus and the other hood were simply shot to pieces. Whether Gus had winged the killer was unclear, since witnesses reported him walking easily as he left the scene.

The case belonged to the Thirteenth Precinct, but Laddy McClain declared it a gangland slaying, probably related to the killings of Tupman and Sedlacek. Mulheisen was called at home, where he had gone that afternoon after the death of Bonny Lande. By the time he arrived downtown at the scene, McClain was telling a television reporter that it appeared there was a gang war in progress. Neither Mulheisen nor Andy Deane took that view, but they didn't say so to the reporters. All three crimes had involved different modes of killing.

Dennis Noell of the Big Four had arrived. A very pretty young black woman standing before a camera, shielding her helmet of hair from the rain with something that looked like a pizza take-out box, managed to snag this big, handsome detective and asked, "What kind of weapon could inflict this incredible carnage, Sergeant Noell?"

"Easy," said Noell with great relish; "it had to be an alley sweeper. Well, that's a sawed-off twelve-gauge automatic shotgun, loaded with double-ought cartridges, ma'am. You could take out a platoon with a couple of them." He went on to describe the victims as "just a buncha dope dealers and whores. Looks to me like some good citizen has done us all a favor."

Mulheisen watched this with disgust, then signaled to Jimmy Marshall. They got into Mulheisen's Checker and sat there in the flickering glow of emergency-vehicle lights. It was raining steadily and dawn was many hours away. Mulheisen lighted a cigar and puffed it while Jimmy sat silently, waiting. A thought popped into Mulheisen's mind—who exactly had he mentioned to Lande, all those weeks ago at the restaurant, as people whom he could do without? He wasn't sure, but he thought it included Frosty Tupman and Billy Conover. And hadn't he mentioned something about Captain Buchanan?

"I think we've got a problem, Jim," he said.

"You mean Dennis?"

"Dennis? Well, yes, . . . Dennis." Mulheisen tapped on the steering wheel for a minute, watching the bodies being removed. There wasn't much of a crowd, and the television people had gone. Mulheisen sighed and said, "Not just Dennis. You heard what the cabby said."

"One man? A little guy?"

"That's the one."

"Must have been Little David," Jimmy said.

"Bonny died this afternoon," Mulheisen said.

"I know . . . I called the hospital. They said you'd gone."

"Did you talk to Lande? No? Well, there was no reason for you to. I wonder where he is right now."

"I guess we better go look," Jimmy said.

"Yes, we better go look."

On the way back to the Ninth Precinct, Mulheisen pondered aloud—"To what extent can we, or should we, contain the suspicions we have about Lande?"

Marshall considered and replied, "We really don't have any more on him than we had before, Mul. It's all speculation. If you're thinking about a warrant, I don't know if a judge would listen."

Mulheisen agreed. From the precinct he called all the numbers he had for Lande, including the hospital, but drew nothing but blanks. The hospital was very interested because Lande had left not long after Mulheisen, without leaving any instructions for the disposition of Bonny's remains. They were holding the body in their morgue. Mulheisen promised to contact them as soon as he learned anything.

He and Jimmy drove separately to Lande's apartment and the Doc Byte office, then met at the Briar Ridge Golf and Country Club. Neither had seen any sign of Lande. The parking lot of the golf course was empty, and there was a soggy, handwritten sign taped over the sign at the gate that said "Closed until further notice." Another sign was taped to the door of the pro shop, saying essentially the same thing but advising vendors and delivery people to contact Eric Smith in case of emergency and giving a Detroit phone number. It was 3:00 A.M. before Mulheisen was able to get the young pro on the phone. He had just rolled in from a date, he said, and he hadn't seen Lande in several days. He was sorry to hear that Mrs. Lande had passed away. He guessed that the course would remain closed for the time being, but he expected he'd hear from Lande soon, and he'd sure let him know that Mulheisen wanted to see him.

"There's nothing much going on out there anyway," Smith said. "The membership list is just about nil, and Gene told the grounds crew to take a holiday for the time being. To tell you the truth, Sergeant, I don't know if he's ever going to reopen. He was pretty down when I saw him. He was talking about taking a vacation with his wife, to the islands, to recuperate. I didn't realize she was that bad off."

Mulheisen sent Jimmy home for a few hours with instructions to be at Doc Byte when it opened, to talk to Alicia Bommarito and to check on the shipment. Jimmy was to call Mulheisen at Laddy McClain's office as soon as he found out anything. Then Mulheisen took himself to the cot in the squad room for a couple hours' sleep. It was a sleep troubled by dreams of coots and ducks and the banging of shotguns.

By eight o'clock he was in Mc-Clain's office downtown. McClain was not in a great mood, having slept little and now furious at the sight of Dennis Noell on television. Mulheisen had never known McClain had a television in his office; it must have been buried under the piles of reports and old newspapers.

"Look at this idiot," McClain said, wielding a remote device. "One of the guys taped it earlier." He punched a button and the screen got furry. When the tape started again a very pretty blonde was saying, "Now we're going to show you some pictures that the kids probably shouldn't see. We're going to Gina Woodridge on Cass Avenue." Then the black woman came on, the camera angle somehow excluding the pizza box as she gestured at the ambulances and the body bags. Shortly they cut to the interview that Mulheisen had partially witnessed. The reporter was looking up at the incredibly handsome Noell. His voice was deep, and he sounded remarkably articulate as he described an "alley sweeper" and even demonstrated how to saw off the barrel on a Remington shotgun. The interviewer was wonderfully sexy, standing up under Noell's great shoulders, looking up at him with delight. She said, "They call you Dennis the Menace, don't they?" And Noell replied frankly, "I'm not the real Dennis the Menace."

"Can you believe it?" McClain said. "Describing an alley sweeper! 'I'm not the real Dennis the Menace.' What is he, arming the home guard?"

"Dennis believes very strongly in the right to keep and bear arms," Mulheisen said.

"I'd like to tear off his arms and beat him over the head with them," McClain snarled. "This is real bad stuff, Mul. I just hope it doesn't make it onto the evening news. Some cluck is going to think the cops say it's all right to sweep the streets of drug peddlers, like our shooter did last night."

"I wanted to talk to you about that," Mulheisen said. "I was a little disturbed about what you were telling the reporters."

"Me?" McClain was indignant. "I didn't say anything."

"You said it was a gangland slaying," Mulheisen reminded him, "and you linked it to the Big Sid and Tupman cases. I'm not so sure of that. In fact, it looks pretty clear that we've nailed down the guy who killed Sid."

"This Iowa guy? I saw your report on that. But so what? So they took him out, too. It's still mob stuff, right?"

"Maybe," Mulheisen said, "maybe not. Now I'm on to this guy Lande, who was originally picked up near the Sid killing. Little bits of information keep popping up that link him to all of these guys, but nothing really strong enough. The thing is he's not a mob guy."

McClain obviously knew nothing about Lande and was curious about Mulheisen's take on the man. Mulheisen filled him in as much as he felt he could, making only vague references to the part Bonny had played in his investigation. He said he'd talked extensively to

Lande and had become convinced that the man was at least peripher-
ally involved. The point he wanted to press, however, was that now
would be a good time to tell the press that they had essentially solved
the Sedlacek case. It might help to ease media pressure, and it could
conceivably be used to separate this spate of slaughters in the public
mind, to mitigate the effect of Dennis's sensational revelations about
alley sweepers, for instance.

McClain nodded. It sounded good to him. "But what about this
Lande?" he asked.

"He's disappeared," Mulheisen confessed. "His wife died yesterday. Maybe he's just gone on a bender or something, I don't know, but
I can't find him. I know he had developed some kind of attitude about
the mob . . . holds them responsible in some strange way for his wife's
troubles . . . It would take a better psychologist than me to sort it out."

"You mean he could have done this alley-sweeper thing?"

"I don't know that," Mulheisen said, "but he let drop a few things
to me that make me suspicious. I'd like a warrant."

"For what?" McClain spread his hands questioningly.

"I'd like to enter his apartment, his place of business, the golf club
. . . He's acting strangely, Mac. He left the hospital without making
arrangements for his wife."

McClain pondered this, glancing at Mulheisen suspiciously from
time to time. Finally he said, "I think I can arrange it."

A few minutes later Jimmy called. "The shipment is gone," he
said. "The lady says it was sitting in the back room when she left last
night."

"Meet me at the precinct," Mulheisen said. "I'll have a warrant."

An hour later Mulheisen laid it out for Jimmy. "We've got to do
something about Buchanan, Jim. I know this sounds weird, but I'd like
you to make a call for me."

A half hour later Mulheisen heard a commotion in the hall, and
when he went out, the desk man told him excitedly that they had just
received information from Captain Buchanan's home that an anonymous caller had warned that the commander of the Ninth Precinct
would be "blown away if he showed his slimy snout in public again."

Buchanan looked calm when Mulheisen went in to see him, but his voice was strained. "What do you make of this?" he asked.

"It must be a crank," Mulheisen assured him, "but to be on the safe side, I'd recommend a low profile for a day or two. In fact, it might not be a bad idea if you went home to be with Alice. She'll be worried and, let's face it, she could be in danger herself."

"Oh, Lord, you're right," Buchanan said. "Johnson," he shouted for the blue lieutenant, "get a car out to my house pronto!"

Mulheisen interjected, "If I might make a suggestion, sir, maybe you ought to get the Big Four in on this. They can provide a hell of a lot of security."

Buchanan, doubtlessly thinking of a wall of tall manly flesh standing between him and an assassin's bullet—perhaps an assassin armed with an alley sweeper—nodded judiciously and said, "Good idea. Johnson! Get Dennis."

Nineteen

Joe was having a friendly little chat with Roman Yakovich. They were talking about Germaine Kouras. The Yak had never liked her. He thought a thirty-year-old woman should have more sense than to try to talk a sixty-five-year-old man into leaving his wife and running away to the Caymans. Big Sid wouldn't have enjoyed it for long even if he did go; he'd soon feel bad about Mrs. Sid, and what kind of food could a Greek woman cook for a man like Sid? He wasn't a Greek, he was a Serb. Still, the Yak didn't think Carmine should have iced her.

"Who says he iced her?" Joe asked.

The Yak shrugged. "That's what they say. I don't know."

"Is there anyplace she could be," Joe asked, "that Carmine wouldn't know about? Any special place where Sid maybe used to take her? A cabin? A cottage? Some place private where they used to meet?"

The Yak thought about it. "The boat?"

"Sid had a boat? Where did he keep it?"

"Down there by the Bayview Yacht Club."

Joe had a vague idea where this was, on the Detroit River somewhere around the Chrysler plant. "Did Carmine know about this boat?"

The Yak didn't know.

Joe tried another tack. "The thing is, Roman, there's a lot of money missing, a whole lot of money, and Carmine wants it back.

Now, you know me . . . I don't give a damn about Carmine's money, except that I get a nice percentage of whatever I can recover. Maybe Germaine knew something about it, maybe she didn't. Maybe she's dead; maybe—just maybe—she's still around, hiding out somewhere. I can help her. I'm probably the only one who can help her. If you know anything, tell me."

The Yak didn't know anything. "The boss allus had a lotta money" was the extent of it.

They were sitting in the Yak's neat little apartment over the old stables. It had a military look, with its neatly made bed on an iron frame and the spotless kitchenette. The television appeared to be the Yak's only source of entertainment. There was a doily on the television and on it a silver framed photo of Big Sid, Mrs. Sid, and little Helen standing on the deck of a cabin cruiser.

Joe nodded toward the picture. "What's the name of the boat?"

The phone rang, or rather, it buzzed like an intercom. The Yak picked it up, and as he talked, his face lightened slightly. "I could come over in a minute," he said; "I was just talkin' to Joe. Joe Service. He's a contractor."

"Is that Helen?" Joe whispered. "Let me talk to her."

He took the phone and said, "Miss Sedlacek? Joe Service. No, no, no, I'm not one of Carmine's . . . Miss Sedlacek . . . Miss, . . . look, I'm an independent . . . listen, can I talk to you? Just let me talk to you for a minute; it's important . . . Hey, you can have Roman throw me out on my butt if I'm too much of a pain . . . Yeah, just for a minute. I'll be right over."

The Yak took Joe over to the house. On the way he explained that Helen had wanted him to come play racquetball. The Yak didn't like racquetball; he just wasn't agile enough to play with Helen, but sometimes she needed an opponent, so he went. He suggested that Joe play her. "You kids can play," he said.

Helen Sedlacek was waiting for them in a kind of lounge in the basement of the mansion. She was wearing slacks and a black turtleneck jersey and Joe, who had never met her before, liked what he saw. She was small and lithe with a great mane of black hair, very pretty and, at the moment, torn between anger and curiosity.

"Miss Sedlacek, it's really kind of you to see me. I know that you're not too happy with Carmine, but believe me, I'm not one of Carmine's stooges." Joe gave her the best smile he had. It seemed to have some effect.

"Whose stooge are you?" she asked, with a hint of a smile.

"I'm my own stooge. You can ask Roman, he knows me. Carmine and I get on . . ." he waggled his fingers, ". . . in a way. He hires me because I get results."

The Yak nodded at Helen's inquiring look. "Joe's all right," he said. "He works for everybody, not just Carmine."

"What are you?" she asked, yielding to curiosity. "An investigator for the biz? I never heard of such a thing."

"Why not?" Joe said blithely. "Even the biz needs a detective now and then. I'm a finder, Miss Sedlacek. I find people, money, . . . whatever needs finding."

"So what are you looking for now, Joe?"

"Money . . . and Germaine Kouras."

"I heard she was gone," Helen said.

"That's what I heard, but the way I was told, it was not very conclusive. Maybe she's gone, but I'm not sure, and I can't help wondering."

Helen frowned. "I don't quite understand. What's the mystery? Either she's gone or she isn't."

Joe smiled. "Carmine says she's gone, but he doesn't say where, if you get my drift. I know what you're going to say." He hastened to forestall her. "If Carmine says she's gone, he probably made sure of it." He shrugged. "He could be lying. Carmine lies a lot."

Joe looked about the area with casual interest. Through an open door he got a glimpse of a swimming pool. "Say, quite a layout," he said, walking over and looking into an impressive recreation area. Big Sid had spent a lot of money down here. The swimming pool was forty feet long and lighted from underneath, creating dancing patterns on the low ceiling. To one side, behind a Plexiglas wall, was the racquetball court; there were weight and workout machines, a heavy bag for boxing, and a speed bag, even a little net-draped driving range where you could hit golf balls against a projected fairway or onto a projected green. "Hey, your own court! How about a game?"

Helen laughed. "You're certainly not one of Carmine's usual mugs," she said. "I think we could find you some shorts and a pair of court shoes."

Roman found all the essential gear for him in the dressing room and pointed out the showers, the steam room and the sauna, then vanished. When Joe came out ten minutes later, Helen was waiting for him at the door of the court. He started to ask her where Roman had got to but forgot momentarily. Helen didn't look like Helen. She was slimmer than he had thought, dressed in very short shorts and a black tank top, and looking very much like a teenage boy—the black mane was gone. What she had was practically a shaved head but for a neat, black patch of hair that barely covered the crown of her shapely skull.

Joe's mouth was open.

"Yes?" she asked.

"I, ah, wondered what happened to Roman."

"I sent him back to his TV. He was a little worried for me, but I told him I thought I could handle you. Come on."

Joe was fascinated by this woman. Inside the court she bounced the blue ball for a few seconds and said, "Shall we warm up with a little volley or two?"

She was smaller than he and faster, very lithe indeed, as he quickly discovered when the game commenced. He soon fell behind by several points because he kept watching her instead of the rocketing ball. In many ways she seemed like a boy, almost sexless at first look, but then a subtle sexiness of her body and movements gripped him. She was quite erotic to watch as she spun and leapt and stretched.

Before the game got quite out of hand, however, Joe was caught up in the competitive spirit that she exuded, and he began to concentrate. It was not enough. By the second game, however, he had fully recovered, and he took it by six points. In the rubber game he thought he was coasting to an easy victory after taking an eight-point lead, but then Helen turned on a furious rally, and her stamina overcame him.

They were both drenched. Helen almost staggered off the court and flung her racket to the floor. "Let's swim," she said, scuffing off her shoes and socks. She peeled off the tank top and the shorts, the skimpy halter bra, and ran across the rubberized floor to leap naked into the pool, her tight little buttocks flexing. Joe was with her within seconds. He was a very good swimmer, but it was only his superior musculature that enabled him to beat Helen to the wall on the return lap. After that she swam away from him enticingly, twisting and writhing, and he dove under, pursuing her furiously but vainly, her foot always just beyond his grasp until she allowed him to catch her and they rolled to the surface, embracing and gasping.

They were a beautiful couple, both small and dark and smoothly muscled. Lying on the warm redwood decking of the dimly lighted poolside, with the glittering light moving eerily about them, Joe thought that she was the most naked person he had ever seen. There was not a hair on her body. She was so clean, so simple looking. Her hips were narrow, her limbs so smooth and firm, even her feet were uncomplicated and smooth, as if she had been fashioned out of some miraculous plastic that was both soft and hard at the same time. Nude seemed to him a new word.

She looked cool to the touch, but she wasn't. She was intensely passionate. "Yes, yes," she demanded in a husky whisper, "Do it . . . not there . . . like this," and she twisted in his grasp, presenting her lean buttocks. This was by no means Joe's preference, but he was caught up in the fury of the moment, and he readily complied.

Afterward they sat, or lay, in the sauna, languorously caressing one another until they made love again, in a more conventional manner. And then they went to the showers together. Later they sprawled in thick terry-cloth robes on the couches of the lounge, tearing hungrily at ham sandwiches Helen had prepared in the kitchenette and gulping down painfully cold bottles of Pilsner Urquell. It struck Joe that he had never enjoyed himself so completely, so thoroughly, in his life. He was absolutely stunned by this woman. For the first time ever the thought that he had met his ideal mate entered his mind. It was more than a little scary.

Helen was watching him with much the same look of delight and an almost resentful awe. "Why is it I never met you before?" she asked, when she had swallowed enough sandwich to speak for a second.

Joe chewed, raising his eyebrows and shrugging. "I've been around," he said finally. He drank down the last of his beer and refused another. "I just don't live here. Don't like it."

"Where do you live?"

For some reason Joe did not hesitate to answer this inquiry, which he had always previously evaded. "Out west, in the mountains," he said, "a place you never heard of."

"What place?"

"It's called—don't laugh—Tinstar. One word." He laughed with her. "Sounds like a movie, hunh? It's not. It's just a little town that had to have a name, and that's the one they came up with. I don't live in the town . . . up in the mountains. I'll take you there."

She nodded. It was agreed.

Helen finished her sandwich while he watched her intently. Finally she said skeptically, "I've never heard of a biz detective, Joe. These people, they don't like free-lancers. They don't trust them—hell, they don't trust anybody. It's their weakness. They like people like Roman, people who are bound to them . . . in blood, in marriage, in gratitude and debt . . . or in fear. Mostly in fear."

"Are you bound in fear?" Joe asked.

"I'm not bound to them," Helen said. "I'm bound to my papa . . . in blood, in love."

Joe sighed. "I don't know anything about that stuff. But these people, they aren't crazy about my independence, but they put up with it. They need a guy like me, someone who is in the biz in a way but not allied to any single one of them. You see the way it is? It's no use hiring your own people to find out what your own people are stealing from you."

"But they would never trust you," she protested. "Papa wouldn't have trusted you to take out the garbage."

"I worked for your Papa once," Joe said with a laugh. "It was a while back, when I was first starting out. He thought some bartender was setting up some action on the side, on Sid's turf."

"Was he?"

"Nanh, Guy was boffing one of Sid's ex-girls. That's all it was, but Sid didn't want to admit it to himself, that he was jealous. But I'll say this, when I told him, he saw it and laughed. Most of them don't. Hey, I'm sorry, I shouldn't have said that about the girl."

"Oh, I knew about Papa and the girls. Mama did, too. It's not a big thing."

"Anyway, Sid trusted me. They mostly do. There's nothing at stake, really. If I don't deliver, they don't pay. But a lot of them lie and try to cheat me, Carmine especially. The thing is they want me to find out who among them is a traitor, who is boffing their girl, whose hand is in the till, . . . but they don't want me to find out too much. Carmine doesn't want me to find out how incompetent and lazy and just plain foolish he is, the mistakes he makes, so he lies to me and hopes that I'll find out what he wants to know and maybe, with luck, I'll get my ass blown off, and he'll still get the info without having to pay."

Helen leaned forward, "Are you the one who found Hal?"

Joe engaged her eyes. "Don't ask."

Her eyes blazed back. "Did Carmine set Papa up for Hal?"

"Oh, yes," Joe said. "What was he supposed to do? Ignore the money Sid took?"

Helen started to respond, but then she just slumped back on the couch. She tried to stare him down, but Joe refused to go on with that game. He looked away with a shrug. Eventually she took a deep breath and said, "You say you're independent, Joe. Does that mean you're for hire?"

"Theoretically," he said dryly, "but not in practice. Of course, I entertain all offers; I don't necessarily accept. Are you making an offer?"

Her eyes glittering, Helen slipped to her knees before him. "I don't know what I can offer, . . ." she said with a sly smile. She reached out and opened his robe and caressed him.

Joe bent forward and took her by the arms and drew her into an embrace. They kissed for a while, deeply, and he whispered in her ear, "Oh, you have a lot to offer, sweet little Helen, but I have a feeling that you have even more to ask." He held her closely clipped head in his hands, loving the way that it felt in his strong fingers. He kissed her eyes. Her hair was a tiny patch of silky fur, lovely to the touch.

"I'm my Papa's boy," she breathed and slipped down between his knees.

"Ah. I see." He held her small skull tightly. Afterward she was warm and alive in his arms. So fine. He had never felt anything quite like it. But at last he shifted her to one side and looked into her face. "I think I know what you want," he said. "I have to tell you right now that I'm not in Hal's line of work. I'm a finder. If you want me to find something for you, I'll do it. But if you want me to perform anything more, ah, terminal, . . . put it out of your mind."

She raised her naked face to his. Her lips were a pale pink, and the little black cap of hair suggested a bird, a chickadee perhaps, or a goldfinch. "Oh, that's fine, buddy," she crooned, "I wouldn't want you to go too far . . . to do my job. But if you could help . . ."

Joe didn't say anything for a long moment, then, "It's been done. Sometimes the people I find are dealt with later by my clients. That's not my concern."

"You know," Helen said, "Carmine didn't even come to Papa's funeral. That was unusual. The official word was that he was ill. He sent a wreath and a card. Mama was disappointed. It's a good thing he didn't come. I wouldn't be lying in your arms right now. I'd be in jail. Can you put me next to him?"

"Maybe we can help each other," Joe said. "Do you know a man named Gene Lande?"

Helen sat back abruptly and wrinkled her nose. "Lande? Sure, I know him. Why?"

"What is he, some kind of leper, or something?" Joe asked. "Everybody gives me this look when I mention him."

"He's a good golfer," Helen said, "a big hitter, and almost a machine around the green. He has a beautiful swing, not big and glamorous, but compact and powerful. Really good. Is that better?"

"Gee, you sound like you dig the guy," Joe said. "I'm getting jealous."

"Only his swing," she said. "Do you play?"

"Never," he replied. "Do you?"

"I carry a five handicap."

"Is that good?"

She shook her head in mock rue. "I only know three or four women who can play with me. Mostly I play with guys. Usually I beat them."

"Maybe you can teach me," Joe said. "It can't be all that hard."

"If you've never played, it's too late. I don't know anybody who ever took it up as an adult and was good at it. Papa used to take me when I was just a kid. He never could play worth a darn himself, but he was crazy about the game. He was so proud of me when I won the junior girls municipal tournament. I was thirteen."

"Papa's boy," Joe said, watching her.

Helen smiled. "That time, anyway."

He took her in his arms again and kissed her, long and sweet. "What should I call you?" he wondered. "Hel?"

"Oh, I'll be hell, all right," she whispered, "but call me Buddy."

Twenty

"**A**re you sure the Sweet Home is the right place for your friend, Mul?" asked Carlotta Bledsoe. She was a trim woman of thirty with light brown skin and a taste for extremely large spectacles that covered half her face.

Mulheisen was puzzled. "Why not?"

"It's very unusual," she said. "We've never had a white woman here. Folks tend to take their loved ones to their own people."

Mulheisen had never given a thought to this aspect of it. The Sweet Home Funeral Parlor was the only private mortuary where he knew the people. His father and Doc Bledsoe had been fishing pals for many years, and Mulheisen had known Carlotta since childhood; it had not occurred to him that there was a racial dimension here. In funeral parlors? But now that the idea had been presented to him, he could see that it was bound to be, given the ornery nature of man, although it still seemed bizarre.

Carlotta's suggestion only gave a momentary check to his scheme, however, which was to move Bonny from the hospital mortuary to a private one. He hoped it would flush Gene Lande out of hiding. The suggested impropriety of placing her in a—what? a "black"? a "non-white"? (even the terminology seemed laughable)—funeral home seemed irrelevant beside the ethical implications of—to be blunt—using her corpse as a decoy.

He thought he'd considered all the arguments—foremost was that

if Lande had indeed been the assassin in the Conover and/or the
Tupman massacre, almost any action was justified in securing the arrest
of such a dangerous man, in the interest of public safety. Beyond that,
if Lande weren't dangerous to others, he might be dangerous to himself
or in danger of being harmed by others, including the mob.

There was a further, compelling consideration: the hospital was
prepared to send the body to the Wayne County Morgue as unclaimed.
Legally they couldn't hold it much longer, even if they had the space
and the inclination. Mulheisen had spent too much time at the morgue
to bear the thought of Bonny on one of its slabs. He was not a
sentimental man, but the morgue was not the place for someone he
cared about.

He had been thinking about Bonny a lot, naturally, and some of
his thoughts had not been comforting. He found he could still not shake
his self-assumed lifelong obligation to look after her, starting with that
day on the playground in the sixth grade. Well, it wasn't over . . . yet.

No, no, he would not permit Bonny to be removed to the county
morgue. He bullied the hospital into releasing the body into his custody,
and it was transported to the Sweet Home, Carlotta's misgivings notwithstanding. The hospital would of course inform Lande of the disposition of the body, if he called, and they said they'd try to notify
Mulheisen if that happened. The body was not to be embalmed, he told
Carlotta, but held in storage until further instructions. Carlotta con-
sented to this.

In the meantime Mulheisen, Jimmy Marshall, and other detectives
from the Ninth Precinct ransacked Lande's office, his home, and the golf
club but found little of interest. There was no documentation, for
instance, on the shipment of computer equipment to Grand Cayman
Island. Alicia Bommarito insisted that Lande himself had handled it. "It
was personal," she said, "something to do with the golf-resort deal he
was working on." What that deal was she didn't know; Lande had
never discussed it with her.

At Lande's home there was nothing of immediate interest; some
personal papers in a filing cabinet might yield something eventually, but
Mulheisen was not disposed to take the time now to analyze them. He
stood in the Landes' bedroom, gazing at the inevitable champagne

decor. The large bed was unmade; a heavy satin bedspread and some of Lande's soiled clothing lay on the deep pile of the champagne carpet, but otherwise everything was quite neat and orderly. Presumably Lande had not slept here for several days.

It was curiously moving to look upon the intimate personal belongings of a woman whom one has . . . well, loved. Bonny's clothes hung in the closet; shoes were lined up primly, the ones she used frequently, anyway—there were a lot of shoe boxes. With a sigh Mulheisen knelt and went through them all. There were nothing in the boxes but shoes, Bonny's shoes. He rose and looked about. Her toiletries were carefully arranged on the vanity. They looked useless. They were useless now. Throw them away.

On a pale, Scandinavian-style dresser was a photo of Bonny in a bikini, reclining against the windshield of what appeared to be a large cabin cruiser. Dimly visible through the glass of the windshield, peering over the boat's wheel, Lande's goofy mustache bristled behind Bonny's head, his grin glowing in a shaft of light. Bonny looked great, almost as spectacular as in the famous centerfold. From the way she looked—the hairstyle, her face—Mulheisen thought the picture may have been taken as recently as a few months earlier, perhaps when the couple was in the Caymans for Christmas.

Mulheisen picked up the photo and stared at it. No doubt about it, Bonny was a beautiful woman. And then in the background he noticed a familiar landscape—the distant shoreline of Ontario. At least it looked like the shoreline he had seen a thousand times—it sure wasn't a tropical setting. He supposed the boat could have been anchored in one of the many little bays of either Peach Island or Harsen's Island. And it was probably taken last summer, evidently a hot day, considering that Bonny was practically falling out of her bathing suit.

Mulheisen took the picture with him.

At Briar Ridge there was no sign of anyone having been near the place in days. There were again some potentially interesting files in the little office, but nothing to grip Mulheisen's attention. He walked out onto the deck. It was a sunny day at last. He looked out over the course. It looked great, but he supposed that the fairway grass was getting a little high. It would need mowing soon.

Back in the precinct by the end of the afternoon, Mulheisen found that there was no further sign of Eugene Lande, and he was considering a full-scale manhunt instead of the cautious effort he had thus far put forth. But he wasn't depressed by any means. He felt confident even if he couldn't say why. He was glad that Buchanan was safely out of the way, with the Big Four engaged in his defense. And he was glad that Bonny was at Sweet Home. There was one setback, however—Sergeant Maki reported that Lande did not and had not owned a boat. Certainly there was no boat registered in his name in the state, no insurance company had insured such a boat, nor could any of the yacht clubs or boat liveries in the Detroit-Windsor area say that he had ever kept a boat. So the picture must have been taken on someone else's boat; not an unlikely conclusion, since someone else had taken the photo. Who the photographer was, however, was not evident. The enlargement had been made from a snapshot, at a photo shop in a mall near the Landes' home, and paid for by Lande. It had been originally developed at the same shop, from film brought in by Mrs. Lande the preceding September. End of story. Mulheisen abandoned this avenue of investigation—if it weren't Lande's boat, it was not likely he would be hiding on it.

About eight o'clock Mulheisen wrapped up a meeting with his detectives, advising them that if nothing had developed by tomorrow morning, he would push for a full-scale manhunt. He was tempted to stop in at one of his favorite watering holes on the way home, but he drove on. It was a warm night, and it occurred to him that the Tigers would be opening the baseball season in a couple of days. This thought lifted his spirits. Baseball was not, after all, a thing of great consequence, and for this he was grateful. He longed for something of no great consequence to occupy his mind, if only temporarily, something nonetheless quite fine and pleasurable after this long, bitter spring.

The protest signs were gone from the site of the development when he turned down his road. He wondered if this were good or bad, but his mother was not home to enlighten him. She had left a message on the refrigerator, concerning the presence of a cold meat loaf that could be warmed in the microwave, with a PS—"I'm at Eastern Star." He had just decided on a cold meat loaf sandwich instead and was slathering the thick slice with ketchup when the phone rang. It was Carlotta.

"Your man was here, Mul," she said, "just a few minutes ago. My, he's a handful, isn't he? He came in here ranting and raving about how I had to release his wife's body to him and I told him, 'Fine, you get me Mulheisen on the line,' and I held out the phone to him, but he said he didn't have to go through no police to get his wife. So when I started to dial you myself, he split. I followed him outside, and he jumped into one of those little Japanese pickup trucks and peeled away—I mean, he burned rubber. I didn't get the license number—it was all covered with mud—but the truck had a sign, or a logo, on the door. It was some kind of coat of arms or something—it was all mud splattered, too, so I couldn't see what it was for sure, but I think I saw the word *Briar*."

Mulheisen thanked her and apologized for the disturbance, which she verbally waved off, then he immediately called the young pro Eric Smith. He told Mulheisen that he had occasionally used the truck, but several days earlier the head grounds keeper, Dennis McMillan, had come by his apartment to get it—no reason given. He had assumed McMillan needed it for maintenance work at the course.

McMillan was home. "Yeah, the boss drove me by Eric's. I drove the pickup back to the club, and the boss drove me home. I thought we were going to get back to work on the course, but the boss said to hold off for a few more days. Jeez, I don't know how much longer we can wait. We gotta jump on those greens and get after that fairway grass before it goes to hell. The guys on the crew don't mind—they're getting full pay doing nothing—but we gotta do something about the drainage in front of number eight . . . all this rain—"

"Where is the truck usually kept?" Mulheisen interrupted.

"Out to the equipment shed," McMillan replied. "It's over between five and thirteen. You take the little road that goes down the hill—about a quarter mile down the road from the clubhouse if you're coming up Briar Ridge Drive. There's a little white gate there, says GOLF COURSE, PRIVATE ROAD—you can't hardly see it 'less you're looking for it."

Mulheisen thought he could find it, but he didn't recall seeing an equipment shed. Was it visible from the road?

"Oh, no," McMillan said, "it ain't even visible from the club-house. Actually it's more like a lodge or a cabin. It's tucked back along that clump of woods that separates the thirteenth fairway from the fifth. It's a real pretty building, fieldstone and timber. Part of it is a shelter and a snack bar—they sell sandwiches and beer there in the summer. The boss seen one like it in Scotland and had it built a couple years ago. The equipment shed is tacked onto the back end."

Mulheisen called Jimmy. Yvonne told him, with no attempt to conceal her annoyance, that Jimmy had gone to the store for her, and "couldn't it wait until the morning?" Mulheisen told her it couldn't, she should send Jimmy to Briar Ridge as soon as he returned.

It was already dark when he found the gate, after first driving by it. It was securely locked. There were recent-looking tire tracks going in. Mulheisen clambered over the fence and began to walk down the graveled road. There was a glow in the sky from the distant city, and there were even a few stars. He stumbled on, down a steep rutted and muddy grade. After a few minutes he reached flatter ground, and a moment later he crossed Clabber Creek (or, as he thought, Petty Creek), on a bridge made of timbers and railroad ties. A few paces on, however, he was afraid he'd got lost. But then he realized that he'd been deflected by a path used by golfers in golf carts, and he backtracked to find the road again as it passed behind an elevated tee. He walked on, more cautiously now, wondering if it wouldn't be a lot smarter to just go back to the car and wait for Jimmy. But then he thought he perceived a darker patch in the night.

Must be the lodge, he thought, and stepped off the noisy gravel, turning toward the trees for a few paces. He eased the Smith & Wesson out of its hip grip and stood quietly. It was pitch-black unless you looked directly upward—he could see tiny stars through the budding leaves. A bird was calling oddly, a kind of nasal *beenp;* he thought it might be a snipe, but he didn't really know. There was no other significant sound, just the distant background static of Yvonne's Greater Detroit Urban Zone. He took three more steps and ran full length into the side of a rough wooden wall. He nearly dropped his gun, stumbling backward until he fell flat on his butt.

Instinctively he felt his nose with his free hand. It wasn't broken, just bumped. His seat was getting wet on the damp earth, however. He scrambled up. At that instant a brilliant light blinded him.

"Mul!" rasped Lande's voice, "what the hell took you so long?"

Lande was holding a heavy-duty flashlight and a sawed-off shotgun. "Just drop the gun there, Mul," he said. Mulheisen looked at the shotgun for a long second and then bent to place his .38 on the ground. Lande opened a door in the wall and turned on a light switch. "C'mon in," he invited.

Mulheisen blinked and entered. They were in a kind of cabin filled with a jumble of boxes and tools. An army cot stood against one wall, and against the opposite wall were built some cabinets with a counter bearing an electric cooker with a coffee pot on it. There was a sink filled with dirty dishes. A grocery sack overflowed with empty tins of chili and condensed soup. Against the back wall was a workbench with two vises, well lighted by fluorescent light and a gooseneck lamp. There were many tools—saws, files, drills, and some bladed instruments that were gouges. There were boxes of cartridges and miscellaneous shotgun shells lying about and something that Mulheisen thought was a shot-shell loader.

Lande waved him to a wooden kitchen chair next to a rickety table covered with coffee-cup rings and bread crumbs, a plate with the remains of dried chili on it, and a cup half-filled with cold coffee that reflected the light like the back of a grackle. There was also a nearly full bottle of Jameson whiskey.

Lande pushed a coffee cup across the table and poured it almost full of whiskey. He stepped back, and holding the shotgun by its pistol grip, he kept his eye on Mulheisen as he took a deep gulp from the bottle.

Mulheisen lifted his cup in toast and drank.

"Took ya long enough," Lande said. "I wunnered how much longer I was gonna haveta hang out here." He shook his head with disapproval. "Jeez . . . some detective you are."

"I've been busy," Mulheisen said. He rubbed his sore nose and took another sip of whiskey. "I guess I should have known about the shed, but I just didn't think of it."

"Yeah. You were thinking about shit like taking Bonny to a nigger

funeral parlor. What the hell 'ja do that for? That ain't no place for
Bonny!"

"What difference does it make? You didn't want her to go to the
morgue, did you? The people at Sweet Home are old friends. I trust
them. Anyway, you left her."

"I thought I could depend on you," Lande complained. He didn't
look well—gaunt, unshaven, his eyes red and glowing madly. Actually
his beard didn't look so bad; if it grew out as it seemed intended to, it
would go some way toward rendering his mustache more respectable.
But his hair was disheveled and much grayer than it had been. Mulheisen wondered if he had dyed it before.

"Dead black people are like dead white people," Mulheisen said;
"you can't do anything to them anymore. What should I have done?"

"Cremation. That's what she wanted. I figgered you knew that.
Hell, yer right. Dead is dead." Lande shrugged. "So, ya figgered out I
was here, but ya figgered I could wait until ya had time to deal with
me." He sounded bitter.

"No, . . . I thought you were gone."

"Gone? Dead, ya mean?"

"No," Mulheisen said, "to the Cayman Islands."

"Cayman Islands," Lande said with disgust. "Yeah . . . that was
gonna be it . . . me 'n' Bonny lying in the sun. Shit! How'm I gonna go
to the Cayman Islands?"

"Why not?"

"Besides never wanting to see the place again without Bon, pro'ly
every cop in Michigan is lookin' fer me. What'm I gonna do, drive
there?"

Mulheisen drained his cup and poured himself another dram. "It's
not my problem," he said. "I figured you had a plan."

"Plan! Sure, I hada plan . . . once't. Me 'n' Bon. But now there ain't
no reason for a plan." He choked and stopped, his eyes glittering with
tears. He picked up the bottle and chugged from it, the shotgun pointed
at the floor. When he regained control, he said, "Sid . . . he was a plan.
But," he flipped his free hand over and back, "ain't no Sid, either. No
Sid, no Bonny . . . just ol' Gene . . . and good ol' Mul. Say," he leaned

forward raising the shotgun provocatively, "how 'bout you 'n' me go to the islands, Mul? Whataya say?"

Mulheisen just stared him in the eye. Lande blinked and stepped back. "Nanh? Guess not." He picked up the bottle again and took another drink. "Good stuff," he said. "I'm 'onna miss this stuff."

Mulheisen wondered what that meant. Two or three possibilities loomed in the hazy distance, none of them cheerful. "So, you're taking off . . . is that it?" he asked.

Lande made a raspy noise that could have been a laugh or a snort. "Yanh, I'm takin' off. Soon's I figure out what to do about you, Mul."

Mulheisen decided to ignore the remark. He took a careful sip of whiskey and said, "You could go by boat, I guess."

Lande cocked his head, frowning. "Boat? What boat?"

"That boat you and Bonny used to go out on . . . last summer."

"Sid's boat, you mean? The *Serb-U-Rite?* How'm I gonna go in Sid's boat, . . . steal it?"

Mulheisen shrugged. "Just a thought. But how will you get the money out?"

Lande waved a hand contemptuously. He must have been drinking before Mulheisen got there, because he was clearly drunk now. Mulheisen wasn't feeling that sober himself. He watched as Lande tottered over to the workbench and laid the alley sweeper down. He just as quickly picked up a .45 automatic, however, and absently checked that the clip was jammed home. He looked over at Mulheisen and thoughtfully racked the housing back, cocking the pistol. He casually gestured with the gun, saying, "I had a good plan, me 'n' Sid 'n' Bonny . . . an' Germaine, a course." He shook his head ruefully. "That damn Germaine . . . Bonny thought I had the hots for her. Can you believe it? Course, Bon didn't know about the plan! Couldn't really tell her, no way. To her it was just me 'n' Sid was gonna buy a golf resort . . . I'd transfer the money . . . no prob."

"A lot of money?" Mulheisen asked simply, raising a brow.

"Oh, yes," Lande said with surprising disgust, "a lot of money . . . too damn much money . . . no end to that damn money . . . sixty-seven million buckaroos, in fact."

Mulheisen was stunned. "So much? Where did it come from?"
Lande shrugged. "Drugs, Sid 'n' Frosty 'n' Billy."

"But I mean, how did they get it?"

Lande clearly didn't share Mulheisen's incredulity. "Maybe you ain't heard—there's a hell of a lotta money in drugs. More than even the mob realized, I guess. Sid tol' me once't he was just amazed when he found out what the biz was worth."

"Well, sure, there's a lot of money," Mulheisen said, "but how could you rip off that much without getting caught?"

"You better ask Sid," Lande said, "speakin' of gettin' caught. Him 'n' Frosty, they figured out that the territories was worth somethin' to the South Americans, sorta like franchises. Only they didn' realize how much at first, . . . which I guess is how come it took Carmine so long to tumble to what they was doin'. You sell a franchise—well, lease is more like it—to the Latinos for a neighborhood for say fifty thousand dollars a month, an' you skim maybe ten percent. But then a rival group comes along and offers you a hundred thousand dollars. An' you take it, but you don't tell Carmine. That's the way Sid tol' it to me, anyways.

"So here's all this money. It just comes pilin' in; you can't turn off the faucet, or somebody'll tumble to the deal, but you gotta get rid of the cash. Cash smells. It attracks rats. So you got Billy, he's layin' the take out in loans . . . phony loans, so Carmine wouldn't wise up, . . . but even that ain't enough. Which is why they come to me."

"Ah, yes," Mulheisen said, relieved to have diverted Lande's attention, no matter how briefly, from the problem of his own disposal. "They would come to you, the computer genius. I'm sure you concocted something suitably brilliant."

Any irony intended was lost on Lande. "Yeah," he admitted. "It took me a little while, but I figured it out. At first I had some notion of gettin' into the banks, you know, crackin' their systems. But then I figured—what the hell, that's not the problem. We already had a bank—some guy who was into Billy for a lot . . . Billy was running loan money through him. An' we already got the money, too much money . . . The problem is how to get rid of it, lay it off. So I just decided to deposit it."

"Deposit it? You can't deposit that kind of money in a bank. The feds would be all over you. What is it, any deposit of more than ten thousand dollars has to be reported to the IRS?"

"That's why I deposited it in thousands of accounts . . . a little more than seven thousand, at about ninety-five hundred dollars per." He cocked his head as if calculating, then nodded. "Yanh, that's about it, in round numbers. Course, I hada make up a lotta names, lotta payments to innavidjuls. The computer did that. I just plugged in about two dozen last names, middle names, and first names—got 'em oudda the phone book. The computer scrambled up all the possibilities—you can get eight thousand different names oudda twenny names from the phone book if you use a middle name and the last name doesn't sound too weird as a first name. You know—Jackson Lewis Arthur or Henry David John or Allen Martin James." He grinned with the pleasure of his genius.

"I had the golf course, a legal corporation, and we had the development company. We could make payments to all these people, and they could make payments to us. The computer does it all. I tried to get them to buy a bank, a savings and loan really, and put Billy's tame banker in there. But Sid thought that was too complicated. So we used the one we had. I just tapped into their mainframe. But you gotta go to the bank once in a while with a bag of money—Billy had the tame banker, so he carried the bag—but it was all paid right back out, wasn't hardly there. The other bank people would never even see it. They never even knew we existed. The computer takes care of it, makes the transfer, then sweeps the tracks behind it. Trouble is there was always this money, this hard cash, comin' in," Lande complained. "An' we couldn't turn it off 'cause it'd blow the plan. Which I guess it must've, once Sid went down."

Mulheisen tried to take all this in, but he couldn't quite get it. It would be something for Jimmy, or the Business Bureau to unravel. What he wanted to know was "Where is the money now?"

"Some of it's in the little accounts," Lande said, "most of it . . . over forty mil. Some of it's already gone to the Cayman bank for the resort account. An' then I got about fifteen mil in cash. It just kept pilin' up . . . What a pain in the ass hard cash is. I can't wait till we go to straight 'lectronic money."

"Where?"

"Hunh? The cash?" Lande nodded toward the rear of the building.
"You have fifteen million dollars here? In cash?"

"Not izzackly. Fifteen mil is an awful lotta cash, even if it's all in
fifties and hunnerds, which it was, 'cause you can't be screwin' aroun'
with twennies and that little crap. Lessee. If it's all hunnerds, that'd be
a hunnerd fifty thousand bills, but ack'shly, with fifties included, you
end up with about two-hunnerd thousand bills, or somethin' like that.
Now, if they was all new bills—you know, in little tight bun'les like the
mint issues—you could prolly cram that much cash inna half-dozen
cardboard boxes, say like they put whiskey bottles in. But what I had
was a couple dozen boxes, 'cause the money was used . . . It's thicker."

"Had?" Mulheisen asked.

"Yanh. It's in boxes, in the shed."

"In the shipment," Mulheisen said.

"What shipment?" Lande said.

"To the Cayman Islands. The computers."

"Computers? Oh, no. I mean, yahn, the computers are in the shed,
but they're just computers . . . Course, they do have the program on the
disk drives, that runs the show. You mean try to stuff the money into
the computers, into the consoles or the drive cases? How you gonna do
that? There ain't enough room. I mean, that's stupid. Nanh, I just put
the extra cash in some old whiskey cartons. I was thinkin' about gettin'
rid of it—dump it in the river, burn it, maybe—but then I got a idea."

"A bright idea," Mulheisen prompted.

"Sure. Whataya think? I'm 'onna git a dumb idea? No, I packed
it all up—well, all but about five mil, which I figgered I could use for
expenses—an' I give it to charity . . . orphanages, neighborhood projecks,
drug clinics, that sorta thing."

"You gave ten million dollars to charity? How?"

"Mostly I drove aroun' at night," Lande said. "I remembered
seein' on TV how these orphanages are allus gettin' babies dropped off
at their doorstep in the night, in a cardboard box. An' I didn' have
nothin' to do—waitin' fer you—so I packed the stuff up and trucked it
aroun' town. Jus' leave the box on the doorstep like other boxes. I

wrapped the shit in old newspapers and old clothes—so it's not too obvious, see. People leave boxes at these places with all kinds a junk, y'know."

"I haven't heard anything about orphanages finding boxes of money on their doorsteps," Mulheisen said skeptically.

"You will. An' if not . . . then, not. Somma the places I dropped it didn't look too cool . . . I prack'ly threw the box oudda the window and split. I got ridda maybe five, six mil that way. Anyways, who cares? It was drivin' me crazy, all that damn cash, but I ain't worryin' about it no more. Yer here."

Mulheisen didn't like the way this sounded, especially with the gun waving around as he said it. He felt he had to say something, anything, to keep this wired-up little maniac from going off half-cocked. "You know," he said, "I promised Bonny I'd look after you."

Lande's jaw dropped open. "You what? When?"

"In the hospital one day, when you were out. She said, 'Promise me you'll look out for Gene.' Didn't you hear her last words? 'Look out for him?' She was just reminding me."

"She said that?" Gene's eyes filled with tears. "An' you promised?"

Mulheisen shrugged. "I felt I had to."

Lande sobbed, a ragged noise that he broke off. "Oh, God . . . this gets harder 'n' harder." He fought for control, his face swept by tortured emotions. He grimaced and twisted his neck. His face seemed to grow larger, distorted, then subsided and shrank. For a moment Mulheisen was reminded of the distortions of Bonny's poor face in the terminal stages.

Lande sagged against the workbench, the .45 wavering toward Mulheisen, then away. "Just a coupla months ago," he said, his voice surging, then waning, then surging again, "everythin' was lookin' great. Fin'ly. I hada great deal goin' with Sid, me 'n' Bon was great . . ." He fought down a deep, welling sob. " 'N' then they hada go 'n' hit Sid. 'N' everythin' turned to shit. Not right off . . . It still looked like it could fly. But Frosty started buggin' me, an' Billy . . . Carmine gets on my case, . . . an' then I met you. Bonny wanted us to be frien's. I thought we could be frien's . . . We was frien's in the hospital, weren't we?" He was pleading. "I tol' you shit in the hospital I never tol' nobody, not even Bon. I wanted to do something for you."

"Do me a favor? You mean Tupman and Conover? That was a favor to me?"

"Yeah, sure." Lande nodded his head repeatedly, as if to convince himself.

"That wasn't a favor to me," Mulheisen said, his face cruel. "You had to take them down. They knew you had the money. They were under pressure from Carmine. If you didn't get them, they'd get you now that you didn't have Sid to protect you. Why, for all I know, Sid was planning to get rid of all of you, clean house . . . Wasn't Hal his friend, his good buddy? He sure hung around a lot, for a hired killer."

"Hal?" Lande was puzzled momentarily, then his eyes grew wide. "You mean the guy at the gate? The one who popped Sid 'n' Mickey?" Lande stared, then shook his head. "No, no. He wasn't a friend of Sid's. I was Sid's pal. I seen the guy pop Sid . . . I seen him in the lockup, later! I hada get the hell oudda there. Those guys, they got secret ways a doin' ya. I wasn't sure if he seen me."

Mulheisen sensed he had stumbled onto something. He had to go with it. "Sure, Hal took Sid down. He was probably supposed to take you down, too, but you hid, and he didn't see you. Then you ran, only the Big Four swept you up. So Sid never told you about Hal? Didn't he tell you he was putting a contract out on Tupman and Conover? No. He wouldn't, even though you were his bosom buddy—because he'd also put a contract on you. You must have known it—maybe not consciously, maybe it was too hard to take—but you knew you had to take down Frosty and Billy. Without Sid to keep them off, they'd want the money, all of it. That's the way it went, isn't it? You were betrayed by your pal, Sid, as usual. Everything was going to hell in a hand basket—Sid gone, Bonny gone. You're left with all the work, left with all the money, too, of course, and left with Tupman and Conover and Carmine breathing down your neck."

"Carmine," Lande said bitterly, "I should of blasted him and that fuckin' Fat Man. You know what they did? Lissena this, this is how they jerk ya 'roun'. Carmine calls me in . . . ack'shly, the Fat Man comes to get me one day with a coupla goons. 'Carmine wants to talk to ya.' We go down there, to the potato chip fact'ry, an' we wait. After a while the door opens to Carmine's office, and Bonny comes out with Carmine, only he steers her out the side door, so she don't see me waitin' with the Fat Man. Her hair is mussed up an' her lipstick's smeared. I don't know what Carmine thinks I'll think . . . Maybe I'm s'posed ta think Bonny's puttin' out for him. Maybe he just wants to show me that he can get to me through Bonny . . . I don't know. But I know Bonny. She wouldn't put out for Carmine.

"Anyways, he gets me in the office. He don't say nothin' about Bon, like she was never there, but we both know, y'know. All he talks about is Sid 'n' Frosty 'n' Billy. He says I should wise up. He knows all about Sid 'n' Frosty 'n' Billy 'n' me. He wants his money back. He's talkin' about ten mil. I hada laugh, but not out loud. He didn' know nothin'. I knew he didn', but I wasn't sure about Frosty 'n' Billy. They might spill it. An' I hada perteck Bon."

"So what did you tell Carmine?"

"I tol' him I didn' know nothin' about Sid's deal with Frosty 'n' Billy. I didn' even know them. Which I don't, hardly—I didn' do any business with them, Sid hanneled that. I tol' Carmine what he already must've knew—I hada deal with Sid to build this golf resort in the islands. Ever'body knew about that. An' I bitched about now I was stuck with it, what with Sid gone, an' I was gonna haveta either bail out or get some new backers. Hell, I ast him to come in with me!" Lande laughed. "He said he'd think about it."

"Why didn't you go after Carmine?" Mulheisen asked.

"Go after Carmine? Are you nuts? Well, maybe I shoulda . . . but how? You can't get close to them big shots. An' if you did, you'd have the whole mob after ya. Frosty 'n' Billy, they don't give a shit. You even said so in the rest'raunt that night. It'd be better for ever'body, you said. I could do you a favor, an' then we'd be frien's. Bonny liked you. I didn' even mind. Anybody else, even Carmine, I'd a popped him. But I could tell you really liked Bon . . . not just after her ass. It was better for ever'body, Mul."

The maelstrom of this mind was too much for Mulheisen. He didn't think there was any way of combing out this snarl of lies and hatreds, of fears and rages and self-deceit. Lande had provided himself with plenty of justifications for killing; if one didn't fly, he'd just put up another. Mulheisen supposed that simply rage and fear at the collapse of his wonderful plans, especially in terms of Bonny's illness and subsequent death, had been enough. He sighed and looked into his cup, then drained it. He poured himself another and held out the bottle to Lande. Lande came forward and took it, still holding the .45 at the ready.

"You see, Mul," he said, putting the bottle down after a long draft, "I'm yer pal. It's funny, eh? You lookin' out fer me an' me lookin' out fer you! That's what frien's are!"

Mulheisen sat back and stared, then he began to laugh—not a great, mirthful laugh but more of a quiet, rueful laugh. "What a life," he said.

Lande laughed, too, but it got out of control and ended in a sob. "You got that right, Mul. What a fuckin' life. An' without Bon it ain't worth shit. Am I right? Hunh? Am I? Who needs it? C'mon Mul, one last drink, right?" He held up the bottle, toasting them.

Mulheisen lifted the cup. Why not, he thought. Could be the last one. He started to put it down but decided to drain it. He was reminded of something his father used to say, a kind of poem, or was it a song?—"When it seems life's joy is up, drain the sweetness from the cup." Or something like that. He wasn't sure he'd got it right. He set the cup down.

Lande drank and set the bottle on the table. His eyes glittered. "I never knew no one like her, Mul. D'jou? She was beautiful, wan't she? I mean, she was really a fine wooman. Right? She wan't no hooer, not really. An' she loved me." He gestured with the gun, soliciting a response. "Right? Am I right?"

"She was fine, Gene," Mulheisen said. "She was beautiful. She was a good woman. The best. And she loved you."

Lande nodded furiously. "Right, right, right. Damn right! You know what, Mul? She was the on'y one who ever loved Eugene Lande. You know that?"

Mulheisen nodded, watching.

Eyes blazing, Lande raised the gun and said, "Good-bye, Mul. You were a good man." Then he stuck the gun into his mouth and pulled the trigger. His face seemed to explode, and the back of his head flew, spattering brains and blood against the wall behind him.

Mulheisen leapt to his feet, his mouth open in shock. Lande's body sprawled against the wall. For a moment he couldn't register what had happened. He rubbed his forehead, dazed. Then he picked up the bottle and walked outside. In the light from the doorway he leaned against a tree with an outstretched hand and gulped the fresh air. He staggered off a ways and found he had a tremendous urge to piss. He unzipped and pissed into the dark grass. Then he drank from the bottle. He zipped up and drank again. The bottle was empty. He reared back and hurled it up into the night, at the tiny, blurry stars. It rattled off some tree limbs, then fell to the soft earth with a thump. The bird he'd heard earlier was making the same weird *beenp*. Mulheisen noticed his .38 lying on the ground. He picked it up and holstered it, then went into the shed. The boxes of computers were there, stacked neatly. There were also a half-dozen boxes bearing well-known liquor labels and closed up in the familiar flap-over-flap tuck that people use when packing, say, books for moving. Mulheisen opened one. It was full of old newspapers. He opened the rest. They were all full of newspapers. He was tired. He sat down on the open tailgate of the little pickup truck and waited for Jimmy.

Time In

"Getting in is not the problem," Joe said. "It's getting out. The Greeks got into Troy, but they knew they were going to fight their way out. You don't want to fight your way out. Now I could dress up like some crazy sculptor . . . You know—beard, long hair, dark glasses, maybe wear a long army-surplus coat, . . . spray-paint you nude with, say, bronze paint—*Helen of Troy*—and wheel you into the office on a dolly . . ."

They both erupted in laughter. They were, as it happened, quite nude, and they did, in fact, resemble Greek statuary—of a particularly flexible, plastic kind.

A few hours later Joe sat up in Helen's bed and snapped his fingers. "Got it," he said.

He explained the whole thing at length to Helen, and she accepted the plan enthusiastically. He warned, "It's dangerous, but you can do it. The thing is—they'll be angry and upset, not thinking rationally. You'll be in a situation that you know, that you've prepared for. You stay calm and go with it. Otherwise . . ."—he smiled sadly—"if I see it isn't going right, I'll have to leave. It's your show."

"Joe, I can do it. Don't worry about me." She kissed him eagerly, clinging like a child and laughing wildly.

They were at Helen's apartment in Bloomfield Hills. Over the following days they rehearsed the show, as Joe called it, until Helen was perfect. During the day, while Helen was at work—putting together a deal to sell her share of Cadillac Communications Consultants to her partner—Joe set about making the necessary preparations. This included renting a small van and shopping in a secondhand clothing store.

One afternoon, as an idle gesture to his irrepressible curiosity, Joe drove out to Lande's golf course. Lande was not in, so naturally he took a look around. There was nothing to see in the clubhouse. On his way back to town, however, almost by accident he noticed the little road to the maintenance building. Someone had left the gate open—in a hurry, he supposed. He drove in. There was nobody in the maintenance building, but there were some interesting boxes stacked up, as if someone were moving. He couldn't resist a peek. The goods were just sitting there, already packed in boxes.

That's the way it goes sometimes, he told himself. You bust your butt to find the goods, and then—voilà! He started to load the boxes into the van, but then it occurred to him that to do so might not be wise. He didn't know anything about this Lande except what he'd been told, but he couldn't imagine that he was the sort of fellow who wouldn't compulsively check on his goods, probably every time he went in or out. If Lande discovered he'd been robbed, it might complicate Joe and Helen's plans. He dumped Lande's money in the van—he figured he could repack it later—and then he refilled the boxes with newspaper from a nearby bin and restacked the boxes as before. That ought to allay suspicion for a while, he thought, and left whistling.

"**W**hat foresight," Joe said at breakfast the following morning. He pointed to the headline: MYSTERY MOB FIGURE DIES, MILLIONS MISSING. "That ingenious sleuth, our old pal Mulheisen, has once again solved the crime," Joe said. "They say this Lande was implicated in the Tupman and Conover shootings. Hmmm."

Helen didn't believe it. "It's all Carmine," she insisted. "He skates again."

Joe lowered the paper and gazed at her. She was wearing her wig and was dressed for work, but she looked mean. She was going to wrap up her business today.

"But not for long," Joe said. That got a smile from her.

An hour later the phone rang. Joe ignored it until he heard Helen's voice on the answering machine: "Joe, pick up." Mulheisen had just called, she said. He wanted to talk to her about Lande and other matters. "I put him off until tomorrow morning," she said. "What do you think?"

"Don't go," Joe said. "With any luck we'll be out of town."

He hung up and went out for a walk. The Detroit Zoo wasn't far. He wandered around the grounds, gazing idly at the caged animals. The serpent house intrigued him, particularly a glassed-in cage that revealed a tree full of pythons. He dodged the kids and wrinkled his nose at the smell, but mainly he pondered his present course of action.

What he was about to do with Helen precluded any notion of carrying out the contract with the Fat Man. It was too bad. Joe had never broken a contract before, but this seemed like a good time to make an exception.

Oh, be honest, he thought, almost every contract has been broken in some sense. A contract has always required bending or amending because of circumstances one couldn't control. This was just the first time he'd decided on his own to break a contract without there being truly mitigating circumstances. It was hard to give up the money once it was in your possession.

He knew the Fat Man and Carmine would be getting antsy. They could read the papers, too. If Lande hadn't had the money, where was it? They would start looking for Joe soon.

He thought about giving them the money—well, some of it, maybe even most of it. That would probably be the smartest thing to do. Then he thought about Helen, about that lithe body, that smooth little head. She was going to be trouble, he knew—he had a curious, bleak feeling in his gut. She could blow his whole life to smithereens. But, nanh, it wouldn't be that bad. It'd be fine. They'd work it out.

But this was definitely a burning of bridges. If he had mused once that he could never go back to Iowa City, well, it was certain that this side of the Missouri River would soon no longer be an appropriate environment for him. He felt no remorse. He'd never liked it in Detroit, even when he'd done well. This time he'd done better.

*   *   *

About midmorning the long brown Cadillac cruised carefully down the narrow side street. It was hundreds of yards from the Krispee Chips factory when, as Carmine's driver had long dreaded, some idiot pulled out of a parking place and the driver had to swerve to avoid him. There was no room. The limo crashed into another parked car, and the idiot halted, blocking the street. Both the driver and the burly bodyguard piled out, angry as hornets. They were confronted by a little guy in a fedora, an old, pin-striped suit, and a full-head rubber Mickey Mouse mask.

The mouse—or the rat, as it were—swung up a sawed-off shotgun. It was over in less than five seconds. Then the rat climbed into the front of the limo and leaned over the back. The gun boomed again and again.

The rat ran down the street in the direction from which the limo had come and jumped into a waiting van. Helen stripped off the mask and flung it into the back, among her luggage and Joe's, which included three large, brand-new duffel bags that were stuffed full. Joe drove them swiftly away.

"My god, I can't hear!" she yelled, holding her hands over her ears. Her clothes were flecked with blood. Joe drove calmly and carefully down the long street and turned onto Jefferson, headed for the Fisher Freeway. He glanced at the woman with concern. Her eyes were wild, and her tiny patch of hair was matted with perspiration, but she was grinning.

"It was perfect!" she shouted. "The little bastard was all squinched up on the floor. I practically had to crawl over the front seat to get him. It was incredible. The noise . . . My ears are ringing! Did you say something, darling?"

Joe laughed and stopped for a light. He rubbed her head gleefully and hugged her. The light changed, and he got into the right lane to take the freeway exit, for their new life.

*   *   *

Mulheisen was still ten minutes away from Tiger Stadium when he heard the announcer say, "Here's the pitch to Phillips . . . He swings . . . and there's a drive to left field . . . It could be . . . It's hooking . . . It hits the foul pole—deflected into . . . It's a home run! It's out of here folks! The Yankee third base coach is arguing, but he won't win this one . . . And the Tigers lead one to nothing in the bottom of the first! That was . . . whataya think, George? An oh-and-two pitch, looked like a curve ball that didn't curve." And George readily agreed, "Inside and low, but it didn't really break, Al. Not a bad pitch on oh-and-two, but Phillips is one of these guys who just won't take a pitch."

"Crap!" Mulheisen snorted. He reckoned it was the only home run he would have had a chance to see off Phillips's bat all summer. But he wasn't really annoyed. What the hell—he was going to opening day. It was fine weather, a little cool, but no clouds. He was determined to think about nothing but baseball today. Even Helen's failure to show for their appointment didn't bother him. He'd checked with her office, and they said she was no longer with CCC. That puzzled him, but he refused to worry about it. Tomorrow.

He wheeled into the parking lot, where a skinny dark man with a tall, sloping forehead frantically waved him away until he saw who it was. "Hey, Fang!" the man yelled, his grin exposing several gaps in an array of otherwise awful teeth, "d'jou hear that! Phillips! Cat got some power, eh?"

Mulheisen exposed his own fangs and said, "That you, Malfitan? Park it, but don't hide it . . . and don't throw a party in it either." Then he sprinted away.

Steeple Head yelled after him, "Ah'mo knock off a piece a ass in the backseat, you jive honky," but Mulheisen was gone. He flipped his badge at the gate and ran in, even though he had a ticket he'd paid for well in advance. He huffed up the ramp to the grandstand over the Tiger dugout and grabbed a Stroh's beer off a vendor as he dropped down the steps to the row where his reserved seat was located. Naturally some clown was already sitting in the seat, but he jumped up and vanished when Mulheisen waved him away.

An overlarge fellow in a Tiger uniform stood at the plate, patiently

waving a bat like a wand as the Yankee pitcher started his motion. The
runner on first was Trammell, and he took off with the pitch. It was a
fatal fastball, and the batter turned on it like a cyclone. The ball arced
up, up, up, up and then began to plane out toward the upper deck in
left field.

Mulheisen didn't sit down. With a roar the rest of the fans rose to
join him as the tiny white pellet crashed into a stanchion, then deflected
over the roof toward Cherry Street.

"Cess-ill!" the people screamed over and over, and Mulheisen
added his voice.

After that they all settled down to that most satisfying of spectacles, a home-team slaughter. By the sixth inning, when the score was
nine-zip, they were all pretty sloshed and hilarious, singing songs and
embracing each other whenever Trammell, or Whitaker, or the Kid on
the Korner snapped a double to the wall or came up with the ball deep
in the hole and lasered a Yankee runner out.

"Is this great, or what!" a vendor yelled. He almost gave away
beer. The fans, including a fine-looking woman in section 27, sprawled
in the sun and took off their shirts. The ushers got the woman to cover
up before any trouble ensued, but the crowd just laughed.

Oh, hell, yes, Detroit was happy. The Tigers were back. It was
spring. Life had begun again.

During the seventh-inning stretch a cop came up to Mulheisen at
the hotdog counter and said, "Mul, didja hear about Carmine? The alley
sweeper got him!"

Mulheisen paused in his glee and said, "No way. Where?"

"On the street, just outside the Krispee plant," said the cop,
grinning.

"They get the guy?" Mulheisen asked, chomping into the mus-
tardy dog.

"It was a rat," the cop said. "An alley rat. Got clean away."

Mulheisen went back to his seat, a little mystified but determined
not to think about it. Today was opening day. He'd deal with the
homicide later, along with the rest of the laborious cleanup of the Big
Sid case. Right now Cecil was stepping into the batter's box . . . One
out and the bases loaded . . . They'd have to pitch to him.

* * *

The following day Mulheisen and Jimmy drove down to the Harbor Bar. They were dressed in jeans and light jackets and they were talking about boats. Jimmy was thinking about buying, and Mulheisen, who had owned both a gaff-rigged cat-boat and a powerboat at different times, was giving advice. He also carried a couple of sealed plastic boxes, a little larger than the boxes that might contain twenty-five Corona cigars. He had picked them up from the crematorium the day before.

"Any word on Helen Sedlacek?" Mulheisen asked Jimmy as they walked into the bar. They ordered beers and sat down by a window that looked onto a dock where pleasure boats were tied up.

"I talked to Roman," Jimmy said. "He hasn't seen her lately, he says. And her home phone has been disconnected."

Mulheisen thought about this. "Another woman flown?" He glanced out the window and noticed a twenty-five-foot cabin cruiser drawn up at the dock. The name on the stern was *Serb-A-Rite*. A woman was loading some bags off the dock, onto the deck, probably stocking up on beer. She was barefoot, wearing shorts and a sweater. She was tall and sturdily built, but she carried herself in a guarded way. Nice looking but not beautiful. Rather strong features. Sunglasses.

"Speaking of flown women," Mulheisen said. "I didn't even have to ask directions." He handed the boxes to Jimmy and walked out onto the catwalk and squatted down next to the boat. The woman looked up at him.

"Miss Kouras?" he asked. Up close she had a worn look, perhaps a little bruised, as if she'd been in an accident but had pretty much recovered.

"Kouras?" she said. She shook her head slowly, her thick hair swinging about her face. "You must have made a mistake."

Mulheisen stared down at her, then looked away. It was a fine day again. Gulls were gliding about as if pulled through the air on strings. The water danced in the sunlight.

"Sorry," Mulheisen said, and he really was. He shrugged and

pulled out his identification folder, holding it open so that she could see. "I have to talk to you."

The woman sighed and said, "Can we talk here?"

Mulheisen looked around. He waved to Jimmy to come over, then said, "Sure. For a while, anyway." And he hopped onto the boat. "Actually, maybe we could take the boat out for a little run. Do you think? I have to drop some friends off."